Yallah

A Journey out of Sanctuary

Sali Mustafic

Published by NLP Devon in 2013

www.nlpdevon.co.uk

Copyright © Sali Mustafic 2013

Cover image Sali Mustafic

ISBN 978-0-9575550-1-3

In memory of
Joan Wilson
of
Budleigh Salterton

who gave me space in which to write.

Yallah

A Journey out of Sanctuary

1

The Beginning Lies in the Past

Heavy heat, low swooping swallows, whispering in the trees - the storm will soon be here. Ria makes her way through the edge of the forest quickening her step to reach the clearing. She has the forest to herself. Everyone else is afraid of the storm while she anticipates it with a thrill. Thunder is rumbling nearer as she stops to pull her dress over her head. She rolls it up tightly and tucks it under a low bush before running to the centre of the clearing to throws herself down, rolling onto her back to watch the sky.

Dirty cream clouds crease against each other, grey piling on purple, turning mid-afternoon to twilight and silencing the birds. An unfamiliar blue shimmers through the tree tops where young leaves shine livid against the bruising sky. The bank of trees between Ria and the clouds is shrouded in grey blue haze.

She waits. *Why am I trembling now? I have searched out storms before. Father's anger is nothing new. I have been to forbidden places and seen things I should not have seen. What is it about this storm, and being here, now? Why does this delicious breeze make me shiver?*

Vivid scratches leap between clouds as a crackling smack stops her breath and she gives herself up to the cold, needle sharp rain. It slaps the earth and bounces off stones. It runs down her body in rivulets triggering a shudder that starts in the pit of her stomach and ripples to her feet, fingers and scalp.

When it is over she lies still, watching the sky change as the ragged edges of storm cloud are sucked away and the delicious heat of the sun spreads over her. *Now I must move.*

Retrieving her dress - still dry in its hiding place - she pulls and runs to the trees making her way to her grandmother's hut at the southern edge of the forest.

As so many times before, she trails her fingers through the branches of her grandmother's rosemary bush, crushing a handful of its twiggy growth and lifting her fist to her face to breathe its powerful freshness.

She lifts the latch and lets herself in to the single room that is the entire dwelling. Here the air is always soft, warm and musky with the mingling scents of wood-smoke and animal skins. Ria loves the colours her grandmother lives with: the red of the clay, sand-gold and many browns. Cushions, pillows, rugs, all dipped and dyed in the colours of the earth, lie against the grey stone walls, hearth and flagstones and the black, grey and white of animal skins. The only wood is the door. Clay bowls, mugs and plates are stored in recesses in the walls. The hut is silent.

Grandmother?

Waiting for you,

Ria walks over to the bed. *She looks so small, like a child sleeping.*

Suddenly Ria is afraid. The hairs in her armpits prickle and her tongue sticks to the dry roof of her mouth. She reaches out hesitantly but recoils before her fingers reach the much loved face. Her legs tremble then buckle and she slides to her knees at the bedside, her forehead resting against the edge.

Grandmother has gone.
Now I have no-one. Now I am alone.

. . . .

'Ria, we know this is difficult for you but you cannot go on living like some wild child in the woods. In three days' time we will bury your grandmother and you must begin to think of the future.'

Her father has spoken and so Ria sits in her room trying to consider the future but all she can think of is the past - the past with her grandmother. *How can he think of a future without Grandmother? Only Grandmother helped me make sense of the past.*

Her first memory.

The ants

How old had she been? Four? Maybe five? She had stumbled over a large flat stone. Looking down she noticed a trickling of tiny creatures emerging from beneath it. She squatted for a long time watching them in and out, in and out, more than she could count, tiptoeing out and around through grass, over twigs and stones, up plant stalks. And some returned to the stone. *Is it some, or do they all return, or have the ones going in come from somewhere different? Maybe they have come from a different stone, bringing messages or*

9

come to collect the children to take them somewhere or teach them something.

She put a stick in their way. Some climbed over it. Some went round it. Some turned back and disappeared under the stone again. *What is under the stone?* Gently lifting the stone she was astonished by the beauty of the tiny world she had uncovered. Hundreds of ants hurried purposefully along smooth earth corridors. Corridors opened out into chambers and each chamber had several passageways leading in many directions. Some ants carried things in front of them. *How?* She turned the stone right over and settled onto her knees, bending low to watch closely. *Some are going out for food. Messengers, explorers. All busy. These little white ones that look softer than the others must be the children and there are the eggs they come out of. The nurses are carrying them away from me, underground. There must be more of their world down there where I can't see. I wonder...*

....

When she returned to her stone the next day Ria had found the ant's nest deserted. Eyes blurred by tears she traced the intricate maze of smooth passages with her finger. *We frightened them away.* Gently, respectfully, she replaced the stone.

As she grew older she wondered why her father was afraid of insects; why he hated her talking about them, stopped her looking for them, why he trembled as he pulled her away. She learned to glance in all directions before taking a closer look at a dragonfly, butterfly or bee.

On another day, she had been lying on her stomach in the grass when she noticed a stalk bent as if weighed down by something. Silently she edged as close as she possibly could, constantly listening for her father's step on the grass around her. On the arching stalk she saw the chrysalis - a tiny castle was how she described it to her grandmother that evening. As she had watched a tiny split had opened up at one end. Ria's first reaction was horrified guilt. *I must have touched it and now it's breaking*, but her curiosity kept her there watching. *Magic* was the only word that came to her as she watched the damp, delicate butterfly crawl out of the castle where it had been sleeping.

I slept in a castle and dreamed I had wings.

Ria had watched the butterfly soak up energy from the sun and send it out invisibly to the tips of its new wings.

How must that feel? How must the moment feel when she knows her wings have all the strength they need to lift her? She knows but she waits for one second more, knowing it is coming but having no idea how it will feel, then a surge of happiness fills her and she knows that she is flying.

Ria ran to her grandmother's hut singing.

I slept in a castle,

And dreamed I had wings,

And when I awoke I could fly.

And now I can tell you

11

Why a bird sings,

He has the key to the sky.

'You have seen another wonder then?' the old woman said, taking Ria's hand gently and smiling as they sat down together and, in the ashes of last night's fire, grandmother drew a circle and, around the circle, pictures. *Grandmother drawing stories and telling pictures.*

She drew a tiny circle 'We'll call it an egg. From the egg a caterpillar crawls and it builds a 'castle', as you call it. And in the castle it sleeps for what feels like a lifetime and when it wakes it has to wriggle its way out into a world where everything has changed because while it slept it dreamt itself wings and changed into a butterfly. The world a butterfly lives in is completely different from the world where a caterpillar lives.'

For a few days after this Ria searched for caterpillars. She wanted to look closely; see if she could detect any sign of the change that would overtake the creature. After several days on her hands and knees, turning over leaves, she found one but it refused to crawl onto her hand or arm *too different,* she thought. She took a leaf from the plant it had been crawling on and crushed the leaf over the back of her hand *to make the caterpillar feel safe.* It still avoided her. *Not enough.* Gathering leaves from several plants she crushed, squeezed, and spread their juices on her fingers, over the back of her hand, into the palm, and then on round her wrist and up pushing back the fabric of her sleeve, past her elbow smearing the slightly sticky, sharp smelling greenness all over her arm. This time, when she laid the leaf across her arm the caterpillar crawled over its edge and onto the back of her hand. Totally absorbed she held her arm close to her face. *Its face is all eyes, two huge eyes. Its bright green body is covered in hairs. All those tiny feet each with toes that cling and tickle.*

She watched as the creature reached tentatively out in front, tapping lightly around the hairs on her arm. *It loops itself up to move - reaches out with its front feet and when they are safe it loops its body and pulls the back feet along. Stretch flat, loop, stretch flat, loop.*

Its touch was so delicate it was hardly detectable and yet she could sense the tickle of it, not only on her skin, somehow it seemed to travel, touching a spot deep, deep inside her while, at the same time, making her aware of the sun, warm on the top of her head. She peered along the creature's back but, flat or curled, she could see no sign of wings.

A sharp and sudden slap stung and shocked her, stopped her breath for a moment. 'Ria!' her father roared. 'What are you doing? How can you behave like this?' He pulled her hand away from her face. 'Cover yourself', he shouted dragging the fabric of her sleeve roughly over her wrist, flinching slightly at the scent and stickiness of the crushed plant. 'This is impure, Ria. You know this is impure. You must be cleansed of this'

Ria tried to hang back. She knew there was no point in speaking. Her father would not listen, would hear only more impurities. She looked down and saw that the caterpillar lay in a curl at her feet. Instinctively she bent towards it.

'Ria!' Her father's voice forced itself into her thoughts as he seized hold of the clean sleeve, careful not to touch her skin, 'Do not touch me, Ria. And do not speak. If we meet anyone, keep this…' stabbing a finger in the direction of her plant stained hand, 'Out of sight and your eyes lowered. I will speak. You will say nothing.'

The rough anger in her father's voice always made Ria feel sorry for him even as it grew louder and harder, even as he tightened his grip until it hurt, she heard herself thinking; *poor father* 'No more Ria. Stop. Leave it and come away.'

'But father,' she had tried to reply. There was always so much she wanted to know, so many questions to ask. But he could never listen. He would only repeat the words she had heard so many times before; the words she already knew by hear

'There is only purity. We do not question purity'. She knew where he would take her and although she always pulled back and tried to wriggle out of his grip she knew that she had no choice. *He will read the words again. He will tell me that I will understand the words as I grow, that they are mysterious and beautiful.* She knew that they held no mystery or beauty for her, that somehow they meant something that she did not want to understand. She would rather watch butterflies and run in the rain.

'There are things we don't do,' he would say 'it is forbidden' as he dragged her towards the chapel.

The air in the cold and dimly lit wooden chapel was damp. 'It smells' she said. Her father's grip on her wrist tightened as he pulled her suddenly nearer and slapped her face with a single sharp slap. 'Remain silent' he ordered in a harsh whisper. 'Kneel!' he began the familiar ritual. She knew enough to kneel in front of the first picture without being told but he always repeated the same words, always pushed her to her knees at the same spots in front of the pictures.

The pictures are the best part of chapel. They are carved into the walls of the building low enough for a child to see as they kneel in the hollows smoothed out by the knees of other children before them. Her father's voice droned in the air over her head as he read from the missal panel above each scene.

'On another continent, in another time, the first community lived a life of peace. This community allowed itself to become corrupted. The good and pure escaped in twelve white and golden ships. For many months they sailed across treacherous oceans. Eight ships and many lives were lost, dragged into the depths by the terrors of the deep.'

Ria could see the ships and the ocean but, as so many times before, she screwed up her eyes to peer into the wavy lines searching for the terrors of the deep. 'Where are the terrors?' She has always wanted to ask. 'What are they?' but she had learned to remain silent.

Each time her father tapped her shoulders, she stood, bowed to the picture and moved to kneel in front of the next. *Grandmother knelt here once* she told herself as she slid her knees into the smooth and reassuring indentations in the floor to gaze at the next picture. Monotonously her father's voice continued the story.

'The last four of the white and golden ships reached sight of land but were lured onto deadly rocks by the beguiling songs of jealous sea dwellers.' *Beguiling songs of the sea dwellers. He spoils the beautiful words with his rough voice.*

And there were sea demons. I wonder if the sea dwellers and sea demons ever came into Sanctuary.

'Only the truly pure survived and reached the shore, pursued to the very edges of the tide by terrible water demons who dared not step out of the water onto this sacred earth. Here the few discovered the Sanctuary of three circles. Here they set about building a new community. Here they devised the Rules of purity. Through purity they earned protection from the evils outside Sanctuary.

Ria looked at the three rings that represented Sanctuary wondering why she didn't feel safe.

'Stand up Ria' her father's voice was louder now 'and come with me'. *And now the rules* thought Ria as he led her further into the chapel to a heavy wooden table where a large book lay open as if waiting for them.

'I will read the rules and you will repeat them' as her father spoke his voice began to return to what Ria called his dream talk.

'The rule of purity will keep us clean, strong, and safe from the dangers outside Sanctuary.' Ria did not need him to read the rules. She knew them. They had practised them every evening for as long as she could remember.

'We will remain inside the rings of the Sanctuary Trees at all times. We will protect ourselves from the contamination of wild creatures. We will shelter from rain and cover our skin to preserve it from wind and sun. We will keep ourselves clean with water that has been three times boiled. Unboiled water will never be allowed to touch our skin. We will learn to live the example of the committee. The committee will learn from the elders. The elders will learn from the Guardian. The Guardian will lead us in goodness and purity.'

Ria looked up at her father and waited for him to smile and say that her mistake would be forgotten but today he spoke without smiling. 'There is a new lesson for you today Ria' he said. 'Today I have been elected to the committee and from now on your behaviour must never undermine my authority. Come with me.' He led her to the front of the chapel, to the foot of a short flight of stone steps.

'Stand here' he said and it seemed to Ria that his voice had changed. *He no longer sounds like my father but like one of those other men, the elders, who read the rules from the platform at the top of the steps every third day with the community kneeling and looking up at them*

'Kneel Ria' her father said in this new voice 'Kneel, look up at me and listen'.

Something has changed my father, and if my father has changed, everything has changed.

'Be thankful, Ria' he was saying in his new voice. 'I am committee now and one day I will become an elder. As my daughter, you will be honoured. Listen' and he climbed the steps and turned to recite to her the words normally only spoken by the elders.

'The Guardian will oversee safekeeping of the community and its history.

On behalf of the Guardian, the chapel elders will ensure that purity is maintained, that the history is preserved, and the sanctity of the chapel upheld. Each elder will be responsible for one quadrant of Sanctuary and the section of our community living within it.

On behalf of the chapel elders, the committee will ensure that the principles and practices of purity are upheld, that the history is revered and that the chapel remains inviolate.

On the passing of the Guardian the longest serving elder will take on the mantle of Guardianship. The remaining elders will elect a fourth from the committee.

The committee will elect a replacement from the community.

The lessons of history and the teachings of the Guardian will be passed by the elders to the committee and by the committee to the community.

....

So when Ria found the beetle, years later, she told no one. It was the most beautiful creature she had ever seen, shiny blue green it fitted in the palm of her hand and didn't move. *It's dead,* she thought. *I will keep it, hide it in the cellar.* She put it in a small wooden box that her grandmother had given her. *Grandmother is the only one who trusts me.*

She crept into the cellar and tucked the box under a pile of logs. The cellar had a brown smell. *The smell of leaf-mould in the evening.* It made her think of twilight, earth-walking with her grandmother, collecting colours and scents.

'Brown is the colour of peace, Ria. It is the scent of autumn and ripeness. It means that winter is coming and nature is ready to sleep, willing to wait for spring. They sang the rhyme together, clapping hands – their own and each other's in turn.

Nuts to pick,

Berries ripe,

Break the stick,

Burn it bright,

Autumn brown,

Winter white.

Sun goes down,

Long dark night.

Wake again,

Morning spring,

Buds and flowers,

Children sing.

It had been a useful rhyme to share with the farm children when the families came to her father's mill in the autumn with their bags of wheat. At about six years old Ria had become conscious of the farm children. They came in clusters of brothers, sisters and cousins, older ones holding onto younger by the hand or arm. Ria noticed the colour of their hands and feet against glimpses of white ankles and wrists. She quickly learned to pull her clothes down and around herself to cover her own colour. But some of them, older than Ria, remembered her. She picked up their whispers as they approached.

'That's Ria. Her skin is coloured - all over.'

Looking into their eyes she saw fear in some, curiosity or envy in others. In a few she found openness. Usually in a child younger than herself, and this would be the one who enjoyed learning Grandmother's clapping games. 'Nuts to Pick, Berries Ripe' was always favourite because the families would have come to the mill along the outskirts of the autumn forest where they enjoyed their first taste of its fruits.

And Ria learned new rhymes in return.

> Down in the sea
> Where the monsters grow
> Deep dark and gloomy
> Are the caves below.
> They will grab you
> And keep you
> And pull you down
> And where you went
> Will never be known.

....

'Grandmother, are you afraid of the sea?' The old woman straightened herself away from the window and moved slowly to the other side of the fire. Her back was hunched at the shoulders, her long hair was grey and her skin was creased, but there was a light in her eyes and her smile was warm.

'No. What is there to fear? My grandmother took me to look at it once and told me stories of how her grandmother had sailed here with the First Ones.'

'I've been dreaming about the sea. Sometimes I am walking away from you along a narrow path with the sea on either side. All I can see is the path in front of me and the sea stretching away on both sides and I know that you are behind me but I can't turn round to speak or see you because there is only room to walk straight ahead.'

After a brief pause Ria slipped into another of her recurring dreams. Leaning back, her eyes half closed, she spoke as if she were only partly awake.

'Sometimes I am down by the sea with steep cliffs all around me and the tide is rushing in. I know I have to get up the cliff quickly - before the tide fills the cove and drowns me. But the path is too steep and sandy, I keep slipping back down and I have to drop all the things I want to bring with me so that I can use my hands to grab at roots and pull myself up.'

'Do you listen to your dreams, Ria?'

'Yes. I know I must listen, but these dreams are difficult. Thinking about them frightens me. When I was young you talked about my dreams and helped me understand them. Can't you help me with these?'

'You do not need me to help you with your dreams now. Listen to them yourself. When you are ready you will understand. You remind me of when I was young - always asking my grandmother questions. Instead of answering them she sang and it was a long time before I understood how her songs could help me find the answers I needed.'

Grandmother began to sing. The tune was simple and melancholy. With each verse, she wove harmonies that echoed around the room and seemed to fill it with an ancient choir;

The deep sea is peace.
Beyond the rocks is peace.
After the storm is peace.
Deep in the soil the forest is rooted in peace.

Beyond the rocks is peace.
After the storm is peace.
Deep in the soil the forest is rooted in peace.
The deep sea is peace.

After the storm is peace.
Deep in the soil the forest is rooted in peace.
The deep sea is peace.
Beyond the rocks is peace.

Deep in the soil the forest is rooted in peace.
The deep sea is peace.
Beyond the rocks is peace.
After the storm is peace.

Between verses, Ria and her grandmother sat, patient and quiet. Wood cracked in the fire and an occasional bird called as it swooped across the clearing around the hut.

'You would have loved my old grandmother, Ria. She told me stories of the land before sailing, taught me sea stories and old songs. All her life she waited for news of more ships but they never came. When I was young I thought I might see them but now I understand and I realise it will be you.'

Straightening herself slowly away from the window the old woman moved slowly across the room to the fire to sit opposite Ria. Without looking at her she picked up a stick from the hearth and began tracing patterns of sparks into the black soot on the stones. 'Time for you to go now.'

She knew. She knew I had been going out of Sanctuary to see the sea. She wanted me to go. Wanted me to see.

....

Seeing the creature dragging itself out of the darkening water had been terrifying. She had gathered the ground-sweeping folds of her dress up above her knees and stumbled away. *I shouldn't have seen it, shouldn't have been here.* The teachings of chapel and committee were in her ears.

'The dangers of the sea; The multitudes of creatures which swim in its fathomless depths; Waiting to pull their victims down; Down until their lungs fill with water and they become too heavy to rise.'

Now she was running with the strangely exciting taste of salt still on her lips, her hair thick with it and her limbs heavy and slightly sticky. All these sensations hovered at the back of her mind as she struggled to run. She might be faster if she pulled off her dress but she felt - for the first time - the need to keep it on, covering her, keeping her safe.

Seeing this creature had disturbed something in her, but Grandmother sang of peace in the sea. *I have seen something I should never have seen. And did it see me? And is it following me? How far can it move from the sea? How fast? Perhaps this is a new dream. Perhaps I will wake, hot and sticky in musty dark. But no, the pain of breathing is too real in my chest and the thump of my feet on the floor hurts right through me. I must keep running, must reach Sanctuary, into the trees, and then I will be safe.*

She dared not look back until she had reached the first ring of trees and scrambled up the bank to Sanctuary. Exhausted she could run no further. Leaning against an ancient trunk she slipped to the ground and sat trying to quiet her breathing, terrified of being heard. As soon as she could breathe easily, she turned to look back from the shelter of the forest edge and the earth rampart and a chant from the chapel came back to her,

'Leave the Sea
Be safe within the Circle
Away from the sea
Live within the Circle
Sanctuary Circle
Save us from the sea.'

Perhaps it would be better if I had never seen the sea – just gone on swimming in the river and stayed inside Sanctuary. Perhaps I should have taken more notice of the teachings in chapel.

....

'Ria, what are you doing?'

'Just thinking,' *Thinking about when I was a child* 'Remembering things.'

'Of course,' her mother's voice softened a little. You are right. Take time to remember your grandmother. You know

24

that once we have taken her to the chapel, and said goodbye, things will change. Her hut will be removed. You will no longer have an excuse to go to the edge of the forest. It is time for us to think about your future. Make some decisions.' Her mother was sitting on the bed, looking into Ria's eyes.

'This is a difficult time Ria. The community is struggling. Of course you must remember your grandmother and all the things she taught you. She taught me too but then I chose to join your father and help him run the mill. She never really forgave me but I think she understood. She lived in the past Ria. Things have changed. You need to be here now.' *But I am here. I don't understand you. Why did you leave grandmother in the forest and move to my father's mill?*

'I know you think I was wrong. You think I should have stayed in the forest with her but there was no future there. Now I wonder whether there is a future here. People are saying the committee is looking outside Sanctuary. Your grandmother said it would happen but I never believed her. But then I never thought I would see buildings falling into their own foundations. Something is wrong, Ria. You must stop living in a dream world and face reality. If you leave it too long no man will choose you and then what will your future be? I want you to have these last days to grieve but after that you must wake up.' *Mother has never been out of Sanctuary. Never seen the sea*

As soon as she was sure that she was alone Ria slipped quietly out of her room, into the mill. No one paid her any attention. *I have to go there one more time. I cannot say goodbye to grandmother in the chapel. She will be waiting for me in the forest, by the river, by the sea.*

She stepped out onto the top of the staircase that spiralled around the outside of the building. There was a hint of sweetness in the breeze that lifted her hair. The mill was one of the community's tallest buildings and from here she could see the other side of the river and across most of the town. *So strange to look out across the town and see holes where there were once buildings. And now they will remove grandmother's hut. Why take a building down deliberately when some are slipping to the ground and no-one knows why?*

She walked around to the other side of the mill and looked to her right where grandmother's hut, the last old hut as many call it, was hidden by trees. The land from the edge of grandmother's forest on her right to the dangerous rocky fall to her left was the farmland. On the river plane the fields were green with ripening crops while on the slopes she could just make out the cattle and sheep. Around it a ring of tall pine trees marked the inner circle of Sanctuary. Beyond them Ria knew there were two more rings and beyond Sanctuary lay the sea.

Trailing her fingers along the wooden walls, feeling the familiar dry roughness of the boards, she made her way down the stairs to the yard. Jumbled phrases wove through her mind. She made no attempt to order her thoughts or quieten her senses.

How would the community manage without the mill? And how would the mill run without the river? Water is good enough to grind their grain. There's that sickly smell again. It turns my stomach, makes my heart beat too loudly, starts that rushing in my ears. It is the town. I would never be happy in the town. The edge of town. Across the stream. The oppression is lifting. They say they keep clean but it is cleaner here.

Fresher. As if the trees clean the air. The rain cleans the forest and runs into the river. The river runs in from outside Sanctuary through the forest, through the three rings, down to the sea. Save us from the circle. Sanctuary Circle. Away from the circle I slip into the sea. She was running now, tears and rain mixing on her face. *Salt and sweet. Goodbye Grandmother but you will never leave me completely.*

She ran to the waterfall pool but did not stop. *Not here? The sea then. Through to the outside, outside Sanctuary, Down the slope of one ring and up the next, through the pine trees where it's always cold and dark and nothing ever grows.* She slithered down as sunlight broke through the clouds and the rain stopped. *It's so close to them all and yet they never see it. And it is so beautiful, so powerful, so real Are you here? I know you are here. I feel the pebbles shifting under my feet. Grey pebbles, grey, grey, grey. One white round pebble Grandmother. This one white round pebble is different from all the others. If it was at the bottom of the sea it would shine and sparkle.* Ria picked up the pebble and, in a sudden and powerful movement she threw it into the sea. It arced through the air, caught the sun, glinted briefly then slipped silently into the waves.   On an outcrop of smooth grey rock she stopped, pulled off her boots and clothes and ran into the sea.

Grandmother, that was for you.

2

New Hope

'Ria, it is time.'

Watching her mother over the last three days Ria has been surprised by her quiet strength and dignity, rising early to go to the clearing in the forest, returning at dusk, saying nothing of what she had done there.

'We have been to the chapel. The women are waiting for you.' Together they go out and stand at the top of the mill steps. A large group of women has assembled, mostly her mother's age, some older. A few she recognises as childhood friends. *The women who came to her for help. They came to her with questions and she answered them with more questions. They came to her with their dreams and she listened.* At the front of the procession four older women share the weight of the woven rush basket. *So small.*

Ria and her mother join the procession, taking their places one each side of the basket. A familiar scent surrounds them. The fleeting sensation of being in the right place, of everything being right. *Grandmother's smells – herbs, leaves, berries* and then the sorrow. Their hands hover over the basket then rest on it as the women begin to move, singing quietly,

The deep sea is peace.

Beyond the rocks is peace.

After the storm is peace.

Deep in the soil the forest is rooted in peace.

The air is full of their harmonies. Ria walks as if in a dream. She had not known what to expect and yet each step now seems so natural, so inevitable. They make their way to the edge of the burial ground. The grave is ready and Ria finds herself standing opposite her mother, clasping hands across the terrible space as the basket is gently lowered. *Into the ground.*

....

'Ria, you are a woman now. No longer a child.'

He waits.

'Ria?'

'Yes father?'

'Are you listening?'

'Yes father.'

'And do you understand?'

'I think so.'

'I blame myself for not speaking sooner. Your mother and I agree. It is time to think of your future. There are things you must give up. Things we should never have allowed. When you were a child we allowed your grandmother to look after you. Now we see that we let things go too far. You knew the teachings. We took you to chapel. But we should have done more'

Grandmother taught me swimming, running in the woods, feeling the sun on my skin.

'Things are changing, Ria. *Their voices are different. Something has changed* From now on you will come to chapel every evening. You will take your place in the community and keep the rules of purity.

....

In the chapel, the first elder moves to take his place in the carved pulpit above them.

'On another continent, in another time, the first community allowed itself to become corrupted.' There is a murmuring, a shocked raising of heads. *The elder has made a mistake. Only the Guardian is permitted to speak these words.*

'No, I am not mistaken. Our Guardian has instructed me to inform you that there has been a sign. He wishes to speak to you of the importance of the moment.'

Few are able to contain a reaction to the breaking of a tradition that has sustained the community through generations. There is shuffling. Someone coughs. The elder bows his head and steps backward from the pulpit. As if the walls had opened from a secret place at the heart of the chapel, a figure appears. Dazzling in white robes with golden embroidery he raises a hand and gestures to them to sit.

Transfixed Ria remains standing; staring at the gleaming purple brooch he wears to fasten his cloak. *The beetle. My beetle. He is wearing my beetle.* A rough shake on one and a fierce pull on the other bring back to the present.

'Sit down' her father hisses. *Why am I trembling again. Am I afraid? Excited? Something strange is happening.*

The Guardian is speaking. 'Throughout our lives we have striven to recreate the life of peace and light enjoyed by the first community, protecting ourselves against repeating their mistakes by adhering to the rules of purity.

'But you yourselves have seen a sign. Three of our most important buildings – buildings at the very heart of our community – have been taken from us, dragged down, disintegrated at our feet. There is an evil force at work here. The dangers outside Sanctuary threaten us. We must be extra vigilant in the shadow of impurity. Keep yourselves pure.' *Am I impure? Will they search me out? How did they find the beetle? What else have I done? Have they seen me swimming?* Ria gathers her cloak and tries to cover her wrists and ankles. *I cannot stay but where could I go?* 'And there has been another sign, seen only by your Guardian and Elders, telling us that the time has come for us to share knowledge of Sanctuary's history with you so that you might understand.' *Grandmother was right when she said there were things we were not being told. Like the stories she learned from her own grandmother.*

Our true ancestors lived across the ocean, in a warm, dry place where food was plentiful and they knew no fear. They worked with a great river, farming, sailing, even fishing. Some were hunters. Some gathered the fruits of the forest. They loved music, sang and told stories. They had no Guardian, no elders, and no committee. Men and women, old and young, would meet to sing and talk and listen and then make their decisions.

'But somehow a seed of evil was sown in their midst. One small group, who revered physical strength above all other qualities, began holding their own meetings. The rest of the community was not troubled. They were happy. They felt safe. As the group grew it took on the name 'Power'. Power began to disrupt decision meetings with intimidation and violence. They raided farms and storehouses, stole provisions and livestock. The community responded with peaceful resistance. Farmers were killed as they stood in front of their homes. Terrified children were hidden in cellars while their mothers offered themselves in an attempt to save them. The community realised that Power had taken control. In a brave and final meeting representatives were elected to sail in search of a place where a new start could be made. Most of the chosen were young and strong men who had enough experience of sailing to crew the ships. Where wives were willing they accompanied their husbands. Children old enough to contribute to the work that would be necessary went with their parents. Younger children remained with grandparents. To each of the twelve ships that sailed, the community appointed a member to a committee whose wisdom and knowledge would be invaluable to those creating a new beginning.

Somehow, after many months at sea, the ships approached new land. Many lives had already been lost. Young men and women had lost their senses and jumped overboard. Illness and accidents had killed others. One ship sank in a terrible storm. As they approached the land they encountered savage rocks that tore great holes in the ships and many more died. The survivors, our ancestors, swam for their lives, crawled out of the waves and made their way inland.

'They believed they had encountered a miracle when they crawled into three rings of trees standing on high circles of earth. As they recovered they found that they had found a place which could provide everything they needed; food, shelter, safety. They called it Sanctuary. At first they returned to the sea, to search for anything washed up from the wrecks. They dragged everything into their new Sanctuary, tools, clothes, boxes, books. But as time wore on they found less and less until only broken, rotten, reminders of their terrible experiences at sea were washed up. Occasionally they would find parts of human bodies, barely recognisable, tangled in seaweed, covered in flies. The sea, and water, came to represent fear and danger and they devised ways of protecting themselves from it. These became the rules of purity.' The Guardian continues but now there is a different tone to his voice. 'Through our understanding of the history your elders and I have known that there would one day be a sign and that the sign would come from the water. On your behalf we have kept watch on the edges of Sanctuary, along the rivers and the sea shore.'

They saw it too.

On your behalf, I have consulted The Book of Guardianship and I offer to you now the portents that I have discovered: It will fall to a small group of courageous individuals to lead us forward. The greater the fear we conquer, the greater the gain. Look again at the place wherein the sign arises for that place will hold the key to the future however much it fills the soul with dread. That sign has come.' Backs stiffen. Hands reach out for reassurance.

A ship was sighted and from that ship a stranger has made his way into Sanctuary. He is the sign we have been waiting for since the beginning. And because he sign came from the sea, it is clear that we must rise above our fears and the dangers of water. It is in conquering the sea and all that lies within it that our future lies. The Book also teaches us:

"There will come a time in every community when change is unavoidable;

A time when fears must be set aside,

A time which calls for a courageous few to lead by example,

To lead their people into the future"

'And this time is fast approaching. The time when Sanctuary will not be enough. The time when we must look to a new beginning. We must prepare ourselves to leave Sanctuary. There is to be a ship. This ship will be our New Hope. Have no fear. Though I will remain here, an esteemed Elder will be selected to lead our courageous people. He will sail on this ship as Guardian to the small community which will sail in search of a new Sanctuary. Soon we will all sail to a new homeland. It is time for courage and strength. A few must go ahead. These few must be strong and pure. They will seek out and map the route on behalf of the community. They will establish a new beginning and we will follow them.'

Taking three steps back the Guardian disappeared into the darkness. People breathed again, tried to avoid being seen looking around at their neighbours, friends, family. All four elders now stood in front of them and spoke in turn.

'It is time for courageous action.'

'We will search out purity and strength.'

'The committee will select, from the good and pure.'

'Those chosen will go ahead to find our new Sanctuary.'

The next day a crowd hovers around the notice board. People linger. Ria watches as they came to talk, wait, walk away, return. It is almost dark by the time the square is empty and she can go down to read without meeting anyone.

To the good and pure of our community

Understand that the Guardian has seen the sign

On the instruction of the Guardian

under the guidance of the Elders

your Committee offers the following information

There is to be a New Beginning

Yallah

It is time for a courageous journey into the unknown

Preparations are under way and selection will begin
immediately

Anyone wishing to be considered

for the voyage to the new beginning

should make their wishes known to the committee

*I will tell my father. He will speak to the committee. They
must let me go.*

3

A New Beginning

Many weeks later, Ria finds herself in a small boat being rowed towards the New Hope.

These are things I have dreamed of. Boats and men who know how to sail them. This huge beautiful ship. I thought the sails were white but now I am close I see that they are brown. They hang from ladders that reach the sky. And are those men climbing amongst the? So small they look, and boys at the top, standing in the air. Their shouts are like bird calls. And the sea, creasing and murmuring, creasing and murmuring. Full of secrets. Leaving Sanctuary. Leaving my parents. Will my mother be strong? I know she believes this is right for me. My father, so pleased that I am leaving, no longer worrying about committee calling on him to explain something I might have done.

'Time to stop dreaming, miss, and climb aboard. Gather your skirts. Second Captain Taylor will meet you at the top.' This Second Captain watches her negotiate the sloping plank. *Have I seen him before? At the mill? In chapel? Wasn't he a committee member?* Then he is shaking her hand and leading her straight to a small wood-lined room.

'Please sit down.' She sits on a wooden bench. He sits facing her, behind a desk. *Everything fixed to the floor.* 'You are Ria, I believe? I am Taylor. Second Captain, but everyone knows me as Taylor. There is much you need to know but I have little time to talk with you as we are in the midst of preparations to sail. I understand you have been ill. We almost sailed without you. The other women have had three weeks of training on board. I will introduce you to Jen. She will guide you during your first days but you will have to learn quickly if you are not to be in the way. A ship can be a dangerous place to someone who doesn't know her. *Her?* Opening a small drawer in the desk he takes out a bell with which he summons a young sailor.

'Yes sir.'

'Bring Jen.'

....

'Some of us sleep in hammocks, some in bunks. The bunks are down at the other end of the hold. I know bunks sound better but it's four to a bunk. At least we get a hammock to ourselves. How old are you?'

'Seventeen.'

'I thought so. Most of the women are about our age, a few younger and just ten or so older, I suppose they thought we might need their help at some point. The hammocks are slung at night, before dark. You sling the head of the hammock to this hook. The hooks are cranked down so that you can lower yourself in. In the morning roll your bedding, lash in into your hammock for stowing. They are numbered so that you can find your own. Yours is a hundred because you are the last to arrive. Mine is at the other end of the hold. Remember to recrank the hook in the morning otherwise someone gets a nasty knock on the head and they won't be best pleased with you. *She speaks as if she has been on a ship all her life. Has she learned all this in three weeks? How will I learn it all? She moves on so quickly.*

'Remember to mind your head everywhere you go and use the rope handrails. The sailors say 'One hand for the rigging and one for yourself.' They mean when they are climbing but it applies everywhere. You soon learn to walk without tripping. Never bump into a sailor.'

Learn the bells. Continuous ringing is fire. If you hear it make for the women's deck. Go there if there is a fire, if we hit rocks, it's called Anchor Stations. Any time you hear 'Anchor Stations' get straight there. One bell sounds the beginning of our day. Eight bells is supper.' *The ship is as big as three mills. It creaks and sways in the same way. It smells of must and damp and tar and baking.* Jen moves confidently and never stops speaking. *So much to learn.*

'This is where we eat. These planks come down off their hooks for tables. The spike fits into the socket to hold it firm. This is the pantry.' *Sweet smell of hot fresh bread.* 'One of us comes here to collect the food. After we have eaten the table and forms have to be stowed and the deck swept. The lifting was impossible at first but we're already used to it. They say the commander wants us all to learn as much as the men so that we can be useful if there's a need. *Where is everyone?*

'Up these steps to the decks. I expect you're wondering where everyone is. They are all in the school room. Kierle speaks to us there every evening. The men call him the surgeon but he was a chapel elder and is to be Guardian when we reach land. This is our deck, for air and exercise. The men are on the other side of the ship.' *I've never seen wood like this before, so hard. And white. There must be hundreds of ancient trees.* 'We wash and polish the deck every day. Everything is inspected. 'Every morning the same worries. Every evening the same problems' is what the men say. Further up there are decks with cabins. They are for the commander. Taylor has a cabin, and the surgeon. I don't know who else.'

Ria goes to the rail and looks around in all directions. She sees land, already further away than she ever expected to be. She knows that somewhere amongst the unfamiliar sweep of trees and mountain is the remains of her home but she feels no connection. *So many questions. But I won't ask them yet.*

'They call that Sanctuary Bay,' says Jen, 'They say it is where our ancestors crawled from the sea. You can't see any sign of the community can you? No-one would know it was there. The highest trees that you can see up there are supposed to be the first ring. I don't know. Anyway all that hardly matters to us now. Down again. Gather your skirt. Hold the rope. *Great knotted ropes everywhere. Why all these ring and bolts? What are these huge rolls?*

'These are the screens for separating spaces. The canvas is rolled up and fastened to the beams when we are not using them. This stair leads down to holds. That's where everything is stored and the animals are kept down there.' *I can hear them, smell them. They smell of fear.* You get used to the sound of them, and the smell. We don't go down there. We see Zak sometimes. He looks after the animals. The rest of the men stick to the other stairs, on their side of the ship.

'Eight bells. That's supper.'

Instantly the ship comes to life. There are shouts and sounds of movement from all directions. *Like the mill, people on every side, people below me, people above me.* Ria and Jen retrace their steps, passing the pantry where people are already queuing for food, men on one side and women on the other.

'Sit here.' On the table are bowls of a meat and vegetable broth and fresh bread. As women arrive Jen introduces Ria to a few but it is clear that their first thought is of food. Even before they are sitting on the bench they have taken a portion of bread, broken it apart and taken a mouthful. They eat as they slide their bowls along the table making their way along the bench.

'Let's sit,' says Jen. Ria follows her, taking a bowl and a small chunk of bread and they slide into place along the bench.

'You'll take more than that tomorrow,' says a woman opposite them and others laugh in agreement.

Ria is struck by the way the women eat. Their noise, and the way they eat and talk at the same time are so different from what she is used to. At the mill everyone would be standing quietly under her father's watchful silence while her mother served the food with slow and careful movements. The mill workers would be quietly passing plates down the table to the youngest new arrival. Only when her father, last of all, had his food in front of him would they lower their heads and wait for him to lead them in the prayer.

'We eat.'

'In Sanctuary,' they replied.

'We work.'

'In Sanctuary.'

'We live.'

'In Sanctuary.'

'Give thanks then for life, work and food.'

'Thanks be to Sanctuary.'

Even when they looked up again, they waited. Once he was seated, they would sit. Once he had begun to eat, they ate, but no one spoke. When her father finished eating, everyone else would stop and wait for him to speak.

'On behalf of our committee, elders and Guardian, I thank you for another day's work in the mill. It is thanks to you that our community has flour for its bread each day.'

Only as he led his family out of the hall would murmured conversation begin. As they made their way up the spiralling wooden steps towards their own living quarters the voices would be rising and Ria would wish she could still be down there joining in the conversation, enjoying the laughter and the occasional song.

Now, snatches of conversation and laughter break into her thoughts.

'No ceremony, no hierarchy, no waiting.' *They are laughing at my thoughts.*

'Don't worry we all thought like you at first. You soon get used to it.'

'So we're supposed to wait for them to make a choice. *Another conversation further along the table* That doesn't stop me looking.' More laughter. 'They're not going to choose me anyway.'

'You hope!' someone shouts in reply causing louder laughter still. Someone else is asking Ria a question.

'What about the buildings? Have any more collapsed? Have they found out what causes it yet?'

This is greeted with loud laughter from several women sitting nearby.

'We know what causes it…' and, amidst lots of laughter, several voices answer in unison:

'Impurity.'

'So has it stopped now they have got rid of us?'

'I'm sorry. I've been ill. My parents have been so determined to get me well enough to join you, I haven't been allowed to leave my room so I haven't seen or heard any more than you.

A slightly older woman leans over the table towards Ria holding out a hand in greeting, 'I'm Nan,' she says. 'Aren't you from the mill? This must all seem very strange to you. But don't worry you will soon get used to it.'

'She'll have to,' the sarcastic voice again 'word is we sail tomorrow.'

'That's Nina,' says Nan. 'She always has something to say'.

Nina continues 'If anyone has any idea of staying behind, this is your last chance to say so.'

Many voices murmur at once.

'Not me.'

'I can't go back.'

'They wouldn't have me.

'So let's make the best of it,' says Nina loudly.

Jen puts a hand on Ria's shoulder. 'We should go and get your hammock slung. It will take you a while to learn how to do it as quickly as the rest of us.'

In the sleeping quarters they find that Ria's wooden box has been brought down. She kneels to put her hands on it and begins to close her eyes but Jen is impatient. 'Open it up, we need your sheets. We must get this done and go straight to the schoolroom. We only have a few minutes while the others are on deck for a last breath of air. Normally we have an hour on deck after supper but this evening we have been called to a meeting. There will be no time later.

Just as they are finishing Ria's hammock two bells sound.

'We must go.' Jen turns abruptly away and Ria follows. Hampered by her long skirts and layers of petticoat she finds it difficult to keep up with Jen's swift movements. She trips on the stair but Jen does not turn back. It reminds her of following her mother to chapel, not wanting to go. Wanting to pull off her clothes, run in the woods, dive into the pool and swim in the river.

She was seven years old again, walking to the chapel with her mother. *It's so tall, so thin. It's trying to reach the sky.* 'It's moving' she whispered.

'No, it's not moving. The clouds are moving. The chapel will never move.'

It seems they are last to reach the schoolroom. The canvas dividers have been fastened up to create a space large enough for the entire ship's company to assemble. Benches have been placed in tight rows. Women are sitting on the right, men on the left. Seeing the men together she realises that they are all dressed in plain white shirts and brown trousers and that the women are all in the long white gowns that she was given before coming on board. Ria follows Jen to sit near the end of the last bench she cannot help feeling like a child again. All dressed the same, the layers of white petticoats. She remembers swinging her legs and feeling the weight of them, imagining peeling them off to run into the river. She remembers not being able to reach the floor unless she stretched her legs, her ankles, her toes; gazing up into the roof, a maze of ladders and platforms reaching up, up. *I wonder who goes up there*

'Ria! Were you listening?'

'Yes sir.'

'Repeat the rule for water.'

'Water must be boiled before touching the skin.'

'Good. Why do we boil water Ria?'

'Because water collects imp, impru, imper…'

'Impurities! Speak clearly girl.'

He is angry now. I must be careful. 'Because water collects impurities. We boil the water before it touches our skin. We boil the water to keep ourselves clean. Water is dangerous. Water must be controlled.'

He moves to question another child. *He is wrong. At the pool near the waterfall, the water is full of bubbles and light. It sparkles and when I swim I feel clean. I feel good. It feels right. I like the smell of the cold earth and the taste of the stones. And grandmother says that scalding the water steals its life. Holding it in barrels makes it stale and tired.*

'Ria,' Now she hears her mother's voice

'Ria,' And now a man speaks, in a hard and authoritative tone, 'Please Ria.' *He is trying to soften his voice.* 'Stand up. We would like to welcome you.' Ria stands and looks around at the women who turn their heads to nod, some smiling encouragement, then turn back to listen to Kierle. The men move in their seats and look first at Ria, then at Jen and then at other women. Their eyes move from one woman to the next until Kierle coughs loudly. As they reluctantly turn their attention back in his direction, Ria sits down again. Someone else has slipped quietly in and is sitting next to her. *A man? No, boy. It must be the boy who looks after the animals. And he doesn't care which side he sits.*

'I'm Zak,' he whispers, 'and this...' He nods towards the man who stands at the front, 'is Kierle, so called surgeon, Elder and our Guardian.' The man in front of them is tall but stands slightly bent, curved at the shoulders *as if for years he has tried not to show how tall he is.* He is older and thinner than the other men on board The New Hope and wears a long blue coat over his white shirt and brown trousers. Even his grey hair is thin. She notices that, where his face is covered by wispy grey beard, the sun has reddened his skin in the weeks on board ship. He appears unsteady as he reaches for the lectern that has been placed there for him but as he speaks he begins to stand straighter *as if his words give him strength.*

'Tomorrow we sail for the future of the community. Behind us our Guardian, elders and committee will lead a celebration of your great courage. At a feast in the Great Hall your names will be read from the panel which has been carved in your honour. You are the New Hope, which gave this ship its name. It is a great honour to have been chosen. The future lies with you.

'It is my duty to remind you that we sail in order to save the community from the impurity that had made its way into Sanctuary. The decay of our buildings was only one of many signs. Your Guardian and elders knew that a time would come when it would be necessary to leave Sanctuary and when the final sign came and they consulted the Great Book they found there the strange truth that had always been there, but, being unlooked for, had never been found. They learned that they must turn their thoughts to the sea. The sea, which had delivered us once, to Sanctuary, will deliver us again.

'And when they pursued this new knowledge, looked deeper into the histories of our people, even before Sanctuary, The Book spoke of the mastery of water and the power of wood. Previously this had been taken to mean our great skill in the building of bridges and buildings such as the mill. But now it was time to look again and among the few precious books in the cased library was found a book that spoke of shipbuilding. We had never needed this book before. But its time had come. And in the final chapter of this book we were told to be patient and look to the sea.

'When our Guardian saw the sign, he understood that it was time to select the courageous men and women who would be entrusted with the most important venture since our ancestors left to seek out Sanctuary.'

Now Kierle is standing up to his full height. He grips the lectern with both hands and looks out over their heads as if he is addressing someone far behind them. His voice grows steadily more forceful and his speech slows so that his words have a songlike lilt.

'And you are the selected ones and this is why your families will be honoured and rewarded. This is why your names have been recorded on the walls of the Great Hall. We are embarked on a great journey. I will be with you to guide you in guarding your purity. And that purity must be guarded above all else for the sake of the future.'

His speech ends but he does not move. He seems fixed in his stance at the lectern, gazing at a point above their heads, breathing deeply until another man, in a long blue jacket and trousers and a white shirt buttoned tightly to the neck, stands up and approaches him. This man is shorter, stronger looking with dark skin. He is clean-shaven and his long curly brown hair is held back from his face by a narrow scarf.

'The Commander,' Zak whispers.

'Ah, Commander,' says Kierle turning away, 'Please,' he hesitates, 'I have... that is I was... no, no, of course, you must speak to them.'

Now Ria sees the ship's commander for the first time and is aware of many things at once. Against the creaking of the ship's timbers and the murmur of the sea she hears a seabird's cry. She smells damp wood and tar and in the flesh of her right hand she feels a splinter of wood from the bench. She licks her lips and thinks *salt* as she sees the captain move forward to speak to them. *Who is he? I hadn't noticed him there before. Was he sitting with the other men? He is different from them and it is not just his clothes. His skin is darker. His hair is longer. He is strange and yet I feel I know him.*

He coughs, a dry cough, holding the back of his hand to his mouth.

'It is a good evening. I have wanted to speak. Forgive me. I should have spoken before and it is important that I do speak.' His words cause the women to exchange glances but the men do not react. 'It is important, this evening.' He coughs again, pauses, stands slightly taller and begins again. 'This is an important moment.' He looks directly towards the women. 'Particularly for you. These men, they have sailed before. They are good men. Good sailors. They are in... they know their ship, your ship, your... New Hope. They helped to build her. You are in good hands. She is well built. *Why does he speak in this strange way?* 'We sail on the... morrow.' There is a murmur and a shifting in seats. I have seen you learning and you have learned well and everything is prepared. You are prepared. Remember all things that you have learned these three weeks. If you are willing there is more that you may learn.

'Now, before we sail, consider your confidence in the sailing. No one should sail who does not wish to sail. Here is your time to speak should you wish to return to your community. I understand that there will be fears. We will sail as swift and safe as the air and the sea will allow.' His speech is interrupted by a bout of coughing which causes him to turn away for a moment but as soon as the coughing passes he turns back towards the women. 'You may not always be comfortable but I believe you will be safe and I believe we will reach a place for you to live and where your family and community will follow.' He turns to Kierle who has been standing beside him. 'Thank you, Mr. Kierle. That is all I wish to say.'

The commander leaves the lectern and, as Kierle holds out his hands as a sign for the men and women to bow their heads, he makes his way between the two rows of benches. As he reaches the back row he notices Ria who is now the only person not bowing her head. While Kierle prays and others answer their eyes meet briefly.

'We will protect ourselves.'

'Through purity.'

'We will defend ourselves.'

'Through purity.'

'We will continue this, our journey to the future.'

'In purity.'

....

By the time they reach their sleeping quarters it is growing dark. The women are undoing the buttons of their long white dresses and petticoats as they walk. They step out of them and, moving freely in their long underwear, open their boxes to lift out their sheets. Ria watches them prepare their hammocks. *They move without needing to think* then pick up their clothes and fold them into the boxes. From somewhere above them comes the sound of a bell and an indistinguishable shout.

'Prayers,' whispers Jen. Ria Follows the example of those around her. She kneels and bows her head. At the sound of another bell, they rise, slip off their shoes and lower themselves into their hammocks.

Ria attempts to copy the women who, all around her seem to be sliding effortlessly into their hammocks while hers swings wildly away. Two women step over and take hold of the hammock.

'Don't try to climb into it,' says one.

'Reach up and then lower yourself in,' agrees the other. 'You will soon learn.'

'Thank you,' she whispers. 'When will the lights be out?'

'We never have lights out,' someone replies 'in case of emergency, a fire or such like. It keeps you awake at first but you soon get used to it.'

All around her people are curling up and falling asleep. Beyond their coughs and snuffles she can hear the animals moaning and kicking and the calm voice of a young man. She cannot make out his words but pictures him reassuring them and enjoys the calming voice. The animals settle. Even their smell is calmer, less sour. *Warm scent of animal skin. How will I ever sleep? If I move I will fall out. The ship moves and creaks more than the mill ever did. And what is that whimpering sound? Someone crying? Or is it the sea? Or some creature in the sea? How would we know if the ship had a leak and it was the sound of water creeping in to drown us all? To drag us to the depths? No, that way nightmares lie. Relax my body, inch by inch as mother taught me in these last weeks. Toes, relax. Feet, relax. Ankles, relax. Slipping into sleep. Slipping into....*

....

It is early morning and the first bell has sounded. Women emerge slowly, leaning against the wooden walls for support. As soon as Ria attempts to sit up her hammock rolls over. She clings to it and although she cannot prevent herself slipping out she manages to lower herself to the floor slowly. *They will be laughing at me, even if I do not hear it.* 'Don't worry,' a voice answers her thoughts. 'It has happened to every one of us.'

Twenty five women sleep in an area barely large enough for ten. In the space between the hammocks there is only room for one person to stand. Each woman has learned to wait for her neighbour to move before she can climb carefully out. Everyone wants to escape the hold where they are surrounded by wood that smalls damp and feels cold.. Wooden floor, ceiling and walls crawl with their own terrors at night. Stomachs roll with the movement of the ship and every step is a balancing act but they must escape the stale air of their sleeping quarters.

A few have learned to cope with the constant movement, but the foul air, the barely stifled groans and the bitter smell of sickness drives out everyone who can move. First they make their way to the wash bay. Those who arrive first drop the canvas screens to create tiny private spaces. Water is strictly limited but each woman takes a small bucket to a wash space. The rituals of purity are changing. Washing so near to another person would have been unthinkable in Sanctuary but here there is little privacy. Just a few weeks ago they would have carefully uncovered and washed every part of their bodies in the strict order laid down by the rules of purity, carefully replacing each item of clothing with clean linen or cotton before removing the next. This morning several women drink from their water ration before they begin. Only a few take a clean item of underwear from their boxes. As Ria watches she finds thoughts, questions, possible answers jostle for attention in her head. She looks for Jen but another woman is approaching her, holding out her hands in greeting.

'I'm Nan.' She speaks very quietly, *not quite a whisper but as if she is being careful not to draw attention.* 'We met last night and I think I know you, from before, but don't worry about that now. Take some water; there is only a little, wait for a washing space. No-one will bother you there as long as you are quick. You will want to wash. You are still used to feeling clean. That's fine but others are forgetting how that feels. They only want to drink the water. Some of them splash their faces but...' She is leading Ria along the row of canvas cubicles. 'Here's a space.' Nan has stepped forward and is holding back a flap. 'Take this one. Don't be long.'

Inside Ria enjoys feeling alone for a moment. *How do they manage living so close to each other, breathing each other's breath, hearing each other's thoughts? And I must manage it too. And purity? Have they given it up so lightly when I have struggled for so long. Perhaps I am no more impure than them? Perhaps* 'Ria,' Nan has remained nearby 'Are you ready?' *So soon? I have not washed at all.* She tastes the water. *It has not been boiled.* She drinks and remembers her grandmother's words, "Boiling it steals its energy. Boiling it twice robs it of life. Boil it three times and it is dead water" but Nan is gently pulling back the curtain.

'Sorry Ria, but if I didn't do it someone else would. They won't wait. We have to get the screens up before we can go on deck and everyone wants air before breakfast.'

On deck the women remain silent until the salt breeze ruffles their hair and gowns and they begin to feel awake. Some go to the rail to look back. Already they are so far out that the bay, which had seemed enormous, and had come to feel like home, is anonymous in the sweeping curve of land. They stretch their arms and legs and arch their stiff backs as they watch the tree covered hills disappear. Others pay no attention to what is behind them. They loosen their hair, bending forwards to run their fingers through, untangling knots, then twist and pin it back up. Around Ria small groups of women meet, clasp hands and move silently to the ship's rail to gaze back. Ria sees Nan approaching two young women who appear to be twins. They are doing their best to comfort a third whose face is streaked with tears. On the other side of the deck an older woman silently hugs a young girl.

Jen approaches, *her lips are smiling; her eyes are not,* holding out her left hand. She takes Ria's hands and holds them together as she speaks. 'It's a beautiful morning Ria. I have been up here longer than most. Already the sun is warm.'

Ria looks up and sees birds circling. She strains to hear their calls in the fresh blue sky, watches them playing, wings spread to gather the breeze which lifts them and carries them briefly backwards.

'Did you sleep?'

'A little. It's hard being so close to so many people. I'm used to being alone.'

'Especially when so many are sick. We have to go back later to sweep up the sawdust and put down fresh. Did I tell you that you will be in my work group? If you feel ready to go to breakfast I can introduce you to Nan and the twins.'

'I've met Nan already. What about prayers?'

'Oh, he will be there waiting to lead prayers before we can eat.'

They make their way across the deck and down a short stair to the women's mess. The women are standing behind the benches, waiting. One group has already been to the pantry and brought them milk and bread. When Kierle comes in all heads turn in his direction. No-one speaks. He inclines his head slightly and stands with arms outstretched, fingertips resting firmly on the table.

'You will bow your heads.' He coughs. *Why does he cough in that dry, unnecessary way? I will bow my head. He cannot know my thoughts.* The surgeon-guardian speaks slowly. 'We will protect ourselves.'

The women respond. 'Through purity.' Each picks up a small piece of root from the table. He waits, watching, as they chew. *Moon Root, Grandmother told me about it, said I would have need of it soon, I didn't believe her but of course no woman would want to carry a child during the voyage.*

'We will defend ourselves.'

'Through purity.'

'We will continue this, our journey to the future.'

'In purity.'

'And now, I commend our new companion to your safe keeping.' He points at Ria and says her name but Ria feels that he has already forgotten her, 'Ria.' The women repeat her name as if responding to something they have heard many times before and are no longer interested in the meaning of his words.

Kierle has raised his eyes and seems to be speaking in a dream. 'Already we have sailed beyond the horizons of the old community. You have learned the ways of the ship and now you will learn how to live at sea. Our commander will ensure your physical safety. Follow his instruction to ensure that the New Hope delivers us to a New Sanctuary.' He slows his speech and raises his voice 'But it is I who will ensure your safety from the unseen terrors that surround us by guiding you in the careful use of purity. From the teachings of the great book and the knowledge entrusted to me by our Guardian in Sanctuary I will lead and you will follow.'

He straightens his back, *grows taller*. 'In purity we travel.'

The women respond 'In purity' and as soon as he turns to leave they step over the benches and sit down. Some lean across the table reaching to pick up a loaf of bread and pull it apart. They pass pieces to those around them. Others pick up a small jug of milk, pour themselves a little and pass it on down towards the bottom end of the table where Jen is introducing the women sitting closest. 'This is Nan,' *I remember her now, the daughter of a baker, older than me but I remember that she liked to play with me when I was still quite young. I remember seeing her at Grandmother's,* 'and the twins, Meera and Beth.' *Are these the same twins who saw me swimming once? I had been to Grandmother's hut with flour, milk and honey and stopped at the pool on the way back to the mill. They are the twins grandmother told me about. The first twins she had managed to deliver.*

'You are the fifth in our working group. This morning we work, tomorrow it will be education while the others work. Mostly it's a case of sweeping and scrubbing but we have been shown how to splice together the broken ends of parted rope and there is talk of us learning more of the ship's work.'

....

Life on the ship reminds Ria of the mill. Every morning the decks are swept, then on their hands and knees, the women scrub the boards of their decks with a large stone sliding on a mixture of sand and water. After rinsing the upper decks dry quickly but on an order from the commander water is kept to a minimum on lower decks to keep them as dry as possible. Even so the very low decks are permanently damp. As Ria scrubs and polishes she is transported by the scent of the wood and snatches of song from men working somewhere above her. She is back in the mill, the steady rhythm of the wheels turning, men singing in time with their work, the scent of the dry wooden floor rising to meet her as she bends to sweep. She is coming down in the morning to the smell of the bread her mother has baked to sell during the day, always keeping a sweet fresh roll on her plate, a mug of fresh milk sweetened with honey, and an apple or a bowl of nuts.

Food on board is a stale dried up version of what she is used to. They know that there will rarely be bread now, just ship's biscuits, and the milk is watered down. Many of the women are happy to drink the pale, watery ale they have been offered but Ria has not yet acquired the taste. Mealtimes are an opportunity for the women to share any information they have gathered about the ship, the men and their journey. Ria listens.

'They say the commander is not from the community at all.'

'That's why he speaks so strangely.'

'So where can he have come from?'

'He has to have come across the sea. How could anyone in community ever have learned to sail a ship? It's not possible. We were not even allowed in the water.'

'I think there will be many more things for us to discover. Things we would never have guessed at. I'm sure the Guardian and his elders, even the committee, selected information to pass on to us.'

'To keep us safe?'

'Or keep themselves safe. I don't know. I'm simply saying there is a lot more to know than they chose to show us.'

'So what about the commander?'

'Well if he's not community he might know things they don't but there will be things he doesn't know too. Things we have grown up with that he hasn't.'

'So who makes the decisions? Kierle or the commander?'

'Well, Kierle rules us. He teaches us whatever he chooses for us to know.'

'But he will not be able to make decisions about the ship, the voyage.'

'Then they must do it together. They make decisions then Kierle teaches us.'

'Is it just the two of them do you think?'

'Well Taylor is known as second captain and I've heard them calling Russell number two. Those are the only names I've heard. The others are called 'men' just as we are called 'women'.

'There's Zak.'

'He's just a boy.'

'Important though.'

'Because he looks after the animals?'

'Well that would make him important wouldn't it? Meat, milk, eggs, it all depends on him.'

'Not that we get much of it.'

'They can't kill the animals just for us to eat meat. They need to start building up herds when we reach land.'

....

4

Dreams and Memories

Lying in her bunk at the end of her first day aboard The New Hope Ria finds it impossible to sleep and is listening to the whispers of those around her.

'How long will we be on this ship? It's beginning to feel like a prison.' 'How many terrible nights must we suffer the impossibility of sleep? Lie listening to the groaning of the ship, snoring women, and the terrifying sounds from the sea?'

'Sometimes I am sure I hear creatures calling to each other, sometimes they are singing, sometimes crying.'

Perhaps this is my punishment. Was it my fault that the mill was destroyed? Was it my impurities that began the destruction of the community? Is that what my father meant? No wonder he hated my bad dreams, all my dreams, but that last one most of all:

She had woken in the dark clammy night, shocked by the sound of screaming, and realised that it was her own voice. The fears she has been keeping deep inside were breaking out and she was screaming with the pain. *Stop screaming.* But it did not stop until it had woken her. Holding a hand firmly across her mouth she stopped the screaming but could prevent the trembling or the moans of fear which crept up from somewhere deep and dark. *So hot, damp under these covers. They stick to me, but I cannot throw them off – cannot let the darkness touch my skin. It is just a dream. It's holding me down. It knows my name. Calling me.*

'Ria, Ria.' *It speaks with my mother's voice.* 'Ria, wake up.' *There is no space between my mother and fear. Tears. Huge soft salt warm tears. Up once more, through one more layer of fear. It is coming up from the hiding place through another layer of fear. It has taken my mother and still growing. Mustn't let it out. Don't let it out. Don't tell.* But fear has started telling its own story.

'A beetle.' She heard her own voice 'I found it at the edge of the forest, on a piece of old wood. Shining blue, green, purple. Hard as stone.' *Stop. Stop telling her.* 'I couldn't leave it there.'

'What did you do with it, Ria?'

Don't tell. 'I didn't even tell Grandmother.'

'Tell me. Wake up and tell me.'

'I wrapped it in a clean cloth and put it in a wooden box. Then I hid it under a pile of boxes and books in the cellar. In my dreams it tries to get out. It whispers my name over and over again.' *Mother's cool fingers on my face. Am I awake?*

'It's another dream. It will be gone by the morning. Don't worry, Ria. You have been ill. It was the shock of your grandmother's death. But I think it is over now. This will be the last of these dreams.' The lamp flickered in the cool air as her mother opened the window. 'I'll leave the lamp.' She turned Ria's cover. Cool cotton against her skin. When she was alone again, cooler, calmer, Ria slipped quietly away from the bed to sit at the open window enjoying the breeze and the calls of the night birds. *It's just a bad dream.*

When she woke, late in the morning, her parents were waiting for her. They watched her drink warm milk sweetened with honey. She had not eaten since the day her grandmother died. Her mother spoke softly. Her voice wavered a little.

'Your father is ashamed of you, Ria. He is angry that you think of no-one but yourself and disobey us so lightly. You are no longer a child. There are many things that must stop. It is not only that you have been going into the cellar. There has been talk about you. That you run in the rain, take your clothes off in the woods. There is terrible danger in behaving like this.'

Then her father spoke, quietly but in a voice trembling with anger. 'Show us your skin' When Ria hesitated he spoke to her mother in the same voice. 'Make her show us.'

Gently her mother took hold of Ria's wrist and turned back a sleeve. Her sigh, at Ria's weather tanned skin, was barely audible. 'Ria' she began, but was interrupted.

'It is true then.' His voice was louder now. He was almost shouting at her mother. 'You knew she was breaking the rules of purity and you allowed it to go on. I trusted you but you have turned out to be little better than your mother and this is her fault.' He turned to Ria. 'Surely you must realise that it is your deceit and guilty conscience that causes these bad dreams? This is impurity at work. No more talk. You will take us to the cellar and we will see what else you have been keeping from us.'

They went down in silence. As they approached the cellar door Ria heard singing and hesitated. *The dream. Was there singing?* Impatient, her father stepped forward, lifted the latch and pushed the door. A rush of warm, sickly smelling air met them. A high-pitched hum swept out of the dark, surrounded them, and then seemed to gather in a cloud before spiralling upwards. Dizzy and nauseous they stood with their hands covering nose and mouth. The sickly scent lingered. Her father shook his head and pulled himself up to his full height before fully opening the door. Instead of stepping inside he groaned then turned to face them. His face was grey and his voice was weak, 'Back!' he barely whispered. As they stepped quickly back the ground trembled and seemed to groan *like the sigh of a forest. He will want us to run.* 'Run!'

Ria ran, tripping on the hem of her skirt, snatching it up without stopping. They ran away from the mill but could not resist stopping to turn and look back. Spreading upwards from the cellar doorway a change was crawling over the building. A web of fine lines spread over the walls as if the building was creasing from its foundations. The tracery surged upwards and out, gathering momentum as it climbed. A living net, whose strands pulsed slightly then swelled to meet each other like a slow moving liquid, engulfed the mill. The building slipped slowly into its foundations with a thunder that subsided to a whispering rush of sickly sweet air.

It is the sound of the ocean rolling against the hull, tilting the ship. *Another dream* Ria's hammock sways in air that has turned sour with sickness. Her groans are lost in those of the women around her.

Lying here in the sour smelling darkness she knows it is morning because she has heard the drumming which calls the men. They have risen with the sun and soon a bell will summon the women. Curling into a tight ball she pulls the white sheet up over her head to seal herself off from the humid, stale air of the other women's breathing. Only partly awake, she lies, waiting to be born into fresh air and sunlight. Her dreams cling to her like smoke with their sickly scent, images of squirming decay and the furious sound of buzzing insects. How did she come to be here?

5

Reality

The bell summons her to crawl out of her cocoon and into reality. Reality is hard to escape on board the New Hope, sailing towards the unknown. Stumbling out of their bunks and hammocks women make their way to water. Some have finished washing are lashing and stowing their bunks. It is difficult to feel clean in these surroundings but she has her grandmother's armour to protect her; memory and imagination. As she splashes herself with cold water she is back in the clearing, beside the mountain stream spending hours climbing in and out of its freezing water, her body tingling with the sudden changes of temperature. *Grandmother?* "Keep your body clean enough girl and learn how to shield your mind. Then you are a fortress."

She pulls on her long white robes wondering whether the commander and surgeon might relax the rules, let them wear fewer clothes, even alter the skirts into short trousers. It would be much more practical on deck, particularly as they learned more skills and shared more of the work.

....

In the two weeks of sailing the evenings have grown lighter. Now that it is warm and light after supper the women return to the deck to sit together sharing memories of their families and the community, telling stories, singing. *Strange that knowledge they discuss is from stories and songs. Things that they were forbidden before everything changed. Before the buildings started to slide.*

'Is it better or worse?'

'Abandoning the rules of purity?'

'Or adapting them to our new circumstances.'

'You sound like Kierle.'

'One of the older women, Elizabeth I think her name is, I heard her yesterday, saying she was falling apart. Everything she believed in being taken away from her and that was all that had been holding her together. She said she felt impure. She's over there now, with the twins. I think they're trying to help her but…'

'I always found myself feeling impure anyway. My mother said I would never be able to live up to the teachings.'

'I suppose that's why they selected mainly younger women. It's easier for us to accept change.'

'And these girls, coming over now, some of them of them are still children. It's hard for them too, in a different way. We have to look after them.' Three of the youngest women on board join the group, continuing their own conversation as they sit crossed legged pulling their skirts firmly around their ankles.

'Like the way they had to choose who came and who didn't.'

'Which rule to keep and which to forget.'

'Never forget the rules,' says someone Ria recognises but cannot name, someone who had visited both her mother at the mill and grandmother in the hut. 'We will need to re-establish purity in the new community.'

'Why? We have to manage without it now, why would we go back to all the rules and restrictions?'

'Everything will be different then.'

'It's different already.'

'Nothing will ever be the same again.'

The women are drifting into lines ready to go down to prayers and breakfast.

'He calls it prayers but it's just a chance to threaten us.'

'To keep us safe.'

'Keep us pure.'

....

The New Hope seems to smaller now. They have adjusted to days which last from first light until dusk, and spend as much time as possible out in the sea air. The acrid stench of sickness has now virtually disappeared from their sleeping quarters, replaced by the tangy sweetness of the fresh sawdust they scatter every morning. Only in the hour before dawn, when Ria lies waiting for daylight has the air become sour with the smells of bodies, trapped in the middle decks thickened by the stink of sheep and pigs kept in the manger below them. Morning prayers have become less and less frequent although Kierle continues to meet half of the women every morning for education sessions and they have learned that he passes on the same information to the men's groups in the afternoons.

This evening the women are on their deck, sitting in groups, their talk has drifted in and out of past and present. They are asking each other why they came. 'I came because my father wanted me to come.' A nodding of heads, murmurs of agreement.

'I didn't want to come,' says another made anonymous by the approaching dusk and the lowering of voices. An uneasy atmosphere is developing. Women glance over their shoulders as they speak. They want this conversation, are hungry for it, but do not want to be overheard.

And Zak has joined them. Zak's skin is dark and his hair is almost white. He wears trousers cut off roughly at the knee and has torn the sleeves from his shirt. He never wears shoes. He runs along the decks and jumps up to swing among the rigging. Ria longs to swing up there with him. She wonders whether he could swim for hours in cold water with her. She watches him now as he listens intently to the women telling their stories. *Soaking up their words* He often sits with the women in the evening until they are given orders to return to their quarters.

Ria realises that someone is telling a story she has never heard before. In the fading light it is difficult to see who is speaking and she does not recognise the voice.

'The Ocean Moth is a creature so rare that few have ever heard of it. Still fewer believe in it. *I have seen creatures that no-one else has seen; ants, beetles that Father didn't want me to see, didn't want me to know.* But it is real. I have seen it.' No-one else speaks. Steadily the ship rises and fall, rises and falls. Masts and rigging creak and an unseen seabird cries in the evening air. 'Its eggs are washed up on the shore amongst the seaweed left on the strand line. The tiny creatures inside can only wait for the tide to return. They feed on the salt water which soaks through the soft egg shell. If the tide does not reach it again within the next day the egg will dry out and the creature will die. Each tide moves it further up the beach and each movement means new danger, the risk of being washed away from the weed which keeps it moist while it grows. As long as the sea covers it twice each day, as long as it lies under moist weeds while the tide is out, it feeds and grows and each tide pushes it higher and higher up the beach.'

Enchanted by this creature, Ria feels her heartbeat quicken. Her pulse races, and the sound of her own blood pounds in her ears. *There are creatures in this world that we know nothing about. Creatures that swim or fly, creatures that call or sing. The sea is full of secrets.* 'Eventually the highest tide leaves the weed stranded in the sunlight and it begins to dry out. Now the creature must fight for its life. It must wriggle out of the shell before the egg dries out completely. A tiny, grey, wriggling thing emerges. Only one in a thousand survives. It will eat the shell that has brought it ashore. It searches the seaweed, swallowing the flies that live in it and finally eats the weed that has been protecting it from the drying heat of the sun. Now it lies perfectly still, drying and hardening until it resembles a jewel, shining black, glinting blue and green in the sunlight, purple in the moon.

'By the time the next spring tide reaches it, it has hardened until it is impossible for any man or animal to break. It is a jewel cocoon, hard enough to float and be carried out to sea where it will be warmed by the sun and washed by sea and rain. Slowly it swells to the size of a man's head then splits open to release the ocean moth – its slender body reflects the colours of the ocean and its wings shine like a silver sunrise.

'The moths are so delicate they are almost invisible. They are carried up, away from the water by warm currents of air, towards the sun. As soon as a male's wings are dry, it turns and swoops back towards the sea in search of an emerging female. He crushes her moist wings as he mounts her and she plummets back into the sea, leaving a trail of fertilised eggs in her wake. Unfertilised females escape to fly towards the sun while the males turn towards the shore to hover over the young delivered by the tide.'

Ria carries the story to her bunk that night and sleeps soundly for the first time since they sailed. In her dreams she is visited by a woman she cannot recognise and yet she is familiar. The woman stands on a stone plinth in the moonlight. She holds out her arms sweeping light in arcs across the night sky. Her hair shifts in the changing lights like so many horns, a crown, and a tangle of weeds. The light swirls where arcs of possibility collide – disturbance, colour, new light. Below her waist a mesh of net protects already strong thighs. At her feet lie fruit, flowers, jewels, and new born creatures. She wakes refreshed and hopeful.

At breakfast the women are asking each other questions, discussing possibilities as they eat the dry biscuits and watered down goat's milk sweetened with a little honey. Ria resists the temptation to slip back into the past, and listens. 'I hope that when reach our new home the days will be warm, the sun will shine, and rain will fall at night.'

'And we will be allowed to live without all the old rituals.'

'Do you think they will allow us…?'

'How will we be pure?'

'We *have* lived without being pure by living on this ship.' Jen often dominates the conversation. 'We all know the old rules. Keep pure, keep safe; to wander away from purity is to seek out danger and once lost you may never return.' But we did not wander away. We were led. The committee, the elders, the Guardian - they led us here.'

'We followed.'

'Willingly.'

'Words!' Nina's anger erupts, 'Try thinking for yourselves instead of all this talk of being led. There is no purity. We are never safe.'

While they are clearing plates and bowls, stowing benches and sweeping up crumbs the women hear the whistle that calls them onto the deck for exercise that the commander has introduced and as they climb the steps Ria's skin prickles.

On deck they breathe deeply and stretch their arms, their legs, their backs. With hands on their waists they circle their hips first one way then the other. They raise their hands in turn, backs arched, a leg stretched out behind them. Zak jumps down from the rail of the deck above them, landing close to Ria and Jen who are exercising together.

'Zak,' says Jen in acknowledgement

Zak grins, 'Jen.' Then turns to Ria and smiles. 'Ria.'

'Zak. How are the animals?'

'Trapped. They don't like it and I have to keep them calm even though I don't like it either. At least I can come out here, climb the rigging, and breathe the air. The only time I can bring an animal out is if it's dead.'

'How do you do that? Keep them calm, I mean?'

'Talk to them, feed them the right things, milk the goats gently, that kind of thing. You can come down and meet them if you like. It would do them good to hear a woman's voice.'

'I'll do that.' Suddenly a chill on the back of her neck tells her someone is watching, Ria turns swiftly and for a second she is surprised to see no-one there. Taylor steps up to the rail of the upper deck and stands waiting as gradually everyone becomes aware and turns to look up at him. He raises his right hand to silence them. 'Mr. Kierle will speak to you now. You may sit if you prefer.'

The women at the front gather their skirts and sit on the deck. This movement spreads back until most are sitting. Preferring to stand Ria steps to the back, Zak on one side of her, Jen on the other. A few of the others remain standing. They face Kierle who stands with the rigging behind him reaching towards the sky.

Ria remembers a visit to the chapel with her father, seeing that the elder who climbed the altar steps, was wearing a beautiful beetle shell on his purple gown. The purple seemed to turn to the colour of night as he reached the top of the altar steps to stand in the light of the window. On either side of him, painted angels flew towards heaven. Angels are like dragonflies, she had thought, as they fly up out of the water. But he had been warning about the dangers of water. 'For there are terrors that creep and crawl in the depths.' He was chanting the Word from The Book or 'Turning words into spells' was what Grandmother called it. The words closed in around her. 'For the terrors in the deep may crawl out towards you. Desiring to drag you down. Stay within the Sanctuary circles. Away from rivers and sea. Collect and boil only rainwater that falls through the light of the sky and use it to keep yourself clean. Keep your skin covered. Keep yourself pure.'

'How do they know about the terrors of the deep?' she had asked her grandmother one evening.

'From stories about the early ones. They say that on their voyage they heard voices from below their ships, deep in the ocean, calling to them to jump into the water and drown themselves. Some of the women jumped over the side of the ships and were never seen again.'

'Why did they jump?'

'Why would a woman jump from a ship into the ocean?' *Grandmother, answering question with question.*

Now it is the surgeon who stands before them and he too has a beetle pinned to hold his gown closed across his chest. He looks directly at Zak.

'You may leave us.' He waits until Zak has gone before speaking again. 'As you know I am here to guide you with the words of The Book and the teachings of our Guardian. I am here for you to turn to if a need arises. Always remember the teachings of the chapel:

'Through purity we save ourselves.
Through sacrifice we purify ourselves.
Through the long dark night we save ourselves
So that light may come again.

'As you know, when we reach our destination, we will begin the task of establishing a new community. As the first step in that task, the process of selection has begun. It is proposed that matches are made and agreements drawn up between individuals while we are still on board The New Hope so that marriages can take place immediately we reach land. The commander and I will, of course, make our selections known first.'

Ria flinches. *As if a bolt of lightning hit me.* The hair on the back of her neck bristles. There is a shifting of bodies on the wooden floor. Women stretch, curl their legs under their long white dresses, some lean against each other. There are murmurs, smiles of encouragement are exchanged, a hand gently rubs a back as someone groans. Ria struggles to remain calm in the face of a strong desire to shout questions at the surgeon. Uncertain whether she has understood, she remains quiet, listening and watching. She is aware of the scent of bodies around her, warm with the musky sweat of a day already hot in the sun.

'You didn't know?' Jen's hand is on her arm.

'Did you?'

'Yes, it was explained to us in the training weeks, while you were ill. Those who didn't agree lost their places and others were introduced. I assumed you had been told.'

Kierle has moved away and there is excitement in the women's voices.

'Which of them gets to choose first?'

'And who will they choose?'

'What if it's you they choose? Which would you prefer?'

'I would take either,' Nina says with a laugh. 'Who wouldn't? What about you, Jen? Who would you prefer?'

'Not either of them.'

'I don't believe that. You wouldn't say no to being up there, with a cabin of your own, fresh food. Who knows what privileges they might have to offer?'

'And what would they want in return?' asks Jen with a shudder.

'What does any man want?' asks Nina loudly. Some laugh with her but Nan replies in a serious tone, 'Not all men are the same.'

Nina's voice is tinged with anger. 'In my experience there's not much to choose between them.'

It is the twins, Meera and Beth who answer her. They speak together, their voices in harmony: Beth's is low and confident; Meera sounds younger, slightly breathless.

'Women are not all the same,' they say together, 'Why should men be?'

'You are young,' says Nina dismissively.

'Sometimes the young say things their elders may have forgotten,' Nan responds.

'And experience teaches us to forget,' says Nina, 'Jen is right. Whoever is chosen will be expected to earn their privileges.'

6

Choices

That night Ria lies awake wondering who will be chosen. *Jen and Nina? They seem to stand out amongst the women. Or Meera and Beth?* From far below her, deeper than the holds, somewhere deep in the ocean, she hears a sound which is a calling, singing cry. A creature is rising up through the water and others answer its song. The ship is surrounded by their strange birdlike voices and now they are calling her name, calling her up onto the deck. Her feet seem to glide over the boards as she makes her way up and over to the rail.

'Ria.' They call from darkness below her.

'Ria.' The answer comes from the other side of the ship.

'Why me?' She tries to call but her voice is silent.

'Why her?' shouts Nina as the other women crowd the stair behind her. 'Why her? Why her?' they chant. The women move slowly towards Ria. *They want to push me over* and their chant has changed 'Why you? Why you?'

Why me? Because I love the water, because I can swim. She leaps onto the rail and up into a high, curving dive towards the water where the creatures are calling her name but she wakes in her hammock with their calling still in her ears.

....

Zak is questioning the women: 'So how was it that you all agreed to come away from the true path? To sail over the home of evil, the dark resting place? What made you agree to this arrangement?'

'There was a sign' says one of the women.

'We always knew there would be a sign' takes up another. 'In all the womens' stories there was always a sign. When the buildings began to collapse we knew it was a sign that things were wrong. The committee had warned that some of us would need to face our fears to save our people.' Jen turns to question Zak in return.

'How is it that you don't know?' she demands, 'Where have you been?'

Zak is undaunted. 'My family lives outside the circle. We farm animals out there and no one ever bothers us.'

Ria is both excited and disturbed by Zak's reply. A shivering mixture of curiosity and apprehension disturbs the group. Questions are fired at him

'How could you live outside the circles?'

'Wasn't it dangerous?'

'How did you come to be outside?'

'Many hundreds of years ago when our people arrived from across the sea, my ancestors were there with yours but when committee ruled that everyone should live entirely within the three circles we chose to say no. The committee ruled that we be given a hundred years to change our minds. Their reasoning was that it would take a hundred years for the great trees to reach maturity. Within that time we would be allowed to come in as we realised our mistake. After that the tree circles would mark the boundary of Sanctuary. Everyone inside would be kept safe from the dangers of sea, forest and mountain. Anyone who chose to live outside would have to fend for themselves.

'We were happier outside the circles than we would have been in. My people are outdoor people. We live by farming land and sea. That's why I was brought on board. I look after the animals below deck because my family are farmers. I live with sheep, cows, goats and pigs. I understand them and they trust me. And I am not afraid of the sea. I know of its power but I also know that it is not evil.

'When I was young I spent my time swimming, climbing trees, exploring the mountainside with sheep and goats. I would never have been happy inside your Sanctuary - however safe I might have felt.

'You may never have questioned the amount of meat and grain available, but do you really think it was possible that you could provide enough for yourselves and the committee on your small area of fields and meadows? We provided them with meat and fish in return for flour and certain tools we could not make ourselves.

'They ate fish?' Nan's incredulous voice breaks the silence.

'Oh yes, as long as we caught it, they would eat it.'

'Living outside I was able to watch the ship being built. We knew things must be changing inside the circles because we knew your rules about leaving Sanctuary and about your terror of the sea. We knew about the signs too. We were waiting for them ourselves. We knew that there was one sign that we would see even before the committee, and I saw him first. My mother told me what to watch for. She used to say, 'A man will crawl from the sea,' and she sang about it'. Never has anyone reminded Ria so strongly of her grandmother as Zak while he is singing

'We saved ourselves from the sea.
We dragged ourselves from the sea.
We lost our ships to the sea
But when a man crawls from the sea
We will turn, turn, turn again
We will return to the sea.'

'So you're not really from the community?' says Nan.

'You're different,' someone adds.

'Different and yet the same,' say Meera and Beth, laughing.

'Maybe everyone on board is different,' suggests Nan.
Everyone is listening now.

'Perhaps they chose us *all* because we were different in some way. Perhaps they needed us to be different, if we weren't we wouldn't have come.'

'Wouldn't have volunteered, you mean?'

'Or been put forward,' Nan answers. 'Not all of us volunteered you know. The committee invited my family to request a place for me.'

'You didn't want to come?'

'I wasn't given a choice is all I'm saying. The committee invited me, my parents agreed.'

The women move closer together and speak more quietly, 'So it was a trap?'

'For me it was escape.' Jen is trembling. She speaks quietly and her voice wavers. 'I couldn't see any other way out of that community with its crumbling buildings and the committee trying to pretend they understood everything, controlling us, keeping us inside Sanctuary, lying to us about what was outside.' As the other women turn to her Jen seems to gather strength and she speaks with growing confidence. 'This is our chance of a different life.' *The rush of air, looking down, dizzy from the height, eyes wide open I see the whole – water, out and out in all directions, reaching only sky arching over ocean, clouds appear; gather and swell out of blue-grey nothing, High above I watch them, I have to get back, concentrate on a single cloud it and rushes up towards me or is it me coming down? down towards the clouds and now I see that each cloud is different, pick one, a wisp of grey-white clinging to itself, changing colour, changing shape, moving, casting a shadow and drawing me to the sea so that I see its greyness is not simply grey; greens, brown, a ghost of purple, a sweep of blue lost under a curling grey wave. Look closely, remember to listen, attention focusing on a tiny speck adrift in the world of restless water – the ship – and on the ship the women and the women are talking, the twins;*

'Well now we are here there is no escape.'

'We could make them turn back.'

'To what? The community is sick. Why go back there?'

'Is the community sick?'

'You think it was just the buildings?'

'Or the committee, the elders, maybe even the Guardian himself.'

'But they were all community once.'

'And we are community too.'

'Not any longer. They let us go.'

'And we don't know where we are going, what is going to happen to us.'

'They must have plans. We can find out.'

'How? Do you think they will tell us if we just ask?'

Jen stands up. 'Maybe they do intend to tell us. We have to know at some point, why not now? Kierle was a committee member, and Taylor, I think he knows something. I've seen the two of them going up to the top deck to meet the commander.

Ria shivers and looks up. *Who's there?* Kierle is standing over them at the rail of the higher deck. Awareness spreads, the women shift uneasily, look up at him, Jen lowers herself to sit between Ria and Nan. In front of them the twins slide closer together. *Fear*

'In a way you are correct.' He speaks slowly, choosing his words carefully.

'Each of you was chosen because you have something special to offer the future. Some of you are physically strong, others have knowledge or experience which will be valuable when we reach land. We will need teachers, mothers, healers of the sick. We needed courageous women who would not be afraid of the dangers that might lie ahead, who could be entrusted with the beginnings of our new community, our children

'Always remember that you are here at the invitation of the committee and that I have accompanied you as Guardian. I am here to look over you, protect you. I have the knowledge we need to keep ourselves pure and safe in these exceptional circumstances.

'I have waited to speak and now you are ready. You had much to learn about life at sea but you have proved yourselves well. I was instructed before we left that a time would come when I could share part of our history with you. That time has come and when we meet in the schoolroom this evening I will explain.'

Jen takes Ria's hand and squeezes her fingers as the women begin to move and the surgeon slips quietly away. They help each other to stand and Ria finds herself guided, by a light pressure in the small of her back, towards the ship's rail. As they stand looking out to sea Jen whispers, 'I wonder where Zak fits in.'

....

'I wondered when you would come.' Zak smiles a welcome.

'I expected it to smell.'

Zak laughs. 'The men smell worse than the animals. I change the bedding often to keep it as sweet as I can. It was bad at first, when it was all new to them and they were afraid but they have begun to adapt. I deliberately chose young animals, they cope more easily. It's a terrible experience for them. Animals shouldn't be kept in the dark, no fresh food, no exercise. I'm hoping we reach land before many of the next generation are born. No creature should be born into these conditions.'

'Why did you come?'

'I wanted adventure and when I heard that they were bringing live animals I realised that they needed me.'

'The animals?'

'Well yes, the animals but the crew too. The committee asked my father but he was unwilling to leave my mother and my brothers and sisters. There are five of them. The committee wouldn't let us all come so I volunteered. They wanted one of us to because they know the animals trust us. We can keep them calm, keep them alive even. They need the milk and meat and on land they will want herds built up. It's not as easy as you might think.'

'So how much do you know about the plans?'

'Not much more than you. And if I were you I wouldn't let on to anyone that you know anything special.'

'But I don't.'

Maybe not,' says Zak as he leads her through his deck, passing cows and pigs chained in rows, 'Look down there.' The cows stand with their heads down, raising just their eyes to follow Zak's movements. The pigs are eating noisily with their faces in a shallow trough. 'They're lucky. They're happy to eat just about anything that comes down from the galley. Goats and hens are pretty much the same. It's the cows that really suffer.'

'Where are the goats and hens?'

'They get the best deal. The hens and geese roost in the ship's boats. There'll be trouble if we need them but I'm hoping that won't be until we reach land. The goats are on the forecastle and upper deck. The commander doesn't mind as long as he gets fresh milk every morning. He has a day cabin up there and I think he likes seeing the animals.'

'Mind your skirts as we go down. I don't know how you women can bear to wear those clothes.' He is leading her down to a sweet smelling hold. 'This is my hideaway. What can you smell?'

She stands still and closes her eyes to breathe in the scents but instantly her stomach lurches and she flings out an arm to steady herself. Zak catches her arm and smiles. *Apart from the twins, he's the only person I've seen smiling since we sailed.* 'Sorry. I forgot. The swell feels different down here. You soon get used to it. Try again. I'll hold on to you.'

With Zak holding her steady she closes her eyes again and tries to identify smells. She knows they are familiar but at first she cannot recognise one amongst the many. She realises that she is smiling herself now. Grass, hay, straw.' *It smells of sunlight, like walking into a meadow. Of course he was right, how could we have thought we were producing enough meat for the entire community. There were so few meadows inside Sanctuary. I only ever saw ten or twelve cows at a time.*

'Yes but what else? Keep your eyes closed and concentrate.'

'Herbs.'

'Can you pick any out?'

'Rosemary, bright balm' *Wonderful, my whole body feels lighter for breathing down here* And something else is happening. Something she does not put into words. It disturbs and excites her as she feels the slight weight of his arm around her waist, the warmth of his body pressing against her back. She wants to go on thinking. She wants to abandon thinking. She wants to turn, look into his eyes, ask him. She turns, looks into his eyes, as she begins to open her mouth he leans forward. *no words* She has no words for his mouth against hers, the warmth rushing up inside, the lightness of his touch, the dryness of his lips. Her body moves without words. Words struggle to regain their power, their hold. What is happening? Words pull her back.

'What?'

'We should bring everyone down here. They would feel so much better.'

He smiles again and lets her go. 'Well, no, on two counts. I can't have everyone down here. For a start they would have to come past the animals and that would upset them and secondly we can't have them all knowing what's down here. You and I are going to need this store of remedies. It has to last the entire journey, and the first few months on land, until we can find or grow more.'

'Why do you say 'you and I'? What has all this got to do with me?'

'Ria, our grandmothers were friends. They linked our communities. The committee knew that they were friends. Your grandmother, Old Ria, lived so close to the edge of the community it was easy for her to slip out or for my grandmother to visit her in her hut. There were many huts originally. The old women who lived in them moved in and out of Sanctuary fairly freely as long as it was never spoken of in the community. It was a useful arrangement for everyone.

The old women held a lot of the ancient knowledge. Things that had never been written down, or else it was in books that were lost with the ships. They passed on the true history of our people. Old Ria must have begun teaching you history and medicine?'

'I thought she was just telling me stories, teaching me songs.'

'Well it's those stories and songs that we are going to need. You can help me with the animals but soon it will be more than that. People are going to need these herbs and our knowledge of them. There are more. I will show you them all so that we can work together. But you must keep this to yourself. I have trusted you enough to tell you but I need to know that you will help.'

I need someone I can trust too. 'I have to think but I will not speak to anyone about what you have shown me here. Give me one night. I will talk with you again tomorrow. I think I should go up now.'

'You go back the way we came. I will go up a different stair.'

7

Information

The women are making their way to the schoolroom *but not so meekly. There is a change. Some of them seem taller, are they moving more quickly, talking quietly, asking questions.*

'How long are we going to be on this sailing prison anyway?'

'What will happen when we get there?'

'Let's listen to what Kierle has to say.' Jen is making her way towards Ria, answering women as she moves through them. She holds out her hands in greeting. 'The men have been summoned too. It's going to be crowded in here.' Zak joins them while Jen is speaking. Ria's body responds to his presence *without words*. He smiles.

The benches have been placed so close together that there is barely room to sit without knees touching the person in front. Taylor moves quietly down the rows indicating that they should move up, sit more closely, make room for the men. As he comes near to Zak he looks closely at the three of them, moves forward slightly, *Is he going to speak? To Jen?* But the moment has passed and he has moved purposefully on, signaling with a raised arm to the men to come past the women to sit in front of them. Zak makes a space between Jen and Ria and they watch the men file silently to their places.

At the front Taylor joins Kierle who stands waiting for silence, stillness. 'This evening I will share with you information which has been guarded by the chapel elders in readiness for this time. You will understand how our community has reached this situation, how we came to be here, why you were chosen, what the future holds.'

'Surely you cannot foretell the future?' a woman's voice calls out and all heads turn to look back towards the speaker.

'I understand that you will have questions but I anticipate answering them without the need for their being asked. Trust me as representative of your committee, the elders and our Guardian. I have had unprecedented access to our history and have studied the Great Book in detail.'

Restlessness begins to build amongst both men and women but Kierle stills it by raising his arms, palms facing them. As soon as they settle he resumes, 'We are sailing to our destiny. It is our right and our duty to continue this voyage in the sure and certain knowledge that we are following what was ordained in the Great Book brought by the first ones. That this book survived their voyage and the terrible shipwreck that threw them onto the shore where they found Sanctuary is testament to the fact that it is the true word.

The first ones were courageous people - scholars and warriors who took their chosen wives and sailed in search of the knowledge. They set out to find proof of their understanding of the great message in the book.

Kierle steps slightly to his left where a large book rests open on a lectern carved in the form of two pairs of wings each with a series of intricately detailed veins reaching out from the spine becoming ever finer, so carefully carved that they seem to fade into invisibility.

'The truth is present

And is available to all.

All who have retained purity

As it was given in the beginning.'

'As you know, our predecessors tried to demonstrate the truth but found themselves surrounded by people who were impure, who preferred to live outside the safety of the rules which would keep them in the truth. They had turned their backs on teachings. They were lawless, did not recognise their ascendancy over beasts, their ownership of place. They spoke to animals, worshipped creatures for flying and swimming. They lay with wild beasts. They ignored the supremacy of walking upright, refused to acknowledge ownership of the seas, forests, hills and valleys. They worked with the base and evil nature of the animal world and called upon creatures and elements to turn against us. They would have forced us out but we had already decided to leave. We took to the sea knowing how to keep ourselves safe through rules of purity.

Even so the creatures of the deep tried calling, particularly at night, inducing madness in some, the weaker ones who jumped into the sea. Of course we are no more created to swim than to fly and it was easy for the creatures of the deep to drag them down, drowning them in front of those strong enough to resist. And as those courageous men and women sailed on they carried the cries of their drowning friends and the singing of the creatures in their dreams and memories. They knew that as soon as they found land they could escape the power of the sea and the influence of the terrible creature that lived there and, from that time on, protect themselves from the water and its evils.

Imagine their joy at the miraculous discovery of the three rings of trees. This was the single most powerful sign that they were on the right path. Driven inland by the knowledge that they must escape the sea and the evils that live in water they had discovered Sanctuary, offering them protection. Proof.

They toiled, and it was long and hard that they worked but they built a place of safety for themselves and their children. They added to the trees on the earth circles knowing that this was a place of safety created for their salvation. They felled the trees and used the timber to build simple shelters then more the elaborate committee buildings and the mill and finally the chapel, right at the heart of Sanctuary, which became the safe resting place of the great book. And so I return to the Book for the words which will convince you of the certainty of our endeavour.

'Those of you who know, will know, that you do not need to search, for the truth is safe in your hearts, and others may learn, from your example.'

'It is to us that the community now looks. We sail as representatives of the committee – your committee, your elders, your Guardian. It is not the fault of our people that the buildings crumble. Sanctuary was a temporary resting-place – a place for us to gather our strength. And we have done that. And now it is time for courage again – for the strong and brave few to leave Sanctuary on the next stage of our people's journey. We will find a new haven and the people of Sanctuary will follow us. They will applaud our courage and our names will always be remembered.

We are the ones who know. We are the ones who do not need to search, who have preserved the truth and have been entrusted with the task of carrying the truth to a new beginning.

A man's voice murmurs, 'He really believes it all.'

Someone else calls out, 'If the committee carry the truth why aren't they on the ship?'

'As you know I was an elder myself and it falls to me therefore to carry the truth on their behalf. Holding the wisdom and knowledge makes it essential that they remain in the place created for them, in Sanctuary, until we have prepared the new resting place for the truth. They remain within the central ring to watch over and guide the rest of the community until the time is right for them to follow us. We are the selected ones, chosen for the strengths and skills needed for this unique undertaking. We are creating the future.

Taylor and the surgeon turn together as if to leave but stop at the approach of Russell who greets them with a slight bow before continuing past them. When he reaches the front he stands beside the lectern to speak. 'The commander wishes me to convey to you his assurance that all aboard the New Hope are well, the ship is in good order and our journey progresses according to plan.'

Behind Ria someone murmurs, 'As protection from the deep.'

'It is the commander's wish that I detail some adjustments which will be implemented as from today. It will no longer be necessary for men and women to use separate exercise decks.'

This surprises everyone. Men and women exchange glances. Some smile, others raise their eyebrows. No-one speaks as they watch Kierle turn slowly and return to the lectern which he grips firmly with both hands. Taylor hesitates then follows remaining a step behind Kierle. Russell continues, 'Seamanship groups will be run whenever conditions allow. The trained crew will pass on knowledge and skills to female volunteers. This will enable women to take a more active role in the ship's routines

'The commander wishes you to know that he admires your courage in undertaking this journey, your willingness to learn and your respectful acceptance of his leadership. He sees no reason for separating men and women in either work or recreation activities.'

Kierle is furious. *He didn't know* 'There will be no fornication on this ship.' The women nearest to him flinch as he spits his words in their faces. He does not shout but his voice is fuelled by anger so that his words seem to punch the air. 'purity will be upheld. The New Hope will remain a vessel of purity in order to ensure our safe delivery to the place of the new beginning.'

He seems to grow taller as he towers over them. He raises his voice only a little and speaks with a restrained and lilting fury. His eyes are hard and his clenched knuckles turn white. 'You, who have been selected by the committee, you will remain pure. You, who have been trusted by your community, it is your duty to them to guard your purity. Guard your bodies. Guard your minds.'

Now he begins to tremble and his voice grows louder, 'We are surrounded by evil, with no way of knowing when that evil will strike. Guard yourselves my friends. Keep mind and body pure. You have been entrusted, by our Guardian himself, entrusted with our people's future. The new beginning must be founded on purity.'

Turning to the men he points a trembling finger and pauses to take a deep breath then continues more quietly, just a little above a whisper, 'And it is your duty to deliver these women to our new homeland in a state of purity and grace. If it is the commander's belief that it will be necessary for you to work with them, for our safety and progress, then so be it. He is the commander and we follow his leadership in matters of the vessel.' Kierle is still pointing and as he speaks his voice, still quiet, becomes more forceful. 'But, at all times, at all times, it will be remembered that the responsibility for our purity, and therefore our safety, falls to me.

'Never have our people been closer to the powers that lurk in the deep. Our ancestors proved it possible to survive these terrible dangers. But only the strongest, the most pure, reached Sanctuary. Many were lured to their deaths by temptation, by the calls of those outside the law.' As he leans forward, energy flushes his face. His voice becomes more forceful again but still he does not shout.

'The future of our community rests with you. Yes, of course you will obey the commander. But,' He slows his speech. 'Above all else, keep your selves pure.' He turns and strides away.

Men and women sit in silence, some hesitantly rise, a few filter out, making their way, in unspoken agreement, up towards the open decks. Ria, Zak and Jen move towards the women's deck. Ria feels a strange calm. Words flutter in her head but she does not follow them. Zak touches her arm. 'I think we should listen to what others are saying.'

Ahead of them Taylor and Kierle have crossed the deck and disappeared up another flight towards the top deck cabins. A group of men and women, sitting in a small circle, move apart, making room for them to sit and join the conversation. Meera and Beth are there, a man sitting between them. To the right of Beth, Ria recognises Russell. He catches her eye and smiles. She turns her attention to the conversation.

'Are we to believe that the history we have always been told is untrue?'

'That the committee has lied to us all these years?'

'Maybe not lies. Maybe they were telling us just what we needed to know - for our own safety. For the sake of the community.'

'But what gave them the right to decide what we needed to know? Why couldn't we be allowed to make our own decisions? *At least I feel I have been making my own decisions.*

Nan has joined them. 'The irony of it is, they made the right decision for me in sending me away.'

'We are glad we came,' says Meera. Beth looks at the man on her left as she nods her agreement. The conversation continues.

'But are we safe?'

'We weren't safe there.'

'The community buildings had gone.

'Some say that the chapel history room fell before we sailed.'

'It was only a matter of time before our own homes started to go.'

'Signs.'

'You only have to look at the buildings that went; the committee rooms, the court, the prison.'

'The mill.'

'All the places that ruled our lives.' *The mill ruled their lives?*

'A sign that they were getting it wrong.'

'A sign that we weren't pure enough.'

'So who was it? The committee? The elders? Or the Guardian?'

'What does it matter who was to blame? We have escaped.'

'What about our families?'

'We will send for them once we have built….'

'You believe in the new community then?'

'I believe that we have a purpose on this ship. Look at us all. The kind of people we are.'

'What kind of people?'

'Different.'

'Like being twins you mean?'

'Or outsiders?'

'Not all of us are outsiders.'

'So why would you want to leave?'

'I don't think it will help to fight amongst yourselves.' Russell is talking to the group but looks at Ria.

Zak speaks. 'Russell is right. Let's talk in the morning, see how we feel after a night's rest.'

As others move away, Ria stays on deck in the rapidly cooling air, watching the sun set. *It is only at sunset that the horizon really becomes visible, cutting the slipping orange circle of light smaller and smaller. I could cling to that shimmering sliver of light. It slips away so quickly. At least in the afterglow it is possible to feel that the sea and sky are not one. That we are not simply trapped in a slowly revolving ball of grey – blue nothingness. Strange how, as soon as the sun is gone the air begins to feel damp on my skin and hair. And these clothes are so heavy. And the sea never stops murmuring.*

When she goes down into the warmer air of below decks the smell of women's bodies rises up to meet her. No-one speaks. *Locked in their thoughts.* She reaches her own hammock and lowers herself in. Accustomed to this now she lies still, listening, waiting for sleep. Muttered words, meaningless phrases, sighs. *The air is full of our breath now. We breathe in each other's as we slip, slipping into sleep, surrounded by nothing but sea. But in the sea I could swim. It would be cool and fresh. I would feel clean. My skin turns pink, fingers grow long and slender, hair floating out behind me as I dive, flying, through weed, down to pebbles, trusting fish swim so close I can see the scales ripple along their waving bodies. And what is this sound so deep under water?*

Singing? Calling? Crying? Creatures approaching, turning back to encourage others, calling them on. Some are crying as they come, others are singing, and Grandmother's voice is among them, she is coming with them. Here I am Grandmother, here, waiting for you, look this way and see me.

A young woman near her is crying. Someone has climbed out of her hammock and is speaking softly.

'I know we can't go back, but I want to go home,' she sobs, loudly now. 'I want to go home.'

'Breathe,' says her friend gently.

Another voice 'There's no going home for any of us.'

'What was there at home anyway? It's all slipping into the ground, rotting. It was all going wrong. Things will be better where we're going. We can learn from their mistakes. They made so many mistakes. There is no way of knowing whether Sanctuary will survive.'

'I just wanted to get away from the stink of rotting buildings and the fear that ours would be next.'

'We can't do anything about all that now. All we can hope for is to reach land and make a fresh start.'

....

Arriving on deck for exercise the next morning they find Taylor ensuring order, directing women to the left. *No sign of Zak.* Their preacher, surgeon, Guardian stands before them, silent and still, watching as they bow their heads. Only Ria looks around. The sun is low and weak, just detectable through a cool white mist. She watches it grow stronger on a patch of restless, glistening water and tries to focus on a flickering near the horizon. It could be something solid but the light dazzles her. She squints, tries to look directly at it, but it is gone. Already the mist is clearing, sunlight growing warm, the horizon a low line of lingering cloud. Soon even that will disappear as the sun climbs and dries the air.

At the top of the highest mast *that must be Zak. What is he doing? What can he see?* a flag dances. She watches Zak swing down, and part of her moves with him, down and along the ratlines. Now she realises that he is not alone. A line of surefooted young sailors make their well-practised way to positions along the yardarm and sit to unfurl the sail which disturbs the air with its rippling and a crack. Heads are momentarily raised. Prayers have been washing over Ria unnoticed but this disturbance brings her sharply back to the present and she realises that she has been murmuring responses with those around her.

'Protection from the deep.'

Now she hears Kierle. 'We will stop our ears to the calling of evil.' She should join in the responses but cannot do so knowingly.

'As protection from the deep.'

'We will follow the word of command without question.'

'As protection from the deep.'

The litany continues. All around her, heads are down in the reassuring posture of prayer. *Closing their eyes. Choosing not to see. I choose to look up. I cannot stop my ears or close my eyes. The sails, unfurled and fastened filling with the breeze, moving us on.* And there, watching the young men, all in step, climbing down, stands the commander. *Watching sky, sea, ship, watching the preacher and the people, watching me. We are all being watched. Each one of us.*

Prayers having finished, Kierle moves away and, as the women begin to eat, Zak appears between Ria and Jen. 'Message for you both. Taylor wants to talk to you.'

....

Ria and Jen stand together, holding the rail, looking out to sea. *Sea in front of me, sea behind me, all around me nothing but sea. I think I understand that you are not here to help me but* Mr. Russell approaches them, interrupting Ria's thoughts.

'Please follow me.'

He leads them across the ship into the area reserved, until this morning, for the men, up a stairway. *Different sounds, rougher coughs, louder voices, and smells, heavier, thicker, overpowering.* They gather their skirts automatically, as they approach a cabin on a high, covered deck. His tap on the door is answered immediately.

'Enter.'

They follow Russell as he bends in the low doorway and straightens again inside the cabin. Taylor stands as they enter. He had been sitting behind a plain wooden desk.

'Thank you, Russell. Please wait outside.' He holds out a hand to greet each in turn. 'Jen, Ria, please sit down.' *No furniture other than his desk and chair and these two benches. All secured to the floor. Nothing.*

'I have some important news for each of you to consider. As you know it is planned that on reaching land one of our duties will be to start families as the beginning of establishing a new community. Our children are to be the first generation.'

'Surely,' Jen interrupts confidently. 'There will have to be a period of building, of farming, of hard physical work, before you can expect women to start bearing children?'

'For most of the women, yes,' Taylor replies. 'Please understand, Jen,' he shifts in his seat to look straight at her. 'These decisions are not mine. I am simply passing on information. I am myself carrying out my own duties, following instructions.' *Whose instructions?*

'Whose instructions?' Jen asks.

'I am answerable to both Mr. Kierle, and the commander.' *Is he a committee member himself?*

'Forgive me asking,' Jen interrupts again. 'But are you a committee member?'

'For the moment, yes. The commander and Mr. Kierle appointed Mr. Russell and myself to the ship's committee.

'Which brings me to the reason you are here: It is true that when we first reach land energies will have to be devoted to building and farming, and that most of us will be involved in that work. However, we also know that the ship will have to return, with a small crew, to guide the community to us. This will require the commander leaving as soon as a return journey is viable. Clearly, it is important that his child be one of the first born of the new generation. This principle was, of course, agreed with the elders before we left. It is important therefore that they each consider their choice and select a wife before we reach land.

'Theirs will be the first marriages, the first homes built. It is a great honour to be selected for such an important role.'
The women exchange glances and speak in unison.

'Do we have a choice?'

'No-one will be forced into anything. It is for this reason that you are being asked so early in the voyage. To give you time to consider the offer being made to you. There will advantages to these positions. You will be given seven days to make your decision. During that time you will have new quarters, your role will be explained to you, and you will be given opportunities to ask questions.'

'Ria, Mr. Russell will escort you.' He stands to lead her to the doorway, opens the door and nods to Russell who is waiting there. Ria turns to Jen who smiles as she sits waiting for Taylor. Ria's stomach lurches. Her skin prickles. *So I am to be confronted with the prospect of marriage to Kierle?*

Taylor interrupts her thoughts. 'You will go with Mr. Russell.'

Her legs are weak but she follows, trying to gather her senses. Thoughts and sensations tumble over each other. *How can I say no? What will he expect of me? What about Zak?* Tripping over the hem of her skirt she stumbles on the stair to an even higher deck. *The boards are so white. The sun so hot. I need a cool breeze. I wish I could dive into the sparkling water. And what would I see beneath the surface? What creatures? What unknown things? What beauties?* She trips again. *This cannot be. I wanted escape and now find myself facing a worse prison than before.* Vaguely aware of s distant rumbling she experiences it as a trembling through her body as Taylor taps on a door.

'Enter.'

He unlatches the door and, as it swings open, steps back for her to enter the cabin then follows her in to introduce them.

'Commander, this is Ria. Ria, the commander.' Between entering the room and looking up at him there is a second in which she is overwhelmed by her senses. She is conscious of the sea rolling against the ship, a distant rumble of thunder, men's voices calling from the rigging, the fierce slap of a sail, and a woman's sudden laugh. There is the smell of wood, a faint scent of leather and she catches a tangy fragrance which she does not recognise. She is aware of her own body, smelling of soap. Her tongue is so dry it sticks to the roof of her mouth. She can feel the dust beneath her fingernails. The ship rises on a swelling wave and she adjusts her feet to keep her balance. The scrape of wood on wood - he is standing up to meet her.

He does not speak immediately and she looks around in the brief silence. She considers the wooden walls; timbers cleverly shaped and locked together, sealed joints, a heavy wooden table bolted to the floor, the curved chair he has just pushed away. The room is brown, his uniform a deep, dark blue. She wonders where the dye was found, berries from the mountainside probably. Her grandmother had talked of the possibility. Feeling vulnerable in her layers of white she wraps her arms around herself and waits.

He stands, as if waiting for her to speak, feet slightly apart, one hand resting lightly on the desk. He coughs - a quiet dry cough with the back of his hand against his mouth. *Muscles throb in his neck, deeply coloured, creased skin, large hands.* He coughs again, keeping his hand to his mouth for a fraction longer than seems necessary, then moves round in front of the desk. She would like to be the first to speak but words refuse to form. When he smiles at her she is surprised by the warmth in his eyes. *Energy and light.* Her eyes are drawn again to his neck and she imagines him swimming, holding his head out of the water then straightening his neck in line with his body to dive. Still smiling he speaks.

'I think it is the time for our first meeting. You must have some doubts of me and there is much I would like to know of you.' Ria looks around and realises that they are alone. Russell has slipped out silently. Flinching as the commander touches her elbow she pulls her arms in tighter around herself.

'I apologise,' he says. 'This is difficult.' Stepping back slightly he holds out his right arm. *Colour, muscles, strength* 'While it is true that I am the commander,' he is saying 'My given name is Randal. I know you are Ria of course.' He is still, holding out his hand, and she is struck by the realisation that he is waiting for her to respond. Relaxing a little, she smiles back and holds out her hand. Their fingers clasp briefly then he releases her. His gesture seems to invite her to sit but as she does so there is another low rumbling and the ship seems to tremble. Almost immediately there is a sharp knock on the door.

'I will be with you in the instant.' He answers, voice raised, projected, to penetrate the door before turning to Ria. *Different voice.* 'Again I must apologise. I am forced to leave you already. A storm approaches. I had hoped to introduce myself more fully. *Is his speech strange?* You will have confusions and there is much I would have you know. But I must leave you for this moment. Of course you are free to go. Or remain here.' Another insistent knock distracts him. 'I repeat; I come in the instant.' He turns to her briefly. 'We will meet again tomorrow. Mr. Russell will escort you.' Then he lifts the latch, opens the door and steps out closing it sharply.

Unexpectedly alone she walks around the cabin, his strange words echoing *'I come in the instant.'* At first she touches nothing but takes note of a huge chest with many shallow drawers and the six deep drawers in his desk, each with a small keyhole. On the desk there is only a bowl of dried fruit and nuts and alongside the desk is a small wooden crate of an unfamiliar yellow fruit. Attracted by its scent *a brightness glinting in the brown* She picks one up and holds it to her nose. Its skin is thin but slightly waxy. Its faint scent tantalises her taste buds. Her tongue curls with longing. She slips the fruit into the deep pocket of her dress, crosses the cabin and lets herself out, closing the door carefully before turning around into fresh air which is already tumbling in the approaching storm. Men and boys are racing to furl the sails. The charge in the air is exhilarating. *If I were a sea creature I would leap and dive in the storm then dive into the deep water where it will be calm.*

The ship is swept up by a heavily rolling bank of water then suddenly dropped amid a roaring crash. Ria lurches forward and grabs a rail as water surges across a lower deck. Men struggle with a loose sail. Shouted orders are whipped away by the rising wind. Out to sea waves are becoming walls of water. Huge curling roars batter her ears. Suddenly the ship feels very small. As a wave half the height of the main mast crashes over the bows, Russell appears beside her, loosens her grip on the rail, shouts into her face. 'Go below.' He pulls her in the direction of the stairs as blue-grey cloud engulfs them in darkness broken only by vivid flickers of white lightning. Men rush around her and she hears snatches of their calls.

'All secure!'

Struggling down she meets other women fighting to stay on their feet while someone shouts, 'Lie on your stomach.' Some women moan with fear, some cry, but most are silent. The air is thick with their fear and sickness. Ria staggers through a doorway and notices a pile of blue clothing. No-one pays her any attention as she gathers up a pair of trousers and makes her way down towards Zak.

She finds him tying terrified animals into the stalls built into their hold. 'Get them to lie down first,' he shouts. The ropes are already in place. 'Tie them tight but keep it simple. We have to be able to untie them as soon as it's over.' A cow, whose head hangs low it almost touches the deck, peers up so that her eyes are almost completely white, tiny slits of brown flickering in fear beneath heavy eyelids. She sets up a mournful lowing sound. 'Talk to her.'

'What shall I say?'

'Anything, just keep a hand on her flank and talk to her.'

'Come on then girl. It's only a storm and it won't last long. At least it will bring us fresh water to drink. We'll all feel better for that.'

The cow falls silent. Staring into Ria's eyes it allows its knees to buckle. *She trusts me.* Together they lower themselves onto the straw. Ria rests her head against the cow's neck, breathing in the powerful brown smell of animal which reminds her of earth but Zak interrupts her thoughts.

'Tie her down. Get the next one settled.'

The storm is directly over them now and the New Hope lurches and rolls. It sounds as if every mast is falling, every timber splitting. Several times the ship seems to fall and lie on one side then somehow rights itself.

'We can't do any more. Stay with them.'

In spite of her fear that the cow will roll over and crush her, Ria slides down and leans against a trembling flank. They seem to calm each other and she begins to feel safe. A sudden scent rushes at her, setting her mouth alive, refreshed by tingling saliva. The fruit has been crushed in her pocket. She pulls it out and turns it over in her hand *the colour of sunlight* then puts it to her mouth. Its bright taste is like waking up in unexpected winter sun.

....

When the storm begins to subside Ria stands unsteadily, takes off her skirts and layers of petticoats and hastily pulls on the trousers. *Strange feeling; so little fabric, so light, except between my legs here; a trapped sensation – enclosed.* Pulling the cord tightly around her waist and knotting it, she looks down. The trousers are too long, dragging at her feet. Zak is beside her offering his knife.

'You do it.' She says holding the fabric taught so that he can saw the trousers off at the ankle. 'Higher. I have had enough of being covered.'

He cuts them again, just below the knee. 'That way you can move freely but they will also keep you warm. Guard against them rubbing, warn the other women about that. They should wear them a little at first, longer each day, but I can't see you going back into skirts in a hurry.' They are both smiling as he hands her the knife. 'Take this. I have another.'

Although the ship is still rolling in the after swell of the storm Ria stands confidently. She picks up the fruit and holds it out to Zak.

'Lemon,' he seems to answer a question she hasn't yet asked.

'We grew them on the mountain slopes. There was not enough sun in Sanctuary. They have been saving them while we have had fruit, nuts, vegetables but we will need them soon, when we find ourselves with only stale biscuits and dried meat to live on. He is moving among the animals, checking and reassuring them, loosening ropes as he speaks. 'You were right about the water too. The storm will have filled the water barrels and now that we are no longer boiling it three times it will go further as well as tasting better.'

'Zak there is something I must tell you.'

'I know the commander has selected you. All the men know. They have been told you will have your own cabin, up on his deck. You will be able to keep an eye on the animals up there and it should give you freedom to come down here more easily. Come with me now.'

As he leads her back to the hold full of herbs Ria is struck by the dryness of the air. She trails her fingertips through leaves. '*Loosestrife,*' her grandmother whispers, '*quietens agitated beasts.*' She bends to inhale the fragrance of each sack she passes. '*shrew ash, chestnut, balm, lungwort*'.

'This is what you will need now.' He reaches into a sack and pulls out a handful of twigs she does not recognise. 'Take it to the women and give them each a small piece to chew. It will help them recover from seasickness. The storm will have stolen the legs from most of them.'

....

He is right. As she approaches the women's deck the acid stink of vomit sets up a heaving in her stomach and throat. She places a tiny piece of the herb twig on her tongue. It is cool in her mouth and as she chews the coolness travels into her throat and spreads down towards her stomach, calming the sickness. The terrible smell loses its power. Now that it is no longer threatening she experiences it as a signal that help is needed.

The least ill of the women raise their heads cautiously. Seeing Nan close by, she approaches her first.

'Chew this. Trust me. It will help. After a few seconds Nan is sitting up, with a hand on her stomach, smiling. She gets to her feet slowly and begins removing her stained clothing.

Ria trims a pair of trousers as she speaks to all the women. 'Pile your skirts here. We have fresh ones for those of you who want them but these are more practical. We do not need to wear petticoats now, store them.'

Handing the knife to Nan she moves along the deck giving a small piece of the herb to each while Nan cuts trousers off at ankle length. Those who are too sick to get up lie still and chew. Gradually their grey green skin returns to its normal colour. They are watching Ria's legs, the colour of them.

'Yes, my skin has been coloured by the sun. I have removed my skirts before. No harm has come by it. You will be no less pure for wearing trousers.'

As more women recover they help each other into trousers. Clothes soiled by sickness are gathered up to be thrown overboard. Some cleaner skirts and petticoats are used to clean the deck, others are stored in the wooden chest each women has below her hammock.

'Thank you Ria.' Some of them are saying.

'Thank you for the herbs.'

'For the clothes.'

'It seems we may all benefit from the commander's choice.'

8

Questions

When Ria makes her way back to the deck and fresh air she realises that Russell has been waiting there for her.

'I will escort you to your cabin.' *I had forgotten* He leads her once again in the direction of the cabin where she had had her brief introduction to the commander earlier in the day but this time he opens a second door, one that she had not previously noticed. 'This will be your cabin. Later you will be invited to meet the commander in his day cabin, which you visited earlier. Allow me to show you; your bunk, your wash basin and chamber pail, fresh water will be brought to you each morning. He moves across to the table. 'Should you choose, your meals can be served here.'

'Thank you but I would prefer to eat with the other women.'

'It is your choice. Should you change your mind, or if there is anything else you require, you have only to ask. I will leave you now.'

He opens the door and steps outside but does not turn away.

'Please, Mr. Russell, don't feel you must wait there for me,' says Ria.

'These are my orders, Miss,' he replies. 'I am here to ensure your safety and to bring you anything you need.'

'But I will feel like a prisoner if I have to have a guard outside my door. I am sure I will be safe and if there is anything I need I can come and find you.'

'Well, if you are sure, I will inform the commander of your wishes. If he is agreeable I will return each morning and evening to check that you have everything you need. In the meantime, if you need me you can ask Zak or any of the men and they will know where to find me.'

'Thank you Mr. Russell. I appreciate your understanding.'

Her cabin is luxurious after the standards of the women's hold. The walls are panelled. Her table and chair positioned under a skylight. At the end away from the door, built against the panelling, and curtained for privacy, is the bunk, made up with fresh linen. Alongside the bunk runs a series of three portholes from which she will be able to see the ocean and horizon. There is even a curtain which can be pulled across these. At the foot of the bunk she sees a wash stand which also contains a chamber pail.

With a polite knock at the door Russell brings her personal belongings from below and asks whether she would like supper brought up to the cabin.'

'No thank you Mr. Russell. I am too tired to eat. I think I would like to sleep now but first I must ask you whether there is anything I should know about the cabin or any special rules about living up here?'

'I don't know of any special rules, Miss. Perhaps that is something you should discuss with the commander. Someone will come every morning to clean and empty and bring you fresh water. They will come while you are at breakfast if you still plan to eat with the other women otherwise they will come whenever you are ready. If there is anything else you need or would like to know I will do my best to help.'

'You are very kind. Are there many cabins on this deck?'

'Yours and the Commander's two, one for his bunk and the other is his day cabin and I have a small cabin at the far end. On the opposite deck Mr. Kierle has two for himself and one for his guest like yourself, and his day cabin. The last is Mr. Taylor's.'

'And is this the highest deck?'

'Yes, there's only the rigging above us. It is quite noisy and may keep you awake at first and you will find the bunk strange now that you are accustomed to sleeping in a hammock.'

'I'm sure I will soon adjust. You have been very helpful Mr. Russell. Thank you.'

'Ria,' says Russell suddenly as he is turning to go. 'There are things...

'Things?' Ria replies, wanting him to go on, but he shakes his head. 'Sleep well,' he says as he pulls the door closed and leaves her.

But Ria has a restless night. Russell had been right about the bunk feeling strange. She also feels very alone and is surprised to find that she misses the sighs, moans and snoring of the other women. The rigging creaks and at times sounds as if it might be splitting. Lying terrified waiting for the crash of a fallen yard arm or mast she drifts in and out of sleep.

....

In the morning she and Jen are summoned to meet Kierle. They meet in his day cabin. Ria is escorted to the cabin by Russell who taps on the door for her and then steps back out of her way.. Kierle's voice is crisp but wavers a little as he answers 'Come in, Ria, 'he says, coughing,' 'and Russell, there is no need for you to remain. You may resume your duties for the commander.'

Ria steps into the cabin and sees that Jen, who glances up at Ria with a faint smile, is already sitting on one of two small benches placed side by side in front of a large table. Behind the table Kierle's own seat is large with ornately carved high back and wide arm rests. The only other furniture is a lectern *where he practices standing over us* and a low stool and table where a large book lies open.

Kierle stands. 'Good morning Ria. We have been waiting for you, Jen and I.' As he says Jen's name his lips almost smile *but his eyes do not* and he looks briefly in her direction without turning his head. *As if he can see us both at once.* 'Please,' he continues, 'sit with Jen and we can begin'.

Ria holds out her hands in greeting. Jen seems surprised for a moment but then stands up and reaches out in return but their eyes do not meet because Kierle coughs loudly and says, 'There will be time for pleasantries later but for now, if you will be seated…' he coughs again. 'There are important matters to be clarified. It is my duty to ensure that you understand.'

'Yours is the highest privilege, the greatest honour.' His voice changes again and takes on the confident, monotonous tone he uses for sermons and teachings. 'Your homes will be the first to be built in the new community, your children the first to be born. You, Jen, will be mother to the next

Guardian. Ria, you will be the example of how our women will live and work. The community will look up to you. As such you will have the best of everything. Your every need will be provided. We have these five days in which to get to know one another. You have five days in which to learn the advantages of your position while we take the time to confirm our choice.

'Jen, please stand and turn around slowly.' Jen stands and turns towards Ria but with her eyes down. 'Lift your head,' says Kierle sharply and she obeys. 'Your posture is good. You can hold your head well and will need to do so at all times. You have pride and confidence. These things are all attractive to me and have helped you secure this opportunity.'

'I assume you would prefer to be seated?' Jen sits and holds her head up. *But it is an effort and why is he so hard when she is so meek?* Allow me to outline my requirements.

I require a physically sound wife capable of bearing, in the first instance, a healthy son. Following this there will be two more children, a girl and another boy. The girl will be your responsibility. She will be your companion and you will educate her in the ways of purity in preparation for a suitable marriage when the time comes.

He turns his attention to Ria. 'You will be required to provide for the needs of our commander. Each of you will be an example to the women of the new community. They will see in you, all that purity can achieve. You will be well cared for, eat the finest food, wear the finest clothes and live in the safest homes.

For the remainder of the voyage I would ask you to avoid contact with the other women. You have each other as companions. Of course there will be no contact with the men apart from Mr. Taylor and Russell. You will, of course, be the epitome of purity in your hygiene, your dress and your bearing. You will be admired by all, an example to your fellow travellers. As I have said, you will be well rewarded. I am sure you will already have realised that there are certain other qualities that are necessary in the wives of the Guardian and Commander. And as surgeon I am well qualified to make the necessary examinations. But we will come to that in good time. In the meanwhile I invite you to experience the privileges that come with the elevated position to which you have been invited. Examine your quarters. It is a rare luxury on board to have a cabin to yourself and you will find a fixed bunk and clean linen much more comfortable than a hammock below deck. Sample the food and enjoy the fresh milk and even a little wine. You will also receive some preparations to ensure your continued good health; a daily balm with scurvy grass; sage leaves each morning for your teeth and gums; Valerian root to soothe and help you sleep. Of course, in the unlikely event of you declining to accept selection, you will lose these privileges and return to life below deck. I am sure there will be someone willing to take your place.'

....

Dawn. Ria climbs out of the bunk, wraps her cloak around her shoulders and goes out onto the deck. It seems very high above the water as she makes her way to the rail and looks over at the waves below but it is still dark and she cannot be sure of what she sees. A small distance away from the ship, just below the surface there is a pale light. As her eyes become accustomed she realises that there are many. They appear to be the eyes of a group of large sea creatures. Gripping the rail tightly she leans against it peering through the darkness trying to make out size and shape. Just as the sun is rising she begins to make out their form but flinches at a sudden, very loud sound close to her. *Daylight drums*

The roll of drumming for daybreak continues until there is enough light for Ria to make out details of her unfamiliar surroundings. She looks back at the grey surface of the sea but there is nothing there. With the sunrise the ship's flag is hoisted and the day has begun.

She returns to her cabin where she enjoys the luxury of washing and dressing in privacy. She then sits on the edge of her bunk and waits for the bell summoning the women to breakfast.

....

When Ria enters she is relieved to see that Kierle is not there. *No prayers this morning.* She looks for Jen and is surprised to see that she has not arrived. *Has she chosen to obey him in all things?* She makes her way down to Nan and the twins, about half way along the bench. They move to create a space for her but as she is climbing over the bench to fit herself in questions are called at her from both sides.

'You still want to eat with us then?'

'Still one of us?'

'How can you come down here, to eat with us, now that you have a cabin of your own, privileges we can only guess at? We are still sleeping in the foul dark, not much higher than the animals, almost below the level of the water.'

'So what have you learned from him, Ria? What do you know about where we are going? What will happen to us when we get there?'

'I haven't learned anything you don't already know.'

'You expect us to believe that?'

Nan speaks 'Surely we should give Ria time'.

'Or give her a list of questions.'

'Demands!'

Ria attempts to answer. 'I can tell you that I think our commander is a good man and…' but her voice is drowned out by more questions.

'But where is he taking us?'

'And when will we get there?'

'And then what?'

Nina speaks from the other end of the table and keeps her back to Ria. 'She can't come down here every morning and expect to sit with us, without answers to some of our questions.'

'Nina's right. If she's sleeping with him he will tell her things. There are things we have a right to know and she can find them out.'

'And what about this one?' Nina demands as Jen appears looking anxiously around the tables. Ria stands up and Jen tries to make her way down behind the seated women to reach her, but her way is barred and she is held by the women she is trying to pass.

Nina stands up and turns towards them. Her face is screwed up with anger, her voice so full of fury that it trembles as she spits her words at Jen. 'What can you tell us from our surgeon preacher? What has he given away about our precious commander?'

Jen answers loudly with her head high but she is trembling and there are tears in her eyes. 'He's not giving anything away. He's committee.'

'And the commander isn't?' asks the woman nearest her.

'I heard he isn't.' As Nina speaks, women around her nod their heads and murmur in agreement. 'I heard he isn't even community. He's the stranger from across the sea. The sign they were waiting for!'

'So if he's from the sea how is it that Kierle trusts him?'

Why are we arguing amongst ourselves?

'Well?' demands Nina. 'What does our self-appointed Guardian say about the 'good' commander?'

'He says nothing, gives nothing away. Only makes demands,' says Jen with a shudder. As she says this the women around her move back into their places and allow her through to climb onto the bench between Ria and Nan.

Resting her hand on Jen's shoulder Ria remains standing. 'Give me your questions,' she says quietly to Nina and those around her. 'I will find out what I can. But Nan is right, I will need time.'

Nina turns to face Ria and speaks more quietly, with a little more control, but her voice is still shaking 'We will have a committee of our own. We will select one now and meet this evening.'

But she is interrupted by Nan who stands up beside Jen to speak. 'No. No committee. We do not need to become like them.'

She turns to the twins and they continue her argument. 'We can all listen to each other.'

'Give each other the right to speak; the right to be listened to.'

'Anyone who has a question should be allowed to ask it.'

'If Ria or Jen can get us an answer, they can tell us. If not, we shouldn't hold it against them. They didn't ask to be selected.'

'It could have been any one of us.'

'It still could. Taylor and Russell will make their choices soon.'

'And we should welcome that as another opportunity for the women to help each other.'

They are so alike but as they speak I can see differences; Meera is more open looking, confident but Beth seems closed down, she holds her eyelids lower, her mouth tighter. Her

posture is slightly more rigid. Every part of her is guarded.
Ria is now sitting next to Jen. Their eyes meet but Jen shakes
her head and looks away. Now Nan sits down with them,
speaking loudly enough for all the women to hear.

'What do you say? Can we give you our questions?'
'Of course,' answers Ria.

'Of course' Jen echoes, her voice wavering.

'So,' continues Nan, 'what are our questions?'

Many voices speak at once, 'Where are we going?'

'How long will it take?

'What will happen to us when we get there?'

'Why were we chosen?'

'Who is he? Where did he come from?'

'Have the committee been lying to us?'

'And what about Zak? Is he telling us the truth about
himself? Maybe he knows some of the answers.'

'I will talk to Zak,' says Ria.

'No need.' Zak answers from the hatchway where he is
sitting cross legged, listening.

'How long have you been there?'

'Long enough. And I know enough to tell you that you will
get different answers to the questions depending on who you
ask. But don't let that stop you asking.'

Nina is back on her feet. 'We will give you seven days. You, all three of you, know our questions. In seven days' time we expect some answers.

9

A Book and a Kiss

Zak has his back to Ria as she makes her way through the animal hold. He does not turn away from the cow he is milking. 'What have you brought for me Ria?' he asks and she thinks she can detect his smile as he speaks. She is not surprised that he seems to know why she has come.

'I have brought my grandmother's book. She gave it to me the last time I saw her alive. I wish I had paid it more attention before we sailed but at least I brought it with me.'

He has turned around and is holding out his hands to take it from her. 'Don't worry about showing it to me. I have one myself, it was my mother's, and my grandmother's and even she was adding to her grandmother's knowledge. Knowledge is like that, quietly building through generations. Sometimes it misses a generation. Bits get lost, passed on incomplete. Other bits are added, and not all of them necessarily true. You and I can bring two threads of knowledge together, you and your book, me and mine. I have brought plants with us not knowing their use but feeling that they were important. My hope is that you might be able to explain some of them to me.' As he speaks he turns the pages of the book while leading her into the hold of herbs.

They sit together on a bale of straw and he reads aloud from the book. 'Lillian Mary - This be my book for passing to Nell. I take this book, now it is Nell's and I will pass it to Rena. I take it with joy and will pass it to Ria. I take it with thanks and will pass it to Elise. I will not take it but with love I return it my mother Ria. And I will pass it to Ria the young one.'

'That was my grandmother whispers Ria, touching the name lightly. I was named for her. Here, you see where it says 'I will pass it to Elise'? Elise is my mother. She didn't want the book. But now it is mine and I am happy to share it with you.'

Their hands close together over the book. Ria is trembling as she looks into Zak's eyes.

'Ria, it was only a kiss.'

'But…'

'You have been kissed before?'

'No.'

'Oh… well… well it was just that, a kiss, nothing more. It was not important. This book, this knowledge, they are important. Many of the plants will be helpful when we reach land but there are some here that we will be using on board. Already I can see that your book names plants which mine does not. We must match the descriptions to the leaves, fruits and seeds I have brought. This page about the shiver tree is almost exactly the same as mine. The Ash sapling, you will have seen the two that I brought when you came on board. We all passed through to be brushed by the leaves. It prevents sea-wasting.'

'Sea-wasting?'

'A terrible illness. I have never seen it but my grandmother told me it affects skin, eyes, and teeth. There is a lot of pain, old wounds open up, men faint or collapse with exhaustion.'

'I missed the saplings. I joined the ship after everyone else had been on board for two weeks.'

'Well we must put that right now.' He stands up and moves over to where he has two young trees planted in half barrels. He drags them slightly apart and directs Ria to walk between them. As she does so he stands to attention, whistles, then salutes. Laughing they link arms, returning to the book which lies open on the straw bale.

Hearing a cough they look up and are surprised to see Russell watching them. He coughs again, looking at his feet, and then looks up with a start when Ria speaks his name.

'Mr. Russell, please don't creep around behind me. What is it?'

'Ria, I have come from the commander. He wanted to know where you were. Says I should be with you, make sure you come to no harm.' As he says this he glances at Zak.

'Please tell him that I am working with Zak. Helping with the animals. I am perfectly safe and will call you if I need you. I will explain to the commander personally that you do not need to spend your days minding me.'

'Well, I think…'

'Please Mr. Russell, give him the message. I promise to explain that it was all my doing and not to trouble you about it. I am sure you have much more important duties to attend to.'

'I will return to him immediately and inform him miss.'

Ria reopens the book continues reading it aloud. 'Mouse holes for cattle disease. What does this mean?'

'Look here,' says Zak, leading her to the wooden walls of the hold. 'I had them cut holes in the planks that line the hold. He lifts a small square of wood away from its place, leaving a hole. There is enough space between them for mice to run about. I have a family of mice. If any of the cattle show signs of disease I put a mouse through the hole. As soon as the mouse dies the cow will be cured.'

'Can they climb out?'

'No, because this fits back into place.' He slides the wooden square back in leaving no sign that it has been removed.

'It seems cruel.'

'But if it saves a cow from disease it means milk on the voyage, and continuation of the herd for the future.' His attention returns to the book as he turns a page. 'This tree that your grandmother calls Trembling Grace, we call the Shiver Tree because of the way its leaves tremble. It cures agues and fevers. She says to pin a lock of hair to the tree. We would take a piece of finger nail and press it into the bark. As the bark grows over the nail the illness passes.'

Ria remembers a rhyme, and as she says it Zak joins in. The only difference is that when Ria says 'Trembling tree' Zak says 'Shiver Tree'.

'Trembling tree, trembling tree,

Shake and shiver 'stead of me.'

'We need to put together what we know, Ria.' Zak sounds excited. 'Let's begin by going through your book and I will tell you my versions if they are different.'

'The Treating of Ailments. I wish I had paid more attention,' says Ria. 'How will we know where to begin?'

'We will simply go through the book. Don't worry. Knowledge is never lost if it is written down. Look at the first entry. Already we have something useful. For Scurvy.'

'What's scurvy?'

'I think it might be sea-wasting. Listen.' He reads: Take the juice of a handful scurvy grass and of water cresses to mix with a whole lemon pulped, skin, seeds, juice and all, the same with slices of horseradish, crushed petals of three rose flowers and stir all into a flagon of strong ale. Infuse two days then draw off a quart.'

'Let me read the next one,' says Ria taking the book back.

'Look. This must be a better one for your sea-wasting:
  If his eyes be sunken and skin be pale,
  Teeth dropping from tender gums,
  If his muscles be wasting and hurting him cruel,
  If he faints and opens old wounds,
  Give him cabbage and onion and scurvy grass ale,
  He's had the last of the life under sail,
  Keep him home, if home he comes.'

She keeps the books and turns a few pages. 'Here's one is for burns. There doesn't seem to be any order to it.'

'If it's like my grandmother's this is the order she learned them in. Just when we thought we had collected every treatment the community had to offer, something new would emerge in a song, or a story, or even in a dream. My grandmother kept a book and just kept adding to it. Read the burns one.'

'For a burn. A handful of houseleek bruised and simmered over the fire to draw out all the juice to which should be added a cup of pig lard and a half cup melten beeswax. Stir all until

almost cold then stir in a good measure of sweet oil.' Ria
lowers the book. 'There are some strange old words here.'

'We can easily work out what they mean,' says Zak. 'I
remember something different for burns. Float nine leaves of
blackberry in hot water. Apply cold. That's good. If one
remedy doesn't work we can try another.'

'Yes, and if we don't have what we need for one, maybe
we will have something for the other. Do you have all these
plants down here, Zak?'

'We haven't mentioned anything difficult yet. Read
another one.'

'Beaten roots of comfrey, spread on leather and lay on
affected place will ease pain and knit up broken bones.'

'That's easy. Strange that it doesn't mention a splint. My
turn?' he asks in a slightly playful tone and Ria taps him on
the head with the book before passing it over.

'It seems to me you are only pretending to need the book
and it is all stored away in this head of yours already'.

'No. No, that's not true. Here's an interesting one. A drink
proved to cause an easy labour. Your grandmother was the
best midwife within and outside the community. Listen to
this: Take two each of root of marsh mallow, parsley, succory,
and one each of root of brown fennel, and mullet. Scrape and
shred lickerish and sweet fennel seeds. Boil all these up in
honey and fresh spring water. Strain and let the liquid stand.
Take a cup full at a time and stir in a little sweet nut oil. Drink
this once each day in all the month before your time. Will you
know succory if I show you my herbs? I think I know what
she means but it would be good to be sure.'

Ria nods. 'I think so.'

'You see, I do need you.'

'Here's another: For The Speedy Delivery of Woman and Child: The liver of an eel killed in the full moon by reason the moon has very great influence over women and especially of woman with child and so also dry it out in the light of the moon but before any sign of mustiness bring it into the sun then bruise it to a fine powder. It must be given in wine or very light ale.

'We might struggle with that one but there shouldn't be any children to be delivered, speedily or otherwise, as long as we remain on board ship.

'Look. This is where the handwriting changes. Someone's daughter has taken over the collecting.'

He hands the book back to Ria, who sighs. 'I wish I knew who had written them all,' she says sadly.

'Don't let it make you sad, Ria. They won't mind that you don't recognise the handwriting but they would expect you to be ready to use the information they collected. Read.'

'Ricketts. Draw new milk. Take sincfoyle, columbine leaves, fennel leaves, strawberry leaves and a handful each of rosemary, lickerish, fennel seeds. Bruise these herbs and spices. Distil them all in milk. Fast in the morning and drink only this. Take the drink also in the afternoon and at bed. You might sweeten with a little honey or not.' She is enjoying herself now and reading with confidence.

'I remember now,' she says turning to Zak and smiling. Sometimes when I was with her, women would visit my grandmother and bring her things. Herbs from the hills and plants from down by the river. She used to say to me "You didn't hear that, Ria" or "You didn't see the women who were here today." Somehow I believed her. I almost remember forgetting.'

'They knew what they were doing,' says Zak. 'Knew how to teach us so that we would remember when it was time. What else is there?'

'Your turn, I think,' says Ria and the book is passed between them as they share their knowledge.

'A powder for the teeth: Gather equally to crush rosemary, sage, leaf of red rose, marjoram, salt and mastic. Take enough wine or very light ale to boil them together gently until they might dry but stir to not have it cleave together in lumps. Crush the all to a powder. Now keep it try til you use it.'

'For Diarrhoea, comfrey.'

'Gentian is a strengthener of the human system.'

'Groundsel for sickness of the stomach.'

'Rub cows udders with buttercups for her to give you more milk.'

'The root of Solomon's seal takes away bruises or blue spots gained by fall or by a woman's wilfulness in stumbling against hasty fists.'

'Rue for repentance or sorrow, rue tea for convulsions, warm sweetened rue for the nervous nightmare, and rue in your posy against diseases brought in by others.'

'Fresh sage leaves and strawberries rubbed in the mouth will cleanse and freshen teeth and gums.'

'The corms of scarlet lady's purse, step on it lady, your babe will be sorry, crush it my lady he'll not see tomorrow, eating it lady before he is born, dead from the womb he will surely be torn.'

'Cowslip for calming.'

'Scurvy grass ale is a tonic.'

'Camomile flowers boiled and drunk cures pains and stitches

'Spearmint allays nausea and vomiting.'

'Valerian root will calm, ease pain, bring on sleep.'

'For attacks from serpents and other venomous creatures and to stop the evil progress of gangrene seek out southern wormwood.'

10

The Journey Continues

Women learn to lash ropes, scrub decks with scouring stones, loose and furl sails. They begin to share the sailors' daily routine. They enjoy being on deck, feeling the breeze lift their hair, kiss their arms, face and neck. They lick their lips, to taste the salt, as they walk the deck, always aware of the eyes of the men, measuring them up, making choices. The sun warms them more each day and everyone begins to relax as the weather improves. It feels as if maybe they are sailing these uncharted waters with hope.

At night life slows but the work continues; half the crew are in their hammocks at the start of first watch as the sun goes down. Four hours later the ringing of the bell signals the second watch. At first the women are exhausted but they adjust to getting only four hours sleep at a time, appreciating the fact that at least they now have double the sleeping space. And at night they hear the singing of sea creatures with less and less fear.

....

Often, Ria joins Randal in his cabin. They sit side by side in his cabin and gradually discover each other's story.

Usually Randal asks the first question. 'So why did you join the New Hope?'

'Escape. I wanted to make a fresh start. I thought it was all my fault. I buried a beetle in the cellar and the mill collapsed. Other buildings were sinking into their own cellars. They started to build again but I didn't feel I could stay. When I heard about a ship sailing to make a new beginning it seemed it was meant for me.'

'You knew you would be expected to marry?'

'No, not straight away but then I thought, better to marry a man who wants adventure. Any man who was ready to leave the community, on a ship, to look for new life must be better than the men who would turn down the opportunity.'

'So are you willing to be my wife?'

'I think I still have some time to make up my mind. Why have you chosen me?'

'Because your skin is dark, your eyes are deep. Because when others bow their heads for prayers you do not. Because you are different from the other women.'

'Does that mean you are different from the other men?'

'I may be.'

'Not just because you are the commander?'

'Maybe not.'

'Perhaps you are the commander because you are different from the others. Do you swim?'

'Why do you ask?'

'Because swimming is forbidden.'

'Of course. Well the truth is, swimming has saved my life on more than one occasion.'

'Tell me how.'

'There was a time in the water when I knew that I was swimming for my life. My ears were full of the sound of my blood while the waves constantly threatened to engulf me. All I could think of was the burning in my lungs and the terrible weight of my limbs. The whole world had become a grey swirling sea.

'I was tired beyond tired and felt I was a child again, a child with my life slipping away in front of me. I remembered an old sailor saying dying was like slipping through a spiral of torches. As long as he could light the next torch he would live. My fire was burning weaker and weaker.

'If I could just stay awake – it would have been so easy to close my eyes in the warm water. *Fight! Fight*! I told myself. I knew that the water must be cold but it felt warm. Warm like a field of poppies, drowsy with poppy scent and familiar voices murmuring nearby.

'Then, somehow, my mother's scream sent alarm coursing through my body like barbed poison in my veins.

'I cursed my stupidity – allowing myself to be seduced by the temptation to sleep. I forced myself to swim harder. Pain kept me awake, kept me alive. I told myself to ignore everything but the pain. Ignore false hope. Ignore the hazy illusion of land. You'll have to swim a lot further than that if you want to feel ground under your feet again. Keep your wits about you.

'I knew I could do it. I'd done it before; talked to myself, held on to pain. I remembered the day the boat turned over, remembered my father's words. 'Don't fool yourself with fear Randal. The water is stronger than us but it means us no harm'

'He had known this would happen. He had prepared me; teaching me to swim, making me swim hour after hour in the freezing cold water. I thought about meeting him again, down there on the ocean floor. If I stopped fighting, let go and sank, there he would be, arms reaching towards me, waiting, waiting, sixteen years of waiting.

'But instead he grabbed me, shook me, slapped me angrily and shouted 'No' into my face. When I opened my eyes in surprise, it was the waves slapping my face. My arms and legs were swimming without my direction and the image of land beckoned me.

'And so I knew. I must go on swimming, must let the sun sink, must swim even in the dark, with my face to the first bright star, must swim straight so that my father could be proud of me and my mother would not have to mourn another life lost to the sea.

'Eventually I began to wonder what my arms and legs were doing as I could no longer feel them. I mistrusted my eyes in the fading light. The beach in front of me looked so real. I shook my head, squeezed my eyes to get rid of the tormenting hallucination, suddenly discovered belief and, in a final burst of strength, hauled my body onto the shingle.

'I heard my own weak laughter and foolish hysterical shouts, 'Find my father. Fetch my mother' before the burning in my chest enveloped me completely and I fell onto pebbles, forgetting to stay awake.

'I saw you,' whispers Ria. 'I was frightened and ran away.' She is surprised to find that she is leaning against him and that he is holding her hand. 'But then I began to believe it had been a dream.'

'It was like a dream,' he answers. 'Many times I tried to wake. It was like fighting my way through a suffocating fog. Even with my eyes closed I could see their trap: that web of fine, sticky rope, stretched from wall to wall, criss-crossing the air just above me. I lay remembering dreams of drowning and then suddenly knew that it had been no dream.

'But I have been talking about myself, my fights and my dreams for long enough. Tell me about your dreams.'

'Not now,' replies Ria sleepily. 'I'm so comfortable enjoying the sound of your voice. I just want hear more of your story. Are you saying the elders held you prisoner?'

'Yes, but at least I was alive. My body ached with life. When I finally managed to open my eyes, the ropes were gone and I was in a small, simple room. The only furniture other than the bed was a table and chair. There was a single window through which daylight eventually woke me. The sunlight on my face made me smile and even smiling was painful. When I sat up and examined myself in the pale warm light, I found bruises on my legs and chest, an ache in my lungs and a pounding that was surely the sea, in my head. Unsure of whether I was on land or on board ship I tried to get to the window. At first it was impossible to walk, or even crawl, but I put my feet to the floor and steadied myself against the wall. Every muscle screamed for rest but I was determined to know. I made my way from the bed to the window. The room seemed steady around me. With my hands on the window ledge I looked out and saw trees. Then I remembered dragging myself out of the water. I sank to the floor, crawled back to the bed and waited.

'There were clues: The plain walls appeared to be clay. The frames of the doorway and window were wood as were the ceiling beams. From the bed, all I could see through the tall window was sky. The calling of sea birds suggested that I was not far from the ocean. Several times I thought I heard men's voices but it was like listening through water. Eventually, was it hours, days, weeks? I discovered that there were clothes at the end of the bed: trousers, a rough shirt, a jacket. Dressing was exhausting. Many times I had to rest and often fell asleep with one arm in the shirt or one leg in the trousers.'

'When I finally found the strength to walk to the door I was not surprised to find it locked. I returned to the bed. I think I spent many days alternating between restless sleep and exhausting dreams. Even when I thought that he was probably awake I felt detached, a spectator to my own experience.

'I watched myself fed by seven silent men who took turns to carry in bowls of warm broth. They put it to my lips and waited for me to be ready to swallow. They brought me stockings and leather boots, helped me put them on and then, seeing my exhaustion, gently took them off again. On a few occasions they tried to speak to me. I struggled to understand but the effort was too great. I shook my head at them and they fell quiet.

'As my strength began to return I ate bread, cheese and eggs although I could still taste nothing and my sense of smell had deserted me. I was living half way between waking and dreaming, lost in a world that was almost familiar. Many times I wondered whether I had in fact died in the sea or had somehow foundered on the shore of a different version of life.

'On three occasions an older man came. He spoke very slowly as if he understood the difficulty of listening through ears that had almost drowned. I gathered his name was Gardin.

'Gradually words became a little clearer. On his first visit Gardin brought me paper, pens and ink. I used it to keep track of the passing days but wrote nothing else. Later Gardin arrived with a collection of badly damaged charts. As I looked at them I felt the floor become more solid beneath my feet. These were plans for building a ship. This was the world I understood. It was my language. I set about redrawing the plans, recreating the parts that were torn off, washed away or indecipherable. The words on the charts became clear to me. They were very close to words that I knew. I wrote in keys and pointers in my own language. Over the next five days it seemed to me that the water was clearing from my head. Sounds became clearer. The previously unintelligible speech of the men who brought my food shifted strangely and I found that I was beginning understand them.

'On his third visit Gardin sat down and, with the charts between us, we found that we understood each other.

'My strength was returning. I was careful to ask only innocent questions, and to give away very little in return, feigning illness and loss of memory as protection. Gradually my life came back into focus.

'My saviour-captors were patient. It became clear that I was important to them. Occasionally reckless with information, they contributed detail to the picture I was steadily building. It took me twenty one days to dispel the dreamlike quality of their speech and begin to work out what had happened.

'I began to taste the food. Regaining my sense of smell felt like a long, slow waking up. In the dry winter sunshine I smelled the dust as floors were swept. I recognised the scent of sap from trees cut to build ships, and the bitter sweetness of the shavings as wood was shaped to fit.

'By the time the elders called me to account for myself I was ready. 'I am called Randal Kapelan,' I told them. 'I am thirty-two years old and was captain of the new ship, Yallah, sent out from my native country to sail in search of descendants of the Reckless Few. It is many generations since the few quit our shores in anger and for many generations my people have searched. Each ten years since their leaving, we have sent three ships in quest of them. Yallah was the last remaining of the three under my command. The other two went down in the terrible seas. Yallah was severely damaged but we managed running repairs and even recovered some of the men from the rowing boats of our sister vessels.

'We sailed on. Our course was set between rising and setting sun but we were impotent against the decay of our repairs. On the day we sighted land we understood that Yallah was fated to sink. But the seas were heavy and the men were reluctant to give themselves to the rowing boats until they saw that sinking was surely our ship's destiny. Their tardy taking to the boats made launching troubleful and I saw many good men lost to the waves as their boats hit the water.

'I owe my life to my father. He had readied me for this eventuality. Surely it was he who taught me to live in the water. Not for the first time, I swam for my life and the incoming tide washed me up on your shore.''

'Did they treat you well?' asks Ria.

'They needed to treat me well,' he replies. 'I came to understand that I was a sort of prisoner-guest of the elders and they behaved as if they had been waiting for me. I realised that they needed me. They had no-one who could oversee the building of a ship, or teach others to build and sail more. They had twenty-five master carpenters and a team of fifty men willing to crew the first ship, which I would command. They hoped that it would carry two hundred men and women and enough animals and supplies for a year. The intention of the committee was that this ship would sail in search of land that could be colonised. Once safely ashore, the passengers would be left to begin building the colony allowing the crew to return to lead further ships carrying the committee and community to the new colony.

'My movements were restricted to a small area near the coast and I met only the men who worked with me. I learned that these were people who had lived in fear of water, particularly the sea, believing it to be full of demons. But a greater fear had driven them to look to the sea as their only chance of a future as their buildings were destroyed and their community began to disintegrate.

'I divided my days between ship building and training the crew. In the evenings I drew charts and plans of land, deep and shallow seas, treacherous rocks, islands. I charted the night sky and mapped weather patterns.

'My first task for the carpenters was to build a raft. Seeing the skill with which they planned, cut, fitted and lashed the wood, plugged and caulked the gaps and pitched the vessel gave me confidence. Together we drew up plans for a four decked ship to carry crew, passengers and animals with provisions for three months at sea and to live six months on land waiting for further ships to arrive. I then felt able to leave the carpenters to work with a minimum of supervision and turned to the training of my crew.

'I supervised training, on the shore, in the water and on the raft. The men began referring to me as the commander. They respected my knowledge and understanding of the sea and began to know that the sea is no more dangerous than the land. As our understanding grew so my speech became more like their own.

'I sent them out on the raft, in teams of ten. They took provisions for three days but I instructed them to stay out for a week and watched and listened as they devised ways of keeping themselves, their food and equipment dry. They improvised additions to the raft, rationed food, collected rainwater and developed working habits that made the best use of each man's strength. I mixed the teams and sent them out for longer. On land I listened to them argue over their experiences and explain discoveries to each other while planning their next voyage.

'Alongside the building of the ship, named New Hope by the committee, I instructed smaller teams of carpenters to build four rowing boats. Completed in thirty days, these become the new training vessels for the crew. I had each boat constructed with a hold, a mast, one sail and a cabin. Divided into four teams the men were given simple instructions.

'Organise yourselves,' I told them. 'Plan the voyage, take everything you need, sail out as far and for as long as you can.

Log, map and chart your voyage and return safely.' From a small cabin built into the shelter of the cliff I watched them set sail and make for the horizon. When they returned I would listen to them, examine their physical condition, question them about their logs, maps and charts and decide who to accept in my crew for the New Hope. I watched for them every day from dawn until dark. That was how I came to see the young woman – the first woman I had seen since the night before Yallah set sail.'

Ria is suddenly alert. She feels the blood rush to her cheeks and hears the sound of her own heart beating. Not wanting Randal to feel her trembling, she moves slightly, lifting her body away from his so that she can see his face. So deeply has he re-entered the memory, he seems to have forgotten that he is talking to her. *Almost as if he is explaining something to himself.*

'I was watching the boats near the horizon on the third day when my attention was caught by the presence of this young woman. She was making her way towards the cliff top on the other side of the small bay.

'Remember that I had been denying myself all thought of women. It had been so long since I touched a woman, felt her soft skin, buried my head in her hair to breathe in her scent. For sixty days on board Yallah before she sank, three days in the water and a hundred and seven days with these elders, I had never allowed myself to think of a woman. Now I was mesmerised. I wondered whether I had conjured her up like a mermaid in the mind of a becalmed sailor, but no, she was real.

'Breathing deeply I leaned against the rock and allowed myself to watch her. While I was cold in the shadow of the cliff, I knew that she would be warm in the spring sunlight, slithering down to the beach. I lowered myself to the ground and lay on my stomach to slide into sunlight. The movement stirred the smell of soil still damp from this morning's rain and I lifted a handful to breathe in its earthy perfume. The sea sang as it rushed towards her and dropped away again leaving petticoat trails of white lace amongst the shingle.

'She bent to pick up a pebble, held it up, glinting in the sunlight. I thought she would hold it up to her face, touch it against her cheek to feel its smoothness, smell it or taste it. Instead, she threw it powerfully into the sea.

'Then, with her back to me she made her way to an outcrop of smooth grey rock unpinning her hair as she walked. It fell in a shining wave almost to her waist. As she sat on the rock she leaned forward to pull off her boots and then straightened again pulling the hem of her dress up over her head. I expected to see layers of underwear but suddenly she was naked. She let her dress fall onto the rock and ran into the sea, leaping in the cold waves and gasping at the shock of the cold, her voice reached me, faint as a lover's whisper carried across the surface of the water. Then she was swimming powerfully away from the shore.

'She stayed in the water for a long time, swimming, lying on her back to gaze at the sky and diving below the surface. At one point she stayed down so long that I thought of a mermaid again then felt a pang of fear that she may have drowned, but she reappeared suddenly, water streaming down her face and hair. She swam so far out that it became impossible to see her between the waves but she returned with a calm, confident stroke. When she finally emerged she walked straight to her clothes, picked up boots and dress and continued to the cliff where she dressed quickly, glanced around her, then scrambled up the cliff and disappeared.'

'You know that was me, don't you?' asks Ria.

'I think I knew' he replies.

A rap on the door shocks them out of their dream-like state. A hoarse voice calls, 'commander, we have a problem on deck.'

Hand to his mouth Randal coughs. 'I will join you in the inst...' He corrects himself. 'In a moment Mr. Taylor,' then looks at Ria and nods his head in a slight bow. 'Apologies. As commander I must always available to the needs of the ship and crew. Before I go there is something I would ask of you. I had hoped for more time to explain, but …… Will you work with Zak? Help him with the animals, share your knowledge? We will talk again tomorrow. Come as soon as you can.'

He leaves her in the cabin with all its books, maps and charts.

He trusts me.

11

Chosen

Nan is in a group of women sitting on deck. She rises and comes to meet Ria, holding out her right hand in welcome then places the left in the small of Ria' s back to push her gently to one side away from the other women. Ria relaxes and allows herself to be guided. She answers Nan's questions:

'The cabin is very plain. He has only the things he needs as commander of the ship; Shelves of books, a desk with deep drawers and a cabinet with many trays. I think the trays contain maps. I can tell you no more than that. The trays and drawers are kept locked. The conversation was simply my answers to his questions; how old am I? Where did I live? What were my parents like? Why did I join the ship?'

'And what was he like?'

'Not what I expected. He asked his questions gently. He listened to my answers. I told him very little. I will meet him again tomorrow.'

'The other women will want to know much more. You are going to have to get into the desk, read his books and maps. You must have something to tell them.' Nan leads Ria back to the group she had been sitting with. They all look in her direction but Nan speaks for her.

'She doesn't know anything yet. Give her time. She will meet him again tomorrow.'

'Thank you, Nan' says Ria. 'It must be hard work for you and the twins without us.'

'The others help us with our work when they have finished their own.'

'I will come and help whenever I can but now I must find Zak. *Ask him about Jen.*'

Ria goes down to the animal hold. 'Zak, why do you think Jen has decided to go along with Mr. Kierle's wishes?'

'What do you mean?'

'He told her not to mix with the other women and she seems to have decided to stay away from everyone.'

'She will have her reasons,' says Zak. 'We all act in the way we see best but I have no way of knowing what her reasons are. I think this is something you should ask Jen. She may tell you the truth. She may not be able to. Either way you may learn something. Help me with this fresh bedding before you look for her. I'm worried about the animals. They need to feel the sun. Their energy is beginning to dwindle.'

Together they drag the bundles of bedding into the animals' stalls. *Even now, the smell of summer meadows I could almost believe I am on my way to Grandmother's hut.*

As soon as the animals are clean and settled she goes to find Jen, gradually becoming aware of a feeling of unease as she approaches the decks. *Do not tell them what you know. But who? Listen first. Listen until they are listening to themselves but do not tell them* Even so she is not prepared for the change she finds in Jen who is sitting on the edge of her bunk with her head in her hands. She looks up briefly as Ria lets herself in. She is pale and trembling, talking even before the door to her cabin is opened.

'I am letting them think I will go on with this arrangement,' says Ria. 'Why would I not? We have our own cabins, privileges. But we have already, haven't we? Assessments, examinations.'

'You mean Kierle?' asks Ria.

Jen looks down as she speaks. 'He has a terrible voice when he speaks to me. It's as if someone else is speaking through him. 'You will do as I command,' he says, 'so that you may command others. I know that you want these things.'

'Is this how the commander treats you, Ria?' she asks and as she speaks she stands up with her head held slightly back and steps towards Ria, scowling and stabbing the air with a pointed finger. 'Kneel and bow your head. Now stand and hold your head high. *She seems to know him so well. It's almost as if she has become him.* 'I want that haughtiness, that strength. You must not diminish yourself with downcast eyes. You were selected for your strength. Having been selected you now have power. Hold yourself straight when you stand before me. Your chin must be level. You must not tremble. You are now mine. You want to be mine and so you stand tall and straight while I test what is mine.'

Jen shudders. *Seems to return to herself for a moment and then goes into a shell.* When she speaks again it is in her own voice *and yet seems far away.* 'He says my back is straight, my hips broad enough, my breasts 'promising'. It's a terrible price we pay Ria, every inch being pried and prodded.'

Trancelike Jen continues, her body shuddering as she recalls each new indignity.

'I never stood naked before, Ria, not even in front of my mother. I kept telling myself that soon it would be over, it would be worth it. His hands were horrible - cold, damp. They crawled over me like heavy spiders, measuring me, 'testing the firmness of my muscles'. We were getting our own cabins. When we land we will have the first homes. And we will have earned it Ria. We won't have to work, clearing the land, building, farming, but none of the others will have to go through what we have endured.'

Jen is shivering now; she twists her fingers together, loosens them, and twists them again.

'I would cut my hair off. His fingers have trailed all through it.' Unaware of her own movements Jen hugs herself, rubs her arms as if to clean them, holds her face momentarily then clenches her fists and shudders, 'Those fingers.' Ria puts an arm around Jen's shoulders. *It might be better if you cried. Let go. Let yourself cry.*

'I won't cry. I won't let them get the better of me. They think I will live with him, carry his child. Well, let them think that. I will take the cabin, the home, the privileges. I have a right to them. The sooner we reach land and he sails away again the better.' *Surely he will stay as Guardian of the new community?* 'It may not be what they want to hear.'

Now Ria realises that her hand is resting on Jen's head. That her grandmother's energy surrounds them; enters her as if through the top of her own head, spreads warmly through her body, down her arms, flowing out through her fingertips to Jen who is still fighting.

'I don't want to cry.'

Grandmother's energy becomes her own as she guides Jen to lie on the bunk, soothes the troubled air around her, around her head, her chest, her stomach, moving intuitively down and around, hardly aware of her own actions, until the light that has been travelling through her ebbs and Jen has cried herself to sleep. Gently Ria pulls the cover over her and moves away. Overwhelmed by exhaustion she makes her way back to her own cabin falls into her bunk and closes her eyes. *Singing? Grandmother and Zak? No, it is the river. The river is singing on its journey to the sea and I am flying over the river, listening to the singing and following. I am sure grandmother's voice is there amongst the others but I look down into the river flowing beneath me and I see my own face with Zak alongside me. I turn to look at him but he has gone; look back along the river now that we have almost reached the sea. Grandmother is in the river but all I see is a swan beating its huge wings, lifting herself away from the water just in time to save herself being carried into the waves, afraid of being dragged down but now I see that she is not a swan at all but some other huge bird folding her wings and diving down under the water. Oh grandmother why didn't you wait and travel with me? And shall I dive in after you? Swimming away from the ship now in the cold and dark, towards a warmer, lighter sea. Through the haze of underwater dawn, strain to see the creatures whose singing is all around and to remember tales of shipwrecked sailors supported by huge fish with skin instead of scales. Surfacing, struggling back towards the air. Waking.*

Crawling from her warm sheets she washes and dresses and wonders what will happen to them - men and women, wonders too, about the ship. She lifts the lamp from its niche to look more closely at the cabin wall. The planks are perfectly fitted and jointed. Sealed together with something thick and slightly tacky they almost appear seamless. There is a sound that she has not noticed before, probably a new creak of the masts and rigging as the ship rocks through gentle swells.

She pulls the cabin door closed behind her as the dawn is drummed into the new day. The air is damp on her face. The sea is only just visible through the bright mist and it to Ria that the sun penetrates the mist onto her body, moving with her. They are sailing in a globe of hazy white light. The sun is a dazzling promise of warmth, a short but vivid pathway into the mist. Even sound has difficulty travelling through it so that a wave rolls calmly against the ship and she is suspended in the momentary hush waiting to hear it. *Hush - whisper - hush. Nothing is certain. The sun may be blazing in the sky. My skin is confused, warm spots in cool air, small patches of warmth on one ankle, one shoulder, the side of my face and yet I am cold, breathing cool into my face, my head, my chest and dampness settles all around me as if my senses are being stolen gently from me, gradually slipping away. I can hear but there is no sound. No scent on the air, just coolness.. There must be salt on my lips but I no longer taste it. All I can see of the ship is a small circle of deck, the bottom of the mast, the low rigging in a curving wall of bright mist as if there is nothing else, just this ship, this water, this uncertainty. And yet I am sure they are out there. They are following us, curious about us, wishing to befriend us. They could be so helpful to us. I will swim with them.*

When the breakfast bell rouses her she joins the rest of the women for breakfast and is surprised that Jen does not seek her out. She sits instead with Nan who asks nothing about the commander. All conversation is about the sounds from the sea.

'They were terrified.' Nan is telling her. 'But I said how can anything so beautiful be dangerous?'

'Not everyone thought it a beautiful sound, Nan.'

'Not me. It was evil. The sound of darkness.'

'I think they are just sea creatures like birds are creatures of the air. Birds sing. We are not afraid of them.'

'Birds don't live under water. These are the creatures of the deep.'

'Calling us.'

'Taunting us.'

'When I volunteered I thought we would be safe. But now...'

'We must try to see these creatures. If we see them we might have a better idea.'

'We will never see them. They will never come to the surface in daylight. They swim under the ship. Following us. Waiting.'

Ria listens, saying nothing. The women are rising now, clearing up, preparing to join their work groups.

....

Later Randal visits Ria in her own cabin. He touches her face as he speaks. His large, strong fingers brush her cheek, trace the outline of her eyes. I have brought you a gift.' It is a sheepskin and she loves it at once. Its oily perfume will transform the cabin into a place of her own, link it to her grandmother's hut. She rests her cheek against then reaches up to brush his cheek lightly with her lips to thank him. *He smells of tar and lemons.* He bows his head, pressing his nose lightly into her hair and breathing in deeply. She enjoys the roughness of his shirt against her cheek, the tang of his breath, the rise and fall of his chest. Their fingers are entwined.

'Here,' he says, stepping back. 'I have brought you my maps and charts. Can you read?'

'Of course.'

'And write?'

'Yes.'

'Read these if you wish. I want you to know that you are free to come and go here. These too, read it all' he says, running his fingers along a shelf of books held firmly in place by leather straps. He lifts one down and opens it for her. *Ship's Log. Dates, times, 'Storm – all safe. New instructions – trousers now available to women. Co-operation.'* He closes the book, returns it to the shelf and slides out a wooden tray. 'And these.' *Night Skies*. For each date he has drawn three charts 'Evening' 'Midnight', and 'Pre-dawn'. *Are the stars in the evening different from those in the morning?* 'Look closely. Each night as we have moved, the stars have appeared in slightly different positions. They will guide us home.'

'Home?' *The cough, the back of his hand against his mouth.*

'I use them to record our route. When I return I will use these charts to navigate.' Replacing the chart he turns to another tall chest of shallow drawers and slides out a tray of large maps. Carefully he lifts one out and smooths it flat on the surface of his desk.

'This is a map of the coastline we have left.'

'And these?' she asks looking at those left in the drawer.

'Other coastlines I have remembered, from my father's collection, from my past.'

'How did your father come to have maps? Who are you really? Where are you from?'

'I am a man of the sea, Ria. All my life I have lived with the sea. It is where I feel at home.' He opens a second drawer, slides out more charts. 'These are maps of the undersea world. There are huge mountains and deep valleys below us, as big as anything is on land. The seabed is full of mysteries, some beautiful, some dangerous, some both.'

'You know the ocean bed?'

'No.' He smiles.

'But I knew of the maps and had studied them. Before we sailed I had time to reproduce them and your committee encouraged me to do so.'

They are standing close together, hands resting on the chart. As he speaks she is entering the undersea world mapped out before her, swimming down into the valleys, exploring the mountains. *There are creatures here we have never dreamed of. What are they thinking as we sail across their sky? That we can fly? That we move across their world as we choose without a thought for them? Perhaps they are afraid of us, waiting to see if we will harm them. Perhaps they are waiting for us to contact them. Perhaps they could help us.*

She shivers. A tremor, ripples through her; the hairs of his arm have brushed against her skin.

'These are the reasons I chose you' he says, straightening up he speaks. 'I wanted to share them with you.

She eases a map from the open drawer.

'My home map,' he explains. 'It shows all I remember of my home. I wish I had explored more, but at least I remember my father's maps, things he taught me. This village,' he points to a bay at the edge of the sea where he has drawn steep banks of pebbles sloping down to the water. Through a broad estuary a river curves its way to the sea. At the other end of the village the pebbles end abruptly at the bottom of tall cliffs topped by trees, 'is where I grew up. Where I learned to swim and fish, build boats and sail them. I never explored the river or went inland to the hills or the forest. It was always the sea for me, following my father. He oversaw the building of a fleet as well as building small boats with his own hands. It was called Sea Village and it was all I ever wanted. They built the ships in the workshops.' He taps the map pointing out a cluster of tall wooden buildings alongside the estuary.

'We launched them on the year's highest tide. The celebrations would start at dawn. We decorated the ships. Everyone went aboard a ship, down into the deepest hold, up onto the top deck. Those who could climbed the rigging. A feast was laid out on tables all along the estuary. Just before high tide the set sail bell would sound and we would all line the bank to watch the ships sail out into the bay.

'Then my father was called to meet our Guardian, on a stage built on the pebbles in the centre of the beach, for the payment for his work and to receive the thanks of the people. They clapped and cheered and sang 'Thanks to the Seafarer'. Then it was down to the water for sea dancing and songs.'

'Sea dancing?'

'Wonderful fun. You would love it. The musicians play from the pier and everyone dances up to their knees in water. They go out in lines, children in the shallows, dancing and splashing and singing, then grandparents, the younger adults go further out and weave around each other along the beach and in and out of the water. The young people go in furthest to mix dancing and swimming with riding the swell. It goes on until everyone is exhausted, or until it is too dark to see, whichever happens first but somehow it seems that the two things always happen together.

'You must have been very happy.'

He coughs. 'Until my father was lost we were.' *When did that happen?* Hearing sadness in his voice, she lifts her head to look directly at him and is struck by the green of his eyes, the unruliness of his eyebrows, the curls in the hair which has escaped the ponytail, tiny beads of moisture which glisten on his skin.

'What happened to your father? He smiles and his fingers tighten slightly on hers.

'I lost him. Or he lost me,' he sighs. *He will tell me.* 'We went out together in our small boat. My mother warned us not to go, I thought it strange, a thing she never did, interfering, but she said, 'Don't take the boy out today.'

'You know he is safe with me,' he said. And we went. We spent the afternoon in the boat and were still out as it begun to grow dark. It was a clear night and he had rowed right out of the bay, away from the lights of the village, to test my knowledge of the stars and moon. We swam in the dark. He had done it many times before, teaching me to stay in the water; use strength and knowledge wisely, find my way home by the stars. Then he said something new,

'Off you go now, swim home. Do it without me to prove that you can. I won't be far away and you will be safe.' And I did. I swam home. I think it took me all night. I don't remember much other than swimming by the stars. I don't remember seeing the village, or finding the beach, or how I got out of the water. They found me there in the morning, with a smile on my face. So they said. My father never came home.'

She moves her face closer to his. *Sea green eyes full of tears.* She kisses his eyes and the salt of his tears is warm on her lips. *Salt on salt on salt then moist and sweet* she tastes his dry salty lips. *A kiss. Thoughts slip away. Body responds, curving, moving closer, sharing mouths and hands, hair and he is beautiful and strong and tastes of salt and sweet strength and he is stars and sea and knowledge we are pulled together and I want to eat him, drink him, swallow him and he wants me and we both know that this should wait and yet we linger in the kiss until our bodies agree to pull slowly apart and I turn as if to look at his maps but with a sweet trembling.*

He tries to speak but has no voice, coughs, then speaks. His voice is barely above a whisper.

'The sea maps are the most difficult because I am trying to remember my father's pictures of places I had never been, things I had never seen.' He is standing very close behind her, their bodies touching. When he reaches to point something out on the map his hand brushes her arm. She drinks in the sensation of his closeness with her whole body.

Now his voice is gradually regaining its strength. 'The star maps are easy because I see stars every night. Land maps are only a little more difficult. At least I am familiar with the landscapes. But the valleys and ranges under the ocean, I can only imagine them.

'When I was very young I thought that he had been down to the depths, seen the ocean floor for himself, known all the creatures that live down there. He used to be gone for months at a time and I believed he took his ship out to the centre of the ocean and anchored it there to dive down, day after day,

162

and explore. I thought that one day I would go with him. I practised staying in the water for hours, diving deeper and deeper, staying down as far as I could for as long as I could.

'That was when I began drawing my own under water maps full of sea eels, jellyfish, crabs, and huge fish that I met far out to sea and deep below the surface. I saw creatures that would have terrified me on land but, down there, in the silent water, any sound was singing, every creature was peaceful. I always felt safe.

....

When she leaves Randal's cabin Ria goes quietly to look for Jen. *Randal's behaviour is so different from Jen's description of Kierle. There are things I need to know. What is Kierle really like? Has she been telling me the truth?* As she approaches the door of Ria's cabin something makes her hesitate and, instead of knocking on the door, she goes towards the small window where she leans against the wall and listens. Kierle's voice is loud and harsh.

'Ah Jen, my dear, I am glad I find you here, waiting for me. I have walked around the decks, considering you. Now I am ready. First we will prepare you. It is necessary. I will remove your undergarments. Trousers do not become you and are not fitted to your position. You will no longer be required to scrub decks, cook or stow your own bedding. You will never be asked to climb rigging or even splice rope. This is why I decided that you would resume wearing petticoats and skirts.'

Ria is curious and does not resist the temptation to continue listening.

'I like this way you have of standing, so still and silent. I think that, for the moment, we will keep just one petticoat for you to wear beneath your skirt. Let me see that these others are clean as I remove them. Do not tremble. Take my arm and I will cover your hand firmly with my own to calm you I have also decided that you no longer need to chew the root distributed amongst the women to prevent their menstruation. It is imperative that your child be the first born of the new community. This will increase your own standing so do not think of challenging me over this. You need tell no one. Have no fear of bleeding. I know that the men have some superstition about menstrual blood on board but it will not come to that. Of course you will tell no one that you are carrying a child. There are too many superstitions amongst these people. We will reach shore before it becomes obvious and by that time we will have selected a woman to tend you.'

'I believe today will be the day you will speak to me as your husband. I wonder how it will be. Will you choose to answer some comment of mine? Or ask a question of your own? I am sure there must be many things I could tell you, things that you will want to know, about your role beside me, as wife to the Guardian and mother of Guardians of the future. But it is also true that there are many things about your role that you will discover without the need for questioning. And now is a good time to start. I have been enjoying our introductions and think we know each other quite well by now. Well enough to begin our task. After today there can be no question of you returning to life below deck. I am sure you understand that. And after this conversation I fancy I will have heard the sound of your voice.

'Come my dear, you know that we do not need you to be quite so covered up for our little talks. That's what we need, for you to offer your undressing to me. We will take off your fine white layers one by one and lay them in a pile at your feet. And as we get closer to your lovely pale skin I am

164

encouraged. Soon I will hear your voice I think. But first I should acquaint myself with your deepest secrets, prepare you for our most meaningful conversation. I see that you are shivering. Don't worry, I will cover you, keep you warm. And as you are trembling I think we will go over to the bunk. Here you can kneel for a moment's rest while I... there, now I too am ready. Allow me to lift you up to meet me. And so we know each other and yes, there it is, a little sound, another? Louder perhaps? If I push you harder? Will you? I think you will if I plead hard enough? What harder? Here then, harder, harder still, a little cry, success. Success. Sweet, sweet, success.'

Ria returns to her cabin but cannot sleep.

12

Calls from the Sea

Just before dawn Ria creeps to the ship's rail at the place where she knows the rope ladder drops down to the water. She pulls off her night-gown, rolls it up and pushes it under the cover of the nearby boat before climbing over the rail and down the ladder towards the dark water. *The cold rush, the shiver, the freedom and I know I am not alone. They are not far away, watching me. Soon they will come, swim with me.* Calmly she turns in the water and sees them, swims towards them. The group disperses. *As if a single thought occurred to them simultaneously.* Disappointed, Ria starts to turn back but a scarcely visible movement catches her attention. One of them has hung back from the group just long enough for her to see him lift his body momentarily out of the water and arch his back into a dive. She rolls in the water and dives after him. First a shallow dive, then a deeper one staying down for as long as she can, allowing ears, eyes, skin, to adjust to being under water. The dark sea is alive. Creatures swim, weaving through each other's clouds to disperse then regroup. And he has gone.

She watches a shoal of fifteen or twenty fish swimming together. Their bodies are speckled with a flickering pale green light and she sees them briefly as individuals before they swim together seeming to create a single creature making its easy way through the water in the direction of another, a sparkling blue creature, much larger and moving faster. As they meet it is as if two bodies dissolve into each other momentarily then re-emerge to find themselves and continue on their way.

Ria looks at her own body. She too has an underwater light – a pale green glow that rises from her skin in thousands of tiny bubbles floating away from her, up, towards the surface. Passing a hand over her arm she sees bubbles rise more quickly.

Needing to breathe, she looks up, kicks and reaches for the surface. Once back in the air she looks for the bubbles of light but they are no longer visible. Treading water she turns her back to the ship and scans the surface in the hope of seeing the group she knows was swimming with her. They have disappeared; extinguished their light by swimming to the surface, or escaped her by diving deeper than she is able, or scattered to render themselves invisible. She cannot see them. It is time to return to the ship.

Climbing the ladder is much more difficult than she has anticipated. *Impossible* She is tired and very cold. Dragging her body up one rung after another she is desperately aware of each sway of the rope, her feet slip, her arms and legs have no strength. Shuddering she looks up to see how much further she has to climb, and is simultaneously horrified and relieved to see someone looking over the rail at her.

'Hold on, miss.' *Russell.* 'Catch hold of this.' He is lowering a rope 'and wrap it round you.' Even though she is stiff with cold she manages to catch the rope and wind it around herself and with Russell's steady pulling she reaches the rail. It is not until he wraps a linen sheet around her that she remembers that she is naked. Russell seems not to have noticed but as they pass the boat he lifts its cover to retrieve her night-dress and comments, 'You'll need this.' She is too cold to smile as he guides her back to her cabin where she falls shivering onto her bunk. As he covers her gently with several warm dry layers he speaks softly. 'I will bring you a warm drink but please don't do that again. It's much too dangerous. And you never know who might be watching you.'

....

Randal is telling Ria more of his own story. 'And then there was my grandmother.'

'Tell me about her.'

'You would have liked her. She was a storyteller. My mother used to say "Don't tell him any more of your stories. Bad enough that his father fills his head with ideas. Already I have trouble keeping him at home without you stirring his curiosity." But I loved her stories. She and I talked about my father's dream to command a fleet of ships, follow those who had left our shore centuries ago and find out what had happened to them.

'His own great grandfather had watched the white and gold fleet sail. On one of those ships his sister was taken as captive wife by one of the captains. He always refused to believe that she was dead. He collected maps and learned about ships and the sea for the day that he could sail in search of her. But the day never came. His collection passed to his son and eventually to me.'

'So it was because of your father that you set sail?'

169

'Partly, but also because of my grandmother's tales. Throughout my childhood she told me stories of the past. Stories about men and women, mountains and forests, rivers and seas. It always came back to the sea. She told me about gold and silver ships and young people tempted, or stolen, from their families to sail in them, about constellations and the star gods who climbed through the night sky to lead sailors safely across the oceans, and sea demons, monsters with many legs that floated effortlessly underwater waiting to embrace any creature who dared go within reach of their inescapable tentacles. Even they called me to the sea.

'My mother did her best to save me. She hoped all the terrible stories would frighten me away from the sea but it was irresistible. I was drawn to it, spent hours out with my father, diving to search out the creatures that lived down there, listening for their calling, their singing. Then that last time I went out with him I nearly drowned and he was lost. My mother was distraught. She blamed the sea. She tried to keep me from it. Begged me not to sail but the more she begged the more trapped I felt. Her love was becoming a prison.

'When I heard that a new fleet was sailing I volunteered immediately and was given the command of Yallah, a beautiful ship, the tallest in the fleet. I combined my father's collection of maps and charts with clues from my grandmother's stories. We sailed in search of our people and we almost reached yours. Yallah was the last of our ships to go down and somehow I managed to swim to land. That was the second time I almost drowned and I promised myself I would get back to my mother and let her know that the sea had not swallowed her son as well as her husband.

....

To feel the early morning sun on her skin, Ria slips off her cotton nightdress and lies naked, stretched out on her window bunk so that the first fingers of dawn can trace its patterns on her body. Lying there watching the sea, welcoming the dawn and dreaming of swimming to freedom she thinks of the creatures who swim alongside the ship. She has come to think of them as friends. As soon as the sun rises above the horizon the swimmers disappear but she knows they will return at sunset; that they are never far away. And now she is aware of one in particular. She sees him from the deck, at dawn drumming. He swims at the front of the group and holds his head up out of the water as if to see her. She stands on the same spot at night and knows that he will be there, swimming, looking in her direction. *How would it feel to be close to him? How would his skin feel? Rough. His skin would be hard and rough. Dry underwater skin that would scratch and graze my own. Taking my hand his fingers would scratch but his palms would be soft. Only when I moved closer, reached out to embrace him would I feel the saltgraze roughness as. I wrapped my legs around him, pulled our bodies together. His kisses would taste of salt. His energy surging through me releasing me to enjoy his freedoms, the enormous cool dark water of the ocean, its green lights, the glowing bodies of the swimmers.*

Another day, Randal is showing her a map of the night sky. Explaining the waxing and waning of the moon and how the stars appear to move, how it is possible to make observations and take measurements in order to follow a steady course,

'Even though we have been at sea for weeks seeing nothing but sea, sky, and more sea.'

Hearing his voice, seeing the stars, feeling the rocking of the ship, she wants his hands on her body, wants to feel his breath on her face, and wants to hold him. 'I know,' she says. 'I know.'

'I brought you these.'

She turns to look at his outstretched fists, turns them over, lifts his fingers one by one to reveal the tiny gifts he is offering her.

'Shells. Once the homes of sea creatures'

'But where from?'

'I have a small collection that I made before we sailed, while the ship was being built. My people believed that shells held great treasure and the deeper a shell lay, the more wonderful the treasure. Every year there was a competition. As young people we trained ourselves to dive deeply, staying in the water longer and longer, searching for the most beautiful shell and always hoping that we would discover the treasure. Whoever stayed in the water longest won a garland, and the throne of shells. It was built entirely of driftwood and decorated with shells from the previous competitions. He or she would sit on the throne to watch the festivities and to eat at the feast on the last evening before handing it over to the new champion. The festival was dedicated to thanking the sea for its bounty - for the fish we ate and the shells we loved, but also for our ancient beliefs that the sea gave us the sun each morning, and the winds which brought us the rain we needed for our crops to grow, for us everything had its origin in the sea. Some even said that people began in the sea. Like these shells.'

'They are beautiful shells,' she says. 'Thank you.'

After he has left she looks closely at the three tiny white shells. At first they seem identical but as she looks closely she begins to see the differences. Each has eight ridges running from the outer edge to a central, slightly raised point. Between the ridges a faint pattern traces a series of pinkish curving lines that loop away from one ridge towards the next. She tries to count these loops, wondering whether they relate to the age of the creature that lived here but they are too faint, too close together. She touches them gently with the tip of her smallest finger. The rough outer edge and the smooth inner. Inside, the largest is pink while the others are blue. One a stormy grey blue, the other the pure blue of a clear sky.

The creatures that lived in them would have known the colour of their own shell, would have had no idea that if they had been living in a different shell their whole world would have been a different colour. We might be born into a pink light, or grey blue, or pure shining blue, a different world, a different life, but how can we know? How many differences might there be? And even our small differences, part of greater differences, part of something we don't know because we cannot see.

....

Ria and Zak are in the hold delivering a cow of her twin calves. Zak is explaining a superstition 'If the crew had realised she was in calf when we came on board they would not have let her on. It's bad enough that they believed the committee's teachings so willingly without having them apply it to the animals as well.'

'I always believed it was for the woman's sake that she was kept away from men while she was pregnant.'

'You believed too much Ria. *I believed too much! And yet I was always told that my questioning was wrong. If I believed too much, what about those who never asked?* It suited the committee to encourage men's fear of women. No man would ever set foot in a birthing house. Pregnant women became such a powerful mystery to them that it fuelled their fear. It was all about fear.

I have been careful not to let them find out, they would throw her overboard, but they will be glad enough of a share of her milk. Lucky there are two. We can get this poor old girl to adopt one and stop her mourning. If she called out through one more night I think she would have ended up as supper for the lucky few. You and Jen are going to have to be careful.'

'I know.'

'I'm not sure you really understand how jealous the other women are Ria. They see you and Jen with privacy, your own cabins, extra rations. . . I know you still do your share of the work but what about Jen? They only see her at mealtimes and even then she barely speaks.'

'We have promised to talk to them when we have something to tell.'

'No, you promised to tell them something in seven days and you have had four days already.'

'I must talk to Jen again. We must decide what we will say.'

'Be careful what you tell them Ria. It may not be what they are expecting to hear.'

....

Each morning now she stands on deck as if to see the dawn. She is meeting him even though he is in the water and she remains on deck. When she sees him first he is at the head of the group, leading them alongside the ship. They are singing quietly and their voices are barely distinguishable from the murmur of the sea. *They have sea bodies, sing with sea voices, they sing to each other but they sing for us too. And he rises out of the water to greet me, dives and reappears away from the group. I feel myself enter the water to swim beside him. We swim closer and closer together. He fits his body to mine, his chest at my back, his tail follows the lines of my legs. His skin is rough and hard with scales. I feel them burning into my skin. We arch and dive then kick and glide as one. I roll in the water to face him, trusting him to hold me on my back as he flies through the water with me in his arms and his breath is cool and the salt of his kiss is far away and I arch my back as I strain to reach him but always he slips away*

....

Randal has brought her a feather.

'Is this the feather of a sea bird?' she asks.

'Yes. Does that trouble you?'

'A little.'

'You do not need to be concerned. The bird was not harmed. The feather floated down from the rigging and as I caught it I thought of you. I have sharpened the end.'

175

'And I have brought you this.' She takes the small clay pot of coloured liquid from him and instinctively lifts it to test its scent *earthy and green plant, juice or crushed berry.*
Carefully she places the small pot onto the ledge built into the cabin wall. When she looks up she catches him smiling, watches the muscles in his neck flex as he lifts his chin a little.

'It is the juice of berries from the hold. Zak found them for me. And here is paper. Use it carefully; we have precious little on board.'

Placing the paper on her table he picks up the quill, dips it into the ink and, in the top left corner of the first sheet he draws a circle. *Purple red, blood.* Then across the circle he draws the feather. Stepping closer to watch she recognises its scent and knows that he is using the same berries that her grandmother had used.

'I cannot stay,' he says 'The heat and stillness of the air is beginning to worry the crew. But now you have something to do. It is boredom more than fear that drives people mad when a ship is becalmed.'

'How long will it last?'

'It is impossible to say but the air always moves eventually.' In spite of the heat she shivers as his hand rests briefly on her arm but he is already turning to leave.

She dips the quill into the ink, stirring up the scent of evenings in her grandmother's hut. At first the nib resists then scratches against the paper. Ria draws a single line down the centre of the page and this line becomes the main mast with three yard poles but no sails. Her pen moves hypnotically as it scratches in the ropes, the shrouds supporting the mast, and the ladder like ratlines between them.

As she sketches she thinks of her grandmother's feathers. She too had used feathers for writing, but also for ornament, for filling pillows, for healing and for rituals. Ria has never before considered the importance of feathers in her grandmother's life but as she hatches and cross hatches the margin of her page she remembers:

'Feathers hold the secret of flight for those who free their mind sufficiently. If you would fly in your dreams, fill a pillow with feathers. A feather at your window can help you learn from your dreams. When you wake at first light and your dream is still new, touch the feather and look through the window. If you have caught your dream it will shed new light on your thoughts as you consider the coming day.

'If you would guard your spirit against the weight of heavy fortune, cleanse yourself, and the air around you, with a feather which you consider beautiful. The size of the feather does not matter, no more the bird it comes from, or its colour. What matters is that it is beautiful to you. No bird must be harmed. If you can collect a feather fallen from a bird in flight its power to lift will be greater, greater still if it is caught before it has touched the earth.

'If you desire to escape the bonds that hold you in your present situation, collect many feathers. Take them to a small room in a quiet place, away from the distractions that will try to hold you. Prepare a small fire and wash an earthenware bowl. Place an ember from the fire in the bowl and hold the first feather over the glowing ember so that the tip of the feather begins to smoulder. One by one your feathers will give up their secrets as they smoulder.

'Do not struggle to answer questions. Hold them in your mind. Breathe them in deeply and breathe them out again. If you have the help of a skilled woman, she will tend the fire and the feathers for you. Breathe in a five question circle of thought until your feathers have burned and the room is full of their secrets. Some secrets will escape and be lifted away but you will have taken in sufficient for your needs.

'You will not immediately know all that you had hoped to know. Continue to be open to new ideas in the days to come.

'You may feel that you have been asleep and are just beginning to wake. You may feel that you have been deprived of sleep and need to rest for hours, or even days.'

....

The heat is becoming oppressive. Men and women grow lethargic as the days lengthen and the ship slows. In the evenings they sit on deck hoping for cool air or a breeze. It has become clear that it was not only Ria who had a secret life in Sanctuary. Some families had been breaking the rules of the community by telling old storied and singing forbidden songs. As the voyage continues, the singers and storytellers become more confident. This evening Ria is surprised to discover that they have been talking about feathers and someone is telling a story of a young boy who was visited each morning by a strange white bird.

This boy was known as Black because of the colour of his hair and eyes. They were as black and shiny as the deepest tar pit. On the fifth morning Black walked towards the bird expecting it to fly away. But its only movement was the comical tilt of its head as it tried to keep an eye fixed on him. Black knelt near the bird and put out a hand. The bird hopped just out of reach. Three times Black reached out and the bird hopped away.

'Black, come and help with the firewood.' At the sound of his mother's voice Black turned his head and when he looked again the bird had gone. There on the ground was a feather, long and white but tipped with grey. Black picked it up and tucked it into his belt.

He and his brother spent the day in the forest collecting firewood and it wasn't until the evening that he thought of the bird again.

'What is that tucked into your belt?' his grandmother asked him.

'A feather from a strange bird I saw this morning' he replied as he handed it to her.

'The feather of sea bird,' she said, 'Look after that, young man. 'If you can fill a pillow with sea bird feathers you will find your way to good fortune.'

'Throw it after the bird it came from' muttered his father. 'No good will come of keeping it.'

At dawn the next morning Black's brother awoke to find the bed next to his empty. He woke his father and they searched the hut, the clearing, the edge of the forest but found no sign. They roused the village and everyone searched all that day and the next day and the next.

When his grandmother found the seabird's feather in his pillow she smiled and said 'Don't worry. He is learning to fly.' In the village some said he had run to the cliff and, believing that he could fly, had thrown himself over the edge and died on the rocks, his body carried away by the sea.

His father and brother gave him up for lost. His grandmother smiled and said 'He will be back.' And every morning his mother went to the cliff to sit and watch for her youngest son. 'However he comes, whether he flies, or walks or swims or whether the sea returns his body, I know he will come back to me' she said. The villagers smiled sadly and said 'It's a terrible thing to lose a son. It takes a mother's mind.'

Three years later a golden ship appeared over the horizon and sailed straight to the cliff where his mother sat and at the prow of the ship stood a captain with hair and eyes as black as the deepest tar pit. The sailors lowered a boat for him to row to the shore and all the while his mother sat waiting. He climbed to the cliff top and she held out her hands to greet him.

Around their hut that evening the villagers gathered and he came out to tell his story. No-one believed that the bird had come back that first night to find the boy who had taken its feather. That the bird had given him the secret of flight for one night and he had flown over the sea and fallen asleep exhausted on the other side of the world. A beautiful young woman had found him and taken her home to her father, a great sea captain. For a year he lived with her family and of course they fell in love and were married. It took another year to build the golden ship that her father gave them as a wedding present and most of the third year for him to learn to sail it.

But however it had happened, the boy with the black hair and eyes had stepped across the sea and back and now that he had family each side of the ocean he spent his life sailing between the two. Many more ships were built and he guided many captains across the oceans in both directions. Families grew and mixed and travelled until the two great countries were separated only by the sea and on each shore there were families who wore a golden feather as a sign of their unity, their ability to step across the sea and back.

....

Ria gets up and crosses the cabin to her wash stand. Her daily ration of rainwater is tiny but she knows it is a luxury, which the other women have lost, until it rains again. At the washstand she pulls off her clothes and sighs as the relief of nakedness allows her to forget the heat for a brief moment. Stretching her arms above her head she releases her hair from its pins allowing it to sweep down her back which arches in response.

She trails her fingers through the water then allows it to trickle down her neck and breasts before stepping over to her bunk where she lies open eyed but looking at nothing. She has no idea how long she has been lying there calming her breathing, relaxing her body, thinking of Randal,
Breathe slow
Breathe deep
Lie calm
Don't sleep

The spell, which had been her grandmother's, is her own now and she uses it well so that she is both relaxed and alert when the door opens.

Suddenly she is aware of many things at once. The air in the cabin stirs slightly as he steps quietly in. He appears calm but his movement is quicker than the heat would normally allow. He leans back against the door as she had on entering the room but rests his head against it as if in relief its weight.

She does not move, not even turning her head to look at him but she senses him moving closer. As he traces the outline of her face with his fingertips she hears his breathing. Brushing her hair away from her face he moves closer and takes her head in his hands. She notices their dryness. Her attention is caught by the closeness of his neck, strong and brown, taught muscles and bold veins. She is aware of the energy flowing through him. As he speaks she watches the movements of muscles and hears his voice as if it were velvet being stroked across her body

'I would like to make a map of you now.' As he speaks she considers reaching up to touch his throat but he seems to know her thoughts. 'Don't move,' he almost commands before beginning to trace the contours of her head and face. His light, dry hands move down her neck towards her breasts. Closing her eyes she swims in an unfamiliar pool. Her skin trembles, cooled by his feather like touch. His controlled energy passes to Ria as a lightning bolt of clarity that strikes head, heart and body instantaneously. Knowing exactly what she wants informs her body totally. She reaches up to put her hands to his throat, slides them round to the back of his neck and up into his hair, pulling his head down until their lips almost touch. A single shudder runs through them both. Their mouths meet and she tastes his salt and lemon sweetness but then he pulls back, 'Ria, I... we should wait,' he whispers and his voice is hoarse. 'You must be free to make your own decisions. I see the way the other women look at you. They wonder about you, are a little afraid of you, but they respect you. I cannot compromise that.'

'It will make no difference to the way the others feel about me.' Taking his hand she slides back to the cabin wall and attempts to guide him into space beside her.'

He breathes the scent of her sleepy body. Outside the rigging is barely creaking, the sails are still. The ship is still. He hesitates, 'I demand restraint on the part of the crew. I must lead by example.'

'You said I must be free to make my own decisions. This is my decision.'

'I am sorry, Ria.' He says, speaking as he moves away from her. 'I should not have come. It was a moment's weakness and it was wrong of me. Forgive me Ria. I must go.'

....

Moments later, as Ria is dressing, Kierle crashes into the cabin. The door slams closed behind him.

'Do not think of Mr. Russell coming to your rescue young woman. Mr. Taylor is with him, even now, explaining why my visit to you is necessary. It is for your own sake and also for the sake of everyone on board the New Hope. It is my responsibility to ensure that we are all protected from the dangers of the deep but you have been beguiled by those dangers, Ria. There is little hope for you but I will not give you up easily. I have come to save you from yourself and in doing so I hope to save us all. You cannot be allowed to endanger The New Hope any further.'

'If you are thinking of the creatures who swim alongside us, Mr. Kierle, I think you are wrong about them. I am sure they mean us no harm. They may even be able to help us; guide us to safety.'

'It is you who are wrong. They are but a small part of the dangers that surround us and they are tempting you. They are not people Ria. They are creatures of the deep. They have deceived you and you think you can trust them, but this is part of their power. This is how they work. They wish to enchant the mind of one of us then leave you to do their work, to serve their purpose. By appearing to you in this way they are affecting us all. You are endangering us all. You are the impure one at the heart of all our difficulties. It is my responsibility to teach you this, to ensure that you change your ways, prevent you causing further harm.

'You are a very dangerous young woman, here to tempt us. You tempt me to the limits of my endurance. You have blurred our commander's vision and led him towards impure thinking; allowing women to show their skin, dress like men, and now encouraging men and women alike to immerse themselves in unclean water, eat fish that have lived in the sea. I fear for the future of this voyage, for our lives. We are in danger of allowing ourselves to be dragged into the depths and where did all this begin if not with you?

'You would lead the other women astray. I know that it is your doing that the women dress like men and show their skin and therefore it is because of you that the men are distracted from their work, tempted by their presence, day and night. There is no modesty, no regard for purity.'

'But those decisions were made by our commander.'

'Under your influence. They are your dangerous, impure ideas. You have seduced him.'

'Have you spoken with Randal about this?'

He steps suddenly towards her, *too close*, and leans over her. She sees beads of sweat on his forehead, tension twitching in one cheek, eyes narrow and hard. She does not look away as he bears down on her.

'You should refer to him as Commander. You are altogether too familiar, too easy.' *Bony face, cheek bones, nose, chin, everything about him is hard, cruel. Hands all knuckle, he would like to hit me, seize me, push me down, but he will not.*

'You think you are clever. You think your trickery will torment me into violence against you, but I am stronger than that.'

He is holding her against the wall and she feels his breath, hot and putrid in her face *anger and fear.* She flattens her body away from him, pressing against the panelling, turning her head *away from the heat of him* towards the sweeter scent of the ship's timbers. *His fury wells up in him, fills him, is streaming out of him* and she keeps her face turned away. *He would pick me up, fling me across the cabin, roar, tear my clothes.* He raises his hands above her, then steps abruptly aside, roars his frustration and brings his fists crashing down onto the table. The table legs, fixed firmly in place, crumple and the table top staggers down unevenly. He regains his balance and strides out, swinging the door violently and slamming it closed behind him.

13

Stories, Songs, and Superstitions

Ria does down to the hold, hoping that Zak will have some calming words for her but now that she is here with the listless animals Ria is hardly able to concentrate on what he is saying. She hears Zak's voice, but picks up only occasional words, 'extra milk, overboard'. Her head is too full of her fears for Jen, her anger at Kierle and now she has Nina's demands to consider as well. She had encountered Nina on her way to the hold and had tried to calm her into waiting a little longer.

'Wouldn't it be a good idea for us all to talk about our hopes and fears? Then I can share them with Randal and Kierle?' she has suggested. *I wanted to listen to the women instead of returning to them with uncertain answers to their questions. But Nina's anger cannot be restrained. She is convinced that all is trickery.*

'You can't keep us waiting for ever, Ria,' Nina had replied in her usual angry tone. 'They have their plans and they think they can refuse our demands. They think they can distract us, prevent us finding out their intentions.'

'This did not come from them Nina. It came from me. I have been listening to women, hearing their thoughts and their ideas as well as their fears.'

'You may have listened, Ria, but these men are not interested in listening or explaining. Perhaps you are as innocent, as naive, as you seem, perhaps it is just pretence, but either way you are cleverly avoiding the facts. The facts are that the men and two men in particular, have the knowledge.

They are in control and we demand to know what the future holds.'

'Don't you believe that we can contribute to our own futures?'

'That is just what I am trying to do, trying to tell you. You and Jen have access to all the information we need. For all we know they may already have told you. Where we are going? How long it will take us to get there? What is going to happen to us there? Don't talk to us about dreams and possibilities. We want facts. You have had long enough.'

Ria tries again to concentrate on what Zak is saying but her thoughts keep returning to Nina's words.. Gradually, as if waking from a deep sleep, she realises that something is wrong. The sounds that reach them down here can be difficult to interpret but she has become accustomed to a certain rhythm and that rhythm has been disturbed. She looks up at Zak as the tone of his voice changes.

'Something is happening up there.' As they leave the animals, the cow bends to nudge her calf and it looks up at her.

The holds are eerily quiet but above them voices, men and women, powerfully urging something, or someone on. There is a muffled thump, a woman's scream, a man's outrage. *Sounds muffled by bodies surrounding, encouraging, venting frustration, heartbeats quickened, energy reawakened in bodies grown unaccustomed but now seizing the opportunity to return to life.* A Woman screams, others groan. Men shout, laugh, snarl.

The sour smell of bodies drifts from the crowd but through cracks in this wall of old air a different scent, of newly spilt blood is refreshing tongues to the memory of fresh meat. The crowd has tightened as men and women have crept forward. A desperate scream flings them back. A few words are distinguishable. Ria hears a man shout, 'Stop her' and a woman is saying 'Bleeding.' From somewhere there is a groan and a deep, resigned moan. The crowd opens up; individuals gather themselves as they see what has happened. Ria and Zak move towards the injured man.

He is lying at a strange angle on the deck, head lolling back, eyes staring in disbelief, mouth half open revealing a trickle of blood already dry. One arm is completely out of sight under his body.

She, *Beth,* stands over him with a knife so heavy she holds it in both hands. Its blade glints clean, pointing at his chest, but she has not reached him, knows that she will never reach him. She stands over him until her arms begin to tremble, her fingers lose their grip so that the knife falls onto his chest and slithers down, its point gouging out a splinter of wood before it slaps flat onto the deck. The trembling has spread through her arms and body and now engulfs her legs so that her whole body is shaking. Her knees turn in and she falls, collapses, over him. Ria and Zak approach her gently, each taking an arm to wrap around their shoulders as they lift.

'Leave her.' They hear Kierle's command but ignore it and continue to lift her away from the man. They lie her on her side. She does not resist, or even respond but lies staring at their feet as they move towards the man.

'You *will* leave him' Kierle orders turning to Taylor, 'Have him lifted.' Taylor looks directly at the two nearest men. He arches his eyebrows and nods. They step nervously towards the man who moans quietly and the crowd breathes in disbelief that he is still alive.

Kierle's voice has an exaggerated calm. 'Mr. Taylor.'

Taylor's is less controlled, wavers slightly as he instructs the men, 'Lift him.' They hesitate.

'Mr. Taylor' Kierle says again.

'Lift him' says Taylor more confidently. They lean slightly towards the man. The crowd watches in silence.

'Mr. Taylor.'

Taylor's voice is unfamiliar, high, stretched, as he orders the men again. 'Lift him.' They flinch but then bend towards the man's shoulders. Each takes hold of an arm, one wincing as if feeling the pain of the broken arm that he struggles to grasp under the body. Both close their eyes as they lift. A scream rises in the man's throat, shows in his face, but all that is heard is a cracking gurgle. The two men hesitate again but Kierle has turned his back and is striding away as he orders 'Bring him to me.' They tug but the body resists, they bend further to gain a firmer hold and pull again. The body comes away suddenly. He had fallen and impaled himself on an anchor hook that had been brought on deck for cleaning. They lift him easily now and, at a nod from Taylor, two more men step forward to help carry him after the surgeon. Taylor turns to follow and the crowd begins to move away as Ria and Zak help Beth to her feet. *No-one speaks. No sound from the sea. It is as still as death. Not a creak from the rigging. No movement in the air.*

Zak and Ria lead Beth towards the animals' hold but as they try to pass the women's sleeping quarters she stops.

'Come down with us,' Ria urges. 'You will be safe. We can look after you there.'

'No further. No further.'

Ria speaks quietly to Zak, 'Go on down. Mix her some warm, sweetened rue with cowslip and valerian root in milk. I will stay with her.' She turns to Beth. 'You and Meera share a bunk don't you? Which one is it?'

Beth lifts her hand a little, gestures towards the bunks at the far end of the hold. 'Show me.' When they reach the bunk, Ria gently presses Beth to sit. She refuses to lie down. *This woman has not slept for days.* 'What happened between you and that man?' Beth shakes her head.

'She cannot cry. She has no tears left.' Meera speaks from behind Ria. As if her head is too heavy to hold up, Beth tips forward.

'What is his name?' Ria asks Beth but Meera replies.

'Kris.'

'Beth, what happened between you and Kris?' Again she shakes her head as Ria looks around. 'Zak should be here by now. You stay with her. I am going to get something to calm her.'

She climbs the stair out of the hold and meets Nan who takes both her hands and speaks quietly, 'The men say Kris is dead. They are saying Beth killed him even though we all saw him fall. She had a knife but she would never have used it on him. No-one seems to know what they were arguing about.'

'Take her this,' Zak has appeared with a beaker of warm liquid. 'I should stay away.

Ria nods, takes the drink and returns to Beth. 'Drink this Beth,' she says, quietly. 'Just take a little sip whenever you can.' Ria begins to stand again but Beth grips her tightly, her trembling beginning again. 'Don't worry. We are not going to leave you here alone. Take another sip. Good, and a little more. I cannot stay with you now, but Meera is here, and Nan.' Beth obediently sips the drink and loosens her grip on Ria's arm. Ria turns to Meera. 'I must find Randal and talk to him about what has happened. Encourage her to drink this and try to get her lie down. The trembling will ease if she can relax even a little, and if she sleeps, don't disturb her.'

…………

She finds Randal in his day cabin, writing in the ship's log. 'I have talked with Mr. Kierle, Taylor and Russell about this incident. It seems that the woman may be pregnant which is particularly unfortunate given that the man has died. We can only assume he was father of the child. The burial will take place tomorrow. Our first burial at sea. I had hoped it was something we might manage to avoid given your people's superstitions about the sea.'

'Superstitions?

'Forgive me. Beliefs. Your people have very strong beliefs about the sea.'

'Beliefs which we were taught as if they were proven truths. It is no wonder so many have difficulty shaking them off.'

192

'Which gives me all the more reason to admire those of you who chose to sail,' he says, taking her hands and smiling gently. 'Look at this. It was amongst the books that Mr. Kierle has brought with him.'

'He allows you to read his books?'

'I have never given him the opportunity to prevent it. Read this, and there are others,' he says indicating a small collection of books on the desk. 'You might find an explanation of how an entire community could come to fear the sea.'

Ria takes the first book and opens it. It appears to be a neatly copied collection of stories and rhymes. The handwriting is small and stiffly vertical. 'Will you sit with me while I read?'

'No. I must check the preparations for the burial.'

'Read it,' he encourages her as he leaves.

From 'A Book of Beginnings'

The sea was here before the people. Creatures crawled out of the sea and learned to live on land. Before that they lived below the water's surface, breathing in the water, swallowing fish and weeds. They were peaceful beings that swam and sang and played in the water. They would swim up to the surface to catch sweet rainwater in their mouths and feel the warmth of the sun on their skin.

A few began to ask why they couldn't have sweetness and warmth all the time. They began to crawl out of the water onto the land allowing their skin to dry in the sun. They found rivers of sweet water that tumbled in to the sea and lost their sweetness. They stayed out longer and longer until some began to demand the right to live permanently in the air.

Their elders listened patiently and explained that staying out of the water too long would mean they would find themselves unable to return. They would lose the ability to breathe in the water. Their skin would dry up and once that happened they would only be able to breathe by swallowing air through their mouths.

For the first time arguments disturbed the underwater currents. Dark ripples spread across the surface as anger grew in the hearts and minds of the few. They accused the elders of trying to frighten them. How could it be proven that dry skin would be unable to breathe? Surely all that would be needed would be to swim again, returning to the water regularly to soften the skin. And, anyway, why would anyone want to return to the sea when the land is so beautiful, so warm and dry and brimming with sweet water?

As their anger grew to rage, furious dark waves built up and ran crashing against the shore. These were the first of many storms, each more terrible than the last.

'Let us go' demanded the few. They began to threaten violence, and the storms spread to the air and the skies above the ocean. Darkness began to eat up the light, which fought to break through in spasms that rent the black.

Always patient, refusing to fight, the elders opened their arms saying, 'Stay, or go. The choice is yours but remain long enough to hear what we have to say once more.'

Refusing to wait, or to listen, the impatient few called, 'We are leaving the oceans to live on dry ground, in warm air, where we can drink sweet water whenever we choose. Come with us now.'

They, and their followers, swam through the great storm towards the land and laughed as the waves tossed them high on to the shore. The tides of that storm were the highest ever reached by the sea into the land. Vicious tongues of water lashed riverbanks, swept down trees, and spread salt across fertile valleys rendering them poisoned so that plants and creatures that had lived there perished.

The storm faded behind them as they made their way across rock and earth to begin their new life but they never forgot the anger of the sea at their leaving and its power to reach inland and destroy. They made their way as far from the sea as they could. They ate whatever food they found. River fish had no taste to their salt ridden tongues. At first the sweetness of berries and nuts burst in their mouths and overpowered their senses so that they lay on the ground, dazed and helpless after eating until they learned to wash their mouths with fresh water. Gradually they became accustomed to these new sensations, but they never forgot those first experiences, never gave up the search for new and greater sweetness.

They encountered a great forest and made their way in with difficulty until they met a wall of rock which they could not climb or get round. It seemed to stretch for ever in each direction. Realising that they could go no further in their retreat from the sea they decided that this was to be their home. The forest would provide them with nuts and berries and it was not long before they began digging and discovered edible roots. Streams trickled to the ground along the edge of the rock face. These streams ran towards the sea, joining forces along the way to create a great river.

Still fearful of the power of the sea they began digging and surrounded themselves with three deep ditches, which they hoped would protect them. Along the tops of the ditches they planted young trees which would spread a protective network of roots deep into the ramparts of what had become their Sanctuary.

What else wonders Ria as she flicks through the book again.

....

The Power of the Sea

The sea has a dark power. It has a voice and it chooses who will hear it. Certain people it calls, calls them secretly. They tell no one but they are drawn, drawn to the sea.

At first they go to the water's edge. It calls them further. They begin to go into the waves. Deeper and deeper they go until their feet are lifted. The sea whispers to them that they are safe, that they can learn to swim like the creatures that live in its depths. And once they have heard the whispers they will not listen to reason.

And always the day comes when the sea calls them so far out, so deep, that they are lost. The sea changes you. The water presses you in, squeezes you. The deeper you go, the deeper its hold on you. And it wants to hold you, wants to keep you down there, to feed the creatures that lurk in its darkness. The dark that is down there is always trying to spread. It would creep up into the light if it could. It tries sometimes, sends a wall of water to suffocate the land, to poison it so nothing can grow. If it can it seizes people, drags them back to the depths, squeezes the life out of them. And when it has taken what it wants it spits what's left, crushed and rotting bodies, spits them back on the shore far from where it found them.

It's the same for those who choose to jump into the water and any that have the misfortune to fall into the waves. It takes them too, drags them deeper, squeezes the life from them. Any who manage to escape will try to get back to the surface but as they rise their bodies fill with life that is not their own. In their desperate race to get to the surface they breathe it in from the water all around them. Their body begins to swell. It rushes through them, up through the face, and bursts out: out of their mouth, out of their ears, even out of their eyes it bursts, shattering their face. If the evils at the ocean floor don't kill them the desperation of their fight to reach the surface will. And if their body is ever found it is unrecognisable, shattered from the inside by the evil rush of poisonous life that lingers in the sea, waiting for its next victim.

....

There are beetles whose wings sing and whose colours
defy the eye.

....

A Song Remembered

Take me to the sea mamma

Take me to the sea

We cannot see the sea daughter

Cannot see the sea

Take me to the sea Dadda

Take me to the sea

You must not see the sea daughter

Must not see the sea

Tell me of the sea Granpa

Tell me of the sea

The sea is full and wide young one

The sea is full and wide

Whisper of the sea Gramma

Whisper of the sea

Deep and wild and true, young one

It waits for me and you

....

And below the seas are other worlds

A world of mud. Mud as deep as the ocean itself. Mud full of squirming. Of violently coloured, wriggling, creeping, seeping things, things that have no need of sunlight, that have no eyes and squirm, sightless, through the cold, stinking mud, absorbing it through their skin to feed. To move they push themselves by swelling and shrinking their foul, soft bodies.

The mud acts as a barrier – a kind of muffler of movement. Beneath the mud lie layers of rock, but rock such as we have never seen. It is living, moving rock. It slips, grinds and crashes against itself. It is this unceasing movement that causes the tides to roll. It pushes the sea, pulls it back, pushes it again. The mud softens the crashing of the rocks but sometimes it becomes so ferocious that rock is lifted up, jagged, through the mud, forcing the ocean into huge waves. As long as it continues waves are formed. A violent storm is created as the waves suck the air behind them causing terrible winds. These storms so disturb the sky that even after the rocks have subsided, the mud settled and the waves died down, clouds continue to move, carrying rain, covering the sun.

It is in the depths, below the sea, below the mud, even below the rock, that our fates are sealed.

....

There are trees whose roots creep from the forest, under the earth, under mountains, under seas, to spring up through fresh earth and begin anew.

....

There is a creature below us which has no bones but a skeleton of gristle that sways as it swims, propelling itself through the water with the powerful side to side sweep of its tail. Its fish skin is covered in thousands of tiny teeth rough enough to scrape off human skin. Its eyes gleam in the deep, dark waters. It has many rows of teeth; Sharp teeth for tearing flesh; Strong teeth for grinding its prey to pulp; teeth that replace themselves when lost or ground down, teeth that are dedicated to killing and eating flesh. Especially human flesh.

This creature's entire purpose is the seeking out of food. It can smell a drop of blood diluted in a million drops of water from a quarter of a mile away. Even if disembowelled it will continue to swim, summoned by the smell of its own blood, and attack and gobble its own guts.

....

The Turning

The sun goes down

To the ocean floor

The sun comes up

To the sky.

As her child gives birth

And a girl is born

Woman looks to her mother

Who dies.

The sun goes down

To the ocean floor

The sun comes up

To the sky.

Man will mourn

But when his son is born

He forgets the past

And sighs

The sun goes down

To the ocean floor

The sun comes up

To the sky

....

Watch Reports

Horizon sighting

One sailing vessel, three masts. Reported by one observer only. Following normal protocol three more observers were summoned. They saw no ships. The first observer reported that the ship had sunk almost immediately after rising from below the horizon. Search parties failed to find survivors.

....

Shoreline sighting

One man crawled from the waves and fell unconscious. If, as suspected, he is a survivor of the sinking reported above, he has been in the water for a day and a half.

The survivor has been carried to the House of Trusted Ones and kept under constant watch. He remained unconscious for three days and nights but has, this morning, revived and taken water.

The man is recovering his strength. He speaks very little but is beginning to answer questions. He seems to understand us reasonably well and answers in a stilted version of our own language. Physically he is almost fully recovered. He is left with a slight irritation of the lungs for which we continue to prescribe the appropriate berries

....

Rhyme

Seed, bud, fruit, seed.

Bird, egg, bird.

Sea, sun, wind, rain.

Day, night, day.

Babe, girl, woman.

Babe, boy, man.

However anything grows,

It goes back to where it began.

....

The Transhue Beetle

The beauty of the transhue beetle cannot be described. Its colour changes so subtly that the changing itself is impossible to see and yet what was blue can become purple or green or shining black. Sometimes it is all these colours at once. It is as if the light falling on it were of shifting colour.

It is a rare creature - unseen by any person outside the circle of the Chosen Ones, Protectors of the Beetle. Theirs is the duty of keeping the sacred colony safe within the chapel at the epicentre of Sanctuary.

Each committee member becomes a Protector, and is given a single beetle which he may pin to his outer clothing or wear on a chain. He may choose to keep his beetle alive, in which case he must go to great lengths to protect it. Alive it is a beautiful, but delicate creature, easily crushed or destroyed by accidental dropping. Or he may choose to allow the beetle to die. The dead beetle is many times stronger than the live. It hardens in the dying process making it easier for the Guardian to preserve it. Care must still be taken however as the dead carapace can be brittle and can therefore crack if not properly cared for.

The most knowledgeable Protectors keep their beetle in a state of living death. This is considered to be the purest state. It is very difficult to attain but the Protector of a living-dead carapace knows that he has achieved the ultimate goal. In a process which can take many weeks, the beetle hardens from within. The Guardian must pin the creature to a piece of well-seasoned oak. The pin must be fine enough to pierce the body without damaging the internal organs. It must be long enough to suspend the beetle sufficiently high that the outstretched legs cannot reach the surface. The constant movement of the legs keeps the beetle alive. It must be fed a diet of the finest possible parings of wood from the innermost ring of a young oak. These must be softened further in fresh rain water in order that the mandibles can chew the oak to a mulch. In swallowing this mulch while unable to move the beetle is slowly committing itself to a solid state. If the suspension of movement and feeding regime were kept in the perfect ratio it is believed that an eternal living dead state might be achieved.

Access to and preservation of the beetle colony is closely maintained and no-one who is not committee would be allowed access to the inner chapel. This inner chapel itself was created specifically to house the beetle colony and The Great Book, containing the history of Guardianship and the Guardians' accumulated knowledge of the transhue beetle.

The chapel is unique in Sanctuary in that the walls and roof are clad in stone. These stone walls have been coloured with the crushed remains of many generations of the beetle. When their Guardian has died, the dead beetles are crushed and ground then mixed with fresh rainwater to form a paste. It is this paste which has been used to paint the stone walls of the chapel. The result is an ever changing ripple of colour - of hues which exist only here.

And there is a walkway around the chapel to which only the Guardian and elders have access. Walking around the chapel gazing directly at these indescribable, shifting hues is said to lead to a trance state, which offers access to certain truths.

Who collected all this and wrote it so neatly? Ria stands up and stretches. *So tired, I should go back to my cabin.* She walks sleepily over to Randal's desk to put the book back with the others and cannot resist picking up another. The handwriting in this one is completely different: It is looser, slopes forward and has some extravagant loops and swirls. *Randal's?*

In spite of the weight of her eyelids and a yearning for sleep, she opens this book at its first story entitled A Mother's Tale and carries it back to Randal's chair, reading as she moves:

I have not seen my son for many, many months. I begged him to give up the sea when his father was lost. He never understood that it was the sea that took his father. He would always believe that it was an accident. But I had seen the signs. I knew I should never have let him take the boy out that day. I wept as they sailed out of the bay but that time young Randal came back to me. The sea had only wanted his father and it threw my boy up onto the beach like a dying fish.

I still go down to the shore every morning, every evening, trying to make my peace with the sea. It gave me my child back once and I believe it will do so again. We were paying the price for the past but the sea is a fair master and I have surely paid in full. It was little enough to do with our generation. Now the debt must have been settled, my son must return.

Five generations have passed since the creature was captured and brought home in the nets and even then it was accidental. None of our people would ever intentionally harm a living being, its part of the agreement. We take what we need to live and we repay the debt by caring for the water; keeping it clean, using it wisely, always giving thanks at Sea Dancing.

She was a being above the fish and our people knew that. They tried to save her by keeping her in the pool. I think they believed that the pool had been created for that purpose. Until then the pool had been a mystery. Some said the waterfall had created it by luck, an accident. But the chapel told us something so beautiful must have been created for a purpose. They said it was proof of a greater power which was beyond our understanding. This power must lie in the water since the ocean rose up twice every day to refill it.

My husband's family is charged with the duty of keeping the pool clean and to visit it after each new tide to give thanks. This is because it was an ancestor of his, five generations back, who had brought her home. His name had been Randal too. That was my husband's mistake. Foolish pride in a name we should have shunned, but no, he would have it for our son.

'The debt has been repaid.' He said, 'It will prove to our people there is nothing to fear from the sea.'

This old Randal, well he was young then of course, had brought her home in his net, lifted her out all battered and broken and instead of putting her back in the sea for her own people he had decided he would save her. He put her in the pool and visited her after every high tide to check that she was still there. How could she get out? The channels are so narrow, only the smallest fish find their way in and none seem to find their way out. That was all she had to live on, the tiny fish that the tides brought in. Of course he took her food, fish that he had caught himself, but she would never touch them. He tried taking her fruit but that wasn't food to her. He took her flowers and scattered the petals on the surface of the pool. He tried coaxing her, asking questions about her life under the sea. She never spoke but he never gave up trying. He went on taking her gifts and talking to her about how he was only keeping her there until she was strong enough to swim back to her own people. His fruits and the flowers spoiled the water. He should have kept it clean but he was afraid that if he tried to climb into the pool with her he would frighten her.

Didn't he realise how terrified she must have been already? I think the truth is he had fallen in love with her and didn't want her to go back. They say that she sang at night. That the best way to hear the song was to swim underwater just after high tide when the returning seawater carried her voice back to her people. I think she was calling them to come and save her but they were helpless. They couldn't live out of the water so how could they come to the pool and they couldn't get up those channels. But they must have heard her calling every night and blamed Randal for keeping her there. What use is love if it is a trap you can't get out of? And she was dying in that pool.

The night that she died there was a terrible storm. Some say it was the storm that killed her, others that it was her dying that caused the storm. We will never know. But while the storm was raging he climbed in to the pool and carried her out. The noise was terrible, thunder and hurricane winds and his wailing, 'She has died,' over and over again.

And the waves were cruel that night, eating away at the shore, they crept right up the river channel, washing away the banks and swirling around the exposed foundations of the wooden houses until people were tipped out of their own homes and into the water.

They said they saw Randal carrying her up onto the cliff, as if he could escape the waves and all the fury of her family come to reclaim her. And then, in a flash of lightning, they saw him jump from the cliff, out into the dark, with her still in his arms.

So, the family is still repaying the debt, but the line has run out at my Randal. He is the last. There are people who say that they have taken him too, as a final payment. But I don't believe it. He is too good a son, too good a sailor. He loves the sea too much and they would understand that. And that's what my husband knew too. He knew the time had come to end the debt.

The night before my husband disappeared he had a dream. In the dream he heard a woman singing, calling him, into the sea. He believed that by giving himself to the creatures of the deep he would release us all, that they would be satisfied; the debt would finally have been repaid. He told me he was sure he had taught Randal enough to be safe from anything the sea might do and that he would prove it to me.

I tried to persuade him not to go. I thought it was some kind of sea madness from being out there day and night, year after year. I asked him to come away from the sea for a while but there was no reasoning with him. When he wanted to take Randal out with him that night I begged him not to. But he said surely I trusted him with the life of our only son. And of course I did. So I let them go. And they will let Randal come back to me. I know he will return. If the sea people wanted to keep him they would have taken him that night. If they were to keep him now they would owe us just as much as we have ever owed them. We paid their price and I trust them to bring him back to me.

14

Woman Overboard

Only when the book falls from her hands, and she realises that it is too dark to read any further does Ria return to her own cabin where she lies on her bunk to wait for the morning. It seems no time at all before the morning bells wake her. Her first thought is of Beth and she goes straight to the women's quarters.

When it is time for the burial Beth allows them to lead her to the top stair but refuses to go onto the deck. They watch the body, wrapped in a sail and weighted head and foot, lifted up to the rail and held there while Kierle speaks;

'His body has been purified and sanctified to preserve him from the evils of the deep. He was a pure man and led a pure life *a tremor through Beth's weak body.* He had high hopes of the new life he anticipated *sobs in silence, no tears,* at the end of our voyage, and it is with great sadness that we let him go. When we reach our destination we will create a memorial. Those of us who sailed with him will always remember that he lost his life in service to the new beginning.

'Enough,' whispers Beth so that Ria turns and guides her back down the stair and away. But not soon enough to avoid hearing the sounds of the slipping of the body over the rail, the slap as hits the surface and the closing of the waves as it is swallowed by the sea. Beth trembles so much that she cannot walk. Nan appears and they carry her back to her bunk. For the first time she submits to lying down and when Meera arrives she smiles to see her sister asleep at last.

'Shall I stay?' asks Ria.

'No,' says Meera. 'I will sit with her.

'Leave me with Meera,' Beth murmurs. 'She understands me best.' Ria returns to her cabin and lies on her bunk without undressing. Confused images and phrases from the day mingle in her mind as she drifts through the beginnings of dreams until the still silence of the ship is shattered by shouts of 'Woman overboard'. Ria rushes out to find Nan clinging to the rail, peering over, into the sea calling 'Beth, Beth.' She turns to Ria

'We thought she was still asleep.'

Beside Nan, Meera does not turn. She stares at the dark water and speaks without moving in a voice that cracks. She wipes away tears with the back of her hand. 'She slept the three hours I sat with her.'

'And the next three' says Nan.

'I thought she would sleep for days.' Meera is weeping now. 'But I allowed my own eyes to close and she slipped away from me. It could only have been a few minutes. She must have been waiting' she sobs. 'I woke up and found her dress lying on the bunk. I ran to the rail. I should have called out but I didn't expect her to… she climbed the rail and just seemed to lie down in the air. I heard the sound of her hitting the water.'

'Return to your quarters please.' *Taylor*. 'There is nothing you can do here.'

'You too Miss,' Russell is saying quietly. 'You'd never find her down there. Let her go.'

Cold and tired, Ria allows herself to be persuaded. *Perhaps it is for the best* Back in her cabin she lies in her bunk and tries to calm herself by listening for the night singing but falls asleep still waiting only to be woken again by an insistent knocking and Zak's voice. 'I think you should come. They are lowering the boat.'

Ria rushes to the boat and climbs into it. No-one tries to stop her. Russell is giving the orders. The boat is bumpily lowered and two of the three men on board lean over to pull Beth out of the water. They lie her on a blanket and wrap another round her. Her whole body is shaking with cold but when she sees Ria she manages to speak. 'They saved me Ria, held me up, carried me on top of the water. I wanted to be down there with him but they held me up.' She repeated herself many times as the boat was pulled back up.

As soon as she is close enough to Russell to speak to him, Ria says, 'Have her carried to my cabin.' but Taylor is there too and he immediately overrules them.

'No. Bring her to Mr. Kierle. He will examine her. Who knows what she has encountered? Our Guardian will know what can be done to purify her of the evils that may have visited her down there.' Ria looks at Russell for support.

'Allow her to be carried to a woman's cabin first,' he says. 'She must be dressed. Ria can give her clothing. I'm sure, Mr. Taylor, you have no desire to set eyes on this woman unclothed.' Taylor hesitates.

'But I have no such fears.' The hard edge of Kierle's voice cuts through their thoughts. 'She is wrapped in blankets. I am

213

quite safe from her impurity. Bring her to me and bring her now.'

Lifting Russell's warning hand firmly away from her arm Ria follows as Kierle leads the way to his cabin. 'Put her down here and leave us. Be assured no harm will come to me. As your Guardian I am purified beyond the reach of any evil which may be present here. He is oblivious to the cabin door left open by Russell's men, and to Ria standing just outside as he pulls off the wet blanket. 'You wanted to be down there with him didn't you?' he is saying viciously. 'Not content with beguiling one of our young men, tempting him with your body, taking his first child then robbing him of his life, you wanted to go to the very depths of impurity.'

Ria turns away and runs across the deck. *I cannot allow this to continue, must go to Randal for help.* She finds him talking to the men who are securing the boat. *I must wait until he is ready to hear me* He acknowledges her presence with his eyes but as she steps towards him he gestures that she wait. *Wait, he must be vigilant for the ship and crew. I must be patient.* At last, when the men are focused on their work and Randal is moving away, she feels she can call out to him, 'Randal, I must…'

'Not now Ria,' *He is distant, something important on his mind.* 'Whatever it is, it must wait. There are things, important things…' *His thoughts have moved away from me.* He steps away from her then as if remembering, turns back. 'Wait for me in my day cabin. I will come as soon as I may.' *He is right of course. The ship must come first and he will come.*

As she is waiting in his cabin, she looks over last night's star chart and Randal's log. Reading 'sea dwellers' she turns back a few pages searching for mention of those she has come to think of as friends. His entries for each day are brief statements of fact.

....

Dawn

Sea dwellers sighted. Animals producing less milk, fewer eggs. Several women learning sail duties - all now able to splice rope. Some can loosen sails. Sun and poor breeze.

Nightfall

Sea dwellers sighted. Progress slowing. Very little wind. Temperature continues to rise. Mr. Kierle repeats his request for action against sea dwellers citing 'evidence from history'.

Incident

Fight apparently between a man, Mr. Kristof and a woman, Beth. Mr. Kierle, unable to save K who has died from his injury, reported that the woman is pregnant.

K's burial.

Considering trial for woman, restrictions unnecessary.

Woman overboard. Presumed drowned.

Body sighted in water. Boat lowered. Beth rescued ?Sea dwellers?

....

Why doesn't he come? 'I am here. There is so much, I must attend to every…'

'I must talk to you about Beth.'

'She is safe now. Mr. Kierle is attending to her.'

Ria steps forward angrily and raises her voice. 'No! You are wrong,' she shouts. Mr. Kierle is threatening her.' Randal steps back in surprise. 'Surely you can see that he cannot to be trusted to care for her.' She is crying now and rushes at Randal, hitting out at him. 'Randal, please… he will, no, no you must…'

Three sharp, knocks interrupt her and without waiting for a response Russell enters the cabin.

Randal takes hold of Ria's hands and looks towards the door. 'What is it, Mr. Russell?'

'Something I must tell you, sir.' *He is trying to prevent it showing in his face. I understand. It is Beth, and Randal will ask me to leave.*

'I am sorry Ria, please leave us. We will discuss these matters later.'

I have failed her.

....

Kierle has called all the men and women together. 'Over these two days we have been offered an important lesson. We have seen the consequences of forsaking purity. I have sad, but surely not wholly unexpected news. The woman, Beth, has died. We will never know exactly what passed between these two young people but of certain things we can be sure. Something that is forbidden took place and each of them, man and woman, was rendered impure.

'We must be thankful that, before we departed on this journey, Our Guardian was aware of the dangers we faced and prepared me for eventualities such as these. You will understand now, even more than before, the importance of following my teachings when I pass on to you the knowledge and wisdom entrusted to me. Through prayer and purity ritual I was able to sanctify Mr. Kristof's body to protecting him from the perils that lay in the depths of the ocean.

The young woman had fallen prey to madness and to the callings of the creatures below. We cannot know what torment she endured from them. It seemed she might be saved and Mr. Russell's men are to be commended for their bravery in going down to rescue her, but she was already beyond our help. She had been exposed to their evils through the hours of darkness. Her mind was no longer her own. And then, the final indignity, they made her their mouthpiece and sent her back to us as a mad woman whose ravings they hoped would persuade us that they were to be trusted. Beware this trickery. We must continue to guard ourselves. And it will be purity that save us. Through purity...'

'Through purity.'

'We will protect ourselves.'

'Through purity.'

'We will defend ourselves.'

'Through purity.'

'We will continue this, our journey to the future;'

'In purity.'

'Mr. Kristof and Beth have died for us; as a warning to us all, of the dangers we face if we fail to obey the rules of purity. This evening my betrothed,' he turns and holds out his left hand to Jen who steps up beside him, *eyes lowered,* 'will perform her first duty. She will be responsible for the purification of Beth's body. Tomorrow we will turn our thoughts to the future, to our voyage, with renewed hope, with purity re-established.

15

Becalmed

Ria is with the women who sit at the wooden tables with ship's biscuits and watered down ale in front of them. Hunger forces them to eat but they do so without appetite. No-one has spoken of, or asked about Beth. Only Nina speaks, and even she seems to have lost the energy to make demands. 'So what have you come to tell us, Ria? And where is Jen?'

Ria answers, slowly and carefully. 'First of all I must repeat what I said to you when you first asked me these questions; I believe that our commander is a good man. It is true that he was not of our community; but he has lived as a member of a community very similar to our own. He honours the principles of purity and respects our beliefs. I believe that we share ancestors.

'I have not been able to answer the question of where we are going or how long the journey will be. If I give you information that turns out to be wrong you will feel I have deceived you. I do know that Randal will do everything in his power to bring us safely to our destination and to do so in the shortest possible time. While the safety and progress of the voyage are his responsibility, any plans were drawn up by the committee, and especially by the elders. They claim that much was drawn from the teachings of the great book and you know as much about this as I do.

'Our commander's greatest wish is to guide us to a place of safety. The climate will be warm and bright with sunshine, we have already noticed that our days are longer and warmer, but there will be plentiful rain. There will be a cove where the ship will anchor and where the running water will be so clean it will not need purification and will be sweet to taste. This water will be plentiful. It will water a green valley where we can grow crops using the seed we have brought with us.

'There will be new experiences for us all. With Zak's help we will build up a herd of strong animals. There will be fresh milk, eggs, enough meat for everyone. It will be a pleasant existence even though there will be a lot of hard work. We will begin by creating shelter but there will be time for celebration too. At first women will continue to chew the root until the settlement is secure and the first harvest is in. Then, following the maps and charts that he has drawn up during this voyage, our commander will return the New Hope to Sanctuary where many more ships will have been built and crews trained in readiness.

'They will bring our committee, our families, and our friends. Once they arrive it will be time for you to take the rest you have earned and build families of your own.

'A new committee is planned. It is to be larger, more representative and many of you will be invited to join it. This is one of the many rewards you can expect in return for the courage you have shown. Your knowledge and experience will be important for the success of the new community in our new home.

'I must say to you that it will help none of us for you to issue ultimatums. In her new position it will be impossible for Jen to speak to us of anything she has learned. Mr. Kierle does not wish her to continue mixing or working with us all. He will allow her to select a companion who will be asked to travel with her. I don't believe there is a woman on board who would wish to take on Jen's role.

'As for myself, I have accepted the situation offered to me and can confirm that I trust our commander and urge you to do the same as we approach one of the most difficult stages of our journey. We are all aware of the quietening wind. The ship is moving less and less. The air is growing still. This will change but we can do no more than wait for the winds to return.

'You asked me to find answers to your questions and I have done as you asked. If I learn more I will let you know. In the meantime we must repair and maintain the ship and guard our spirits.'

....

Later Ria is in the hold speaking calmly to the cow she is milking. 'You knew you had to let it go, and your milk will be so good for us. We will look after you. Zak will.' A cold shudder has crept up her spine. *Zak...* She leaves the cow and hurries towards the decks; towards the place she knows Zak would have chosen where he would not have expected to meet anyone.

A small group of men has gathered on the upper middle deck, hidden from view below the three small boats that sit on cradles attached to beams. It has become known as dead man's alley because this was where the bodies of Kris and Beth were brought to be sewn into sails, and where they lay before their burials.

Ria, sensing danger, moves silently as she approaches the space from an unusual angle, climbing over ropes and anchors, straining to her what they are saying in low, aggressive tones. 'If a ship ceases moving, it is held by a curse, held outside the reach of the winds, no breeze will lift its sails; it will sit on the sea until the source of the curse is removed.' She wonders where Zak has got to and how she might warn him.

'A ship can be cursed by the presence on board of a pregnant woman.'

'We might move then, if that was the curse on us.'

'We aren't moving still.'

Unaware of their presence Zak is moving quietly past the end of the boats with the body of the dead calf wrapped in a sheet.

'Here's that boy, Zak' one of them shouts angrily. 'What does he know of life? What dangers might he have brought on board with his precious animals? A cow in calf? Goats? Sheep? Who knows?' Another of the men stands and moves deliberately to block Zak's path.

'What have you got there boy?'

'One of the animals died.'

'What animal is that? A small one?'

'Yes, a small one.' Other men are looking over, getting up.

'Let's see.'

'It's dead, Mr. Gosse. Allow me to...' but Gosse steps forward and snatches the bundle from Zak's arms. 'No, no,' he interrupts mockingly. '*You* allow *me*.' He turns to the two men nearest him and holds it out to them. They take it and unwind the sheet that Zak has carefully wrapped around the calf.

'This calf is very young?'

'Very young.'

'Have you sacrificed it then?'

'Its mother allowed it to die. It was unable to suckle, born unwell.'

Turning to face the rest of his dissatisfied group Gosse shouts, 'Because its mother was a curse, the curse that caused the winds to abandon us. We should throw her overboard.'

Zak remains calm. 'She is no longer pregnant Mr. Gosse, but she has plenty of milk and her calf is dead.'

'You mean you could be bringing this milk to us?'

'I could bring some of it. The commander, and Mr. Kierle, they will expect fresh milk every morning, but, yes, there will be more than they need. It wouldn't be much and there are many of you.'

'Leave that to me. You bring the milk and I will divide it amongst us.' Zak holds out his arms ready to take the calf back. Gosse's eyebrows go up and he stops Zak with one hand. 'We will dispose of the calf.'

'I must warn you, if you are thinking of eating the meat, it is probably diseased.'

'Do not worry yourself. We will dispose of this while you go back to your animals.' Turning to his men he speaks sharply, 'Take it away.' As they disappear Zak turns to go but Gosse grabs him, pulls an arm up behind his back, forces it up. 'And you would tell us if any more of those animals were carrying young, or any others had died, wouldn't you, Mr. Zak?'

'There will be no more young until we reach land. The animals are in poor condition, anxious.'

Pulling a knife from its sheath, Gosse mocks him again with a harsh laugh, 'The animals are anxious!' The other men join the laughter and close in forming a circle around Zak. They knock him to the deck kicking and punching him as he falls.

Ria starts to move but finds herself held back by Russell's firm hand on her shoulder.

'I have sent a message to Randal,' he whispers. 'There is nothing you can do. Wait now.'

Even as he Russell is speaking, Randal strides towards the crowd of jeering men pushing and kicking where Zak has fallen. The group steps back to let him through to where Gosse has Zak pinned down

'Mr. Gosse, stand up please.' As the other men move quietly back, Randal kneels at Zak's side calling, 'Mr. Russell, Ria, he's going to need help.' But they are already there.

Zak is barely conscious. His legs are slashed in several places and bruises are appearing. The ankle, shin and knee of his right leg are obviously broken.

....

Ria goes down to the hold. She and Zak have often spent time here preparing splints and leather pieces in readiness for accidents on board. She knows where to find the comfrey she will need to help ease the pain and knit the broken bones. And now she is searching for moss to heal his skin and prevent it becoming infected. She closes her eyes and concentrates on finding the tell-tale dry dust scent which will lead her to the grasses, trusting that Zak will have stored them together as she would have done. She finds the deep hessian sacks of moss and, trusting her intuition, pulls out the sack at the bottom of the pile opening it to take the moss at its centre. Pulling the moss apart gently she is testing it for just the dry softness she needs when her fingers find something unexpectedly hard. *Stone?* She eases it out of the moss. *A beetle.*

What is it doing here? Even in the darkness of the hold I can see its shine. What shall I do? This rattling of ideas in my brain. Think Ria. I cannot. Beetles... danger? Is it dead? It is still and cold but is it dead? Has it been here from the beginning? Since before we sailed? Or crawled all over the ship and found itself this place to hide? Hide it. But no, I made that mistake before. She drops the beetle and crushes it with her heel then carries it up to the deck and throws it overboard.

....

While the ship lies hot and motionless in the heavy, damp air, Ria nurses Zak through pain and delirium. Whenever she can leave him she spends her time searching any part of the ship to which she can gain access but finds no more beetles.

Randal is trying to keep men and women busy and they are glad of something to do, to take their minds off the fact that the ship is not moving. The mood has settled to one of resignation. There is no longer singing or storytelling. Mornings are slower. There is no rush now to wash, dress or eat. The food is dry and stale, water severely rationed.

One of Randal's ideas has been the construction of a canvas pool and it hangs now from ropes suspended between a cathead and the lower topsail yard. This fills with seawater. At first only Randal or Ria used it, Ria leaving Russell to watch over Zak while she bathed. Encouraged by both Randal and Ria, Russell was next to try immersing himself in the refreshing water. Seeing this man they know and trust bathe in the water others have begun to join him. Kierle stands on deck, watching in silence. *He knows he cannot prevent it.* 'Affording them his protection while so close to danger' is how he explains it to Taylor.

The women need much less encouragement. As soon as they hear that Ria is using the pool Meera and Nan join her. Groups of women stand at the rail, watching, waiting their turn. As she encourages the others Ria glances up at Jen. Kierle has managed to assert his authority by decreeing that men and women bathe separately and that Jen stands over the women. *Cannot read her clearly; desperately unhappy and yet accepting, almost pleased, satisfied in some way. I will invite her to join me in the water privately.*

But when Ria and Jen come together each morning, to bathe in the pool before anyone else, they are awkward together. Ria tries asking Jen, 'How are you? How do you spend your days? Are you lonely?' But Jen's answers are guarded.

'I will be fine. There is much my husband would have me learn in order that I can share the responsibilities of Guardianship, so that I can lead the other women, help them in the days to come. He has tried to find a way of preventing me joining you or even speaking to you. I use his belief in the authority of Randal as commander to justify my movements.'

Ria is glad when Jen climbs back up to the deck leaving her a few moments in the pool alone. Shortly afterwards Jen will reappear, fully dressed in her long white gown, to give the signal for the women's bathing to begin. Later, after the day's work has been done, the men will take their turn.

This has become the new daily routine; Randal bathes first, followed by Ria and Jen, and then the women. Men and women then work together in small groups many of which have specialised in jobs such as carpentry or sewing. There are still many tasks that require everyone's contribution and women are still learning, climbing the rigging to unfurl sails in the hope of catching any breeze, however slight. A   fall from the rigging would mean serious injury so they are still cautious, using the safe hole close to the mast rather than clambering around the platforms or scurrying along ratlines as the men do. They have been attaching extra sails and bringing down for repair any that were damaged in the storm.

On deck they stitch sails and clothes, repair tools and furnishings, and dismantle empty barrels to save storage space. There is still a lot to be learned and all over the ship men are explaining the lines that control the set of the sail, the storage tags which indicate which yard a sail is made for and the storage system so that any folded sail can be quickly identified. But they are beginning to believe that it is all for nothing, that the wind will never fill the sails again, that they are working simply to fill their time.

....

The ship has not moved for many days. Below decks, the hot, heavy air is tainted once more by the odours of sickness and fear. The moaning of animals is indistinguishable from the low sighs of men and women giving up hope as their energy ebbs away.

Ria's thoughts turn more and more towards Randal. Remembering his cabin as lighter, drier, and cooler, than the rest of the ship she often considers going up the few wooden steps to join him. The decks are littered with small groups of limp figures lying, or sitting against each other. No one bothers her. Ria can now move freely around the ship and in this way she hears the mutterings and whispers of women and crew:

The air must stir.

The creatures in the sea follow us constantly. We do not need to see them to know.

The men need to be occupied with the business of sailing. The sails are fully repaired and furled. The ropes are ready, decks, stairs, rails, scrubbed until they are white. I cannot keep these people busy much longer. Games and exercise will no longer satisfy help. They do not have the energy.

Surely a wind will come soon.

On deck yesterday I glanced out to the horizon and I'm sure I saw more ships. I tried to look more closely but they slipped out of view. That happens out here with no trees, no mountains, no buildings for the eye to hold onto. Things slip in and out of view. I have seen the strange underwater men swimming in our wake or alongside us just out of sight for most of the time. If I glance at them briefly I think I may see them clearly but if I look too hard I lose them. I don't think they want to be seen. They are watching us, waiting to see what we will do. I have heard them calling to each other. It sounds like singing but I know it is their form of speech. They try not to let us hear them, by keeping their distance, but the water carries the sound of their voices and it washes up against the sides of the ship. At night when everyone else is asleep I hear them.

The committee will have sent more ships by now. They will be following us. The commander will have left instructions for them. As each ship is ready it will set sail so there will be a line of us creeping across the surface of the ocean carrying more of what we need. They will arrive soon after us with supplies and news of our families.

This ship is a prison.

Listen to them now. Their singing is beautiful. Beautiful and dangerous. It makes me think they are calling us, telling us how beautiful it is under the water. Down in the depths they must have a world of their own. A world we have never suspected. In the night when I lie in this bunk with the ship creaking and moaning all around me I know we are trapped and the ocean is so huge, so much space and it would be so cool. It is so hot in here, so stifling. The air is thick and sour brown and we are expected to breathe it, filling ourselves with the dirty breath of others. I will creep out one night and lean over the rail to see them. If they are as beautiful as they sound they will save me. I could jump into the water, the cold, clean water, and they could swim to me, hold me up, carry me safely away.

I believed we would find land, reach a new safe place, build a new Sanctuary but now I am afraid. Whenever I close my eyes ropes are knitted around me, they criss-cross above, below me. There is no escape. I tell myself it is just a bad dream but I wake and the ropes are still there and I wake again and again. Each time I am waking back into the dream. Each night the dream pulls me deeper and I have to wake more and more times to reach the surface. Soon the time will come when I am so deep in the dream that I will never get back to the air. I will be trapped forever waking and to find that I am not yet awake.

We must remain vigilant.

It's all very well for them to whisper and plot about refusing to go on but what could we do? How could we sail without the commander? He is the only one who can lead us. As for the surgeon who thinks he is Guardian, what could we do without a surgeon and how could we remove him without the support of everyone on board? Most of them are still terrified of him, they would never dare cross him for fear of their souls. If a few of us were to stand up to him, capture him, how would the others react? Maybe if there was an accident, if he fell overboard. And then what? Make the commander turn back? We could not go back to the committee. Sail on with just the commander then?

When will the rest of us be allowed to start making choices? That dark one, Nan. She's a beauty. Strong too. I've seen her looking at me.

Terrifying cold dark with creatures all head, just eyes and teeth, swimming where everything we have thrown over the edge is gathered waiting for us and when we pull things up all dripping with gore and slime they wriggle on deck and then they expect us to eat them and yesterday they said they would tie him up and lower him over the edge and into the cold and dark full of evil wriggling things and trail him there behind the ship then pull him up the next day for us to see what happens to anyone foolish enough to try to escape in the water.

There is one down there that is giant and squirming made only of head and legs and he lies in wait and all his life he has waited for us and now he wonders whether to reach up and haul us gently, slowly in, savouring the last hours of waiting, entertained by our struggles and fears, or to carry on waiting because he knows that we have nowhere else to go.

These creatures have guided ships for generations.

These creatures are waiting for us to fail.

They are calling me. Soon I will not be able to bear this madness any longer, I will jump, give myself to them. Whatever they do to me cannot be worse than this waiting.

All we wish for is the wind. We have forgotten everything else. Forgotten to worry about what the future holds, where we are going, how it will be when we get there, all we dream of is a movement in the sails, a shifting, a change. We are losing the will to move, to eat, to think.

He may command us against the dangers of superstition but what harm can it do to whistle for the wind? I will whistle and if the wind comes I will have the satisfaction of knowing I called it and if there is no wind we will be no worse off than before.

Sometimes what is necessary is courage.

So he will not allow superstition but how will he know if my few coins drop over the side of the ship? What harm can come of it? I give these coins to the ocean to buy the wind. And if the wind doesn't come, what will I have lost?

He is right about superstition. If we try to buy good fortune with superstition we will soon fall prey to the consequence of accidentally bringing bad luck on ourselves by breaking a rule we did not know.

This sailing is something worse than death. We are in a place of perpetual evil, of shifting truth, where nothing is real. We have ceased to be real. We are simply vessels of suffering gathered together and herded here, to this place which is no place, in a time where there is no time.

This morning I saw stones boil on the surface. We were no longer sailing on water but on waves of boiling stones. We may pray for wind to move us on but in a great wind the stones will be thrust up and thrown at us. Because the water has gone, the ship – and us with it - cannot even sink but will be ground to dust by crashing waves of stone.

How much longer?

I grew up believing that a ship should never carry a pregnant woman. I know they chew the root but I could never risk visiting that on her. Women have been thrown overboard for less.

Do they really imagine that we do not know what happens? Can they expect us to live by their rules, their 'purity', when they do not do so themselves? Why should we deny ourselves when they do not?

The ship must move soon.

I have my eye on Nan and I'm sure she has noticed me. I see her glancing in my direction.

It's Taylor again, looking at me. I suppose he thinks he is next to choose but he will not choose me. I make my own choice. I choose Russell.

We have no idea where we are or where we are going. Yesterday, during morning prayers on deck, I sighted another ship, on the horizon. I knew it was a ship sent out to meet us. Someone knows we are coming. Somewhere out there a part of our history has been waiting for us. Patiently. They knew we would come back, back to our roots, back to where it all began. And they will welcome us. The ship disappeared but it will be back. It has returned to tell them we are on our way. They will send out a welcome party to guide us home and there will be celebrations and explanations and then we will understand.

Ria has forgotten to count the days. She has no idea how long she prowled, as Zak refers to her wanderings, about the ship listening to the beliefs and fears of others and the wanderings of her own mind. Even Zak had sent her away eventually telling her to save her energy. 'Rest' he had said. 'If you watch the animals you can learn a lot. They lie still because that is what their bodies need. Go and lie down.' How many days ago had that been. How long has she slept? She tries to gather her thoughts unsure whether she is awake or dreaming. *The sea sounds as if it is moving, alive, but the ship feels dead in the water. Body too heavy to lift, head heaviest of all, as if it would lag behind the rest of me, stretch my neck, curling it back, but it would snap. That crack. Not my neck but a shock right through me, jolting, waking me, I don't want to lie here and let death creep over me. How to find the strength to lift myself? Go in search of water.* Gripping the wooden bunk side, she prepares to take the weight of her body, lifts her head and shoulders. *The weight follows but it is not me, my heavy shadow trying to drag me back, pull me down.* She tries to lick her lips. Her tongue is swollen, her lips cracked and dry, sticking together, sticking to her teeth. She knows she must find water.

She is sitting up now, already feeling that she has shed some of the darker shadow weight that was holding her down. *Must move again.* She looks down at her legs and feet. *They seem so far away, not part of me. How to move them? Don't wait, act.* Bending forward she takes hold of her left leg, lifts it, expects it to feel dead, but at the touch of her own hands the leg becomes part of her again, moves willingly, the right leg too. They are slow, stiff and aching but they move . For a brief moment she is aware of her body in all its separate parts, a moment of panic, disjointedness – *How to pull all these parts – head, neck, shoulders, arms, hands, fingers, body, thighs, knees, shins and calf muscles, ankles, feet, toes – so many parts, where to be....* Closes her eyes, breathes, a light is travelling through her. From her head a wave of energy swells down, a dissolving of parts into a whole. The panic ebbs. She wonders but resists the temptation to dwell on the fear and feed it with attention, and already she has refocused on her need for water.

16

Rain

Moving carefully, still unsure of her body, she crosses the cabin and opens the door. She is dazzled. The ship shines at her, every surface glistening in a flash of sunlight which has broken through thick black cloud. *It has rained. It will rain again.* The bowls left outside the cabin door more in despair than in hope *How long ago? How long have we lain, waiting?* are full, brimming with sparkling water. She lifts one, sips the water, its sweetness bursts in her mouth, lips and tongue rejoice. She fills her mouth with the coolness and holds it there, swollen tongue softening, cracked lips released from each other, from teeth. She wants to hold it there longer but her parched throat is pleading. She knows she must be careful, but not yet. She swallows and feels it travel, throat, chest, past her heart, towards her stomach. *Coolness, sweet and light. I am coming back to life.* She sips and sips again, soothing her aching body with promises of more. She dips fingers into the bowl and gently bathes her eyes, thinks of pouring it over head and body but *No* she stops herself. *It may not rain again. We must conserve* and even as she thinks it she knows that it will rain again and already it is raining. Her hair is wet, her arms are wet, she lifts her face up to the clouds and her smiling face is wet.

....

At first it is only the women. Gathered together, they sit and someone begins to sing. It is Nan. Her voice is deep and calm. Her gaze is directed downward, slightly to her right. She repeats the tune as if singing a ballad with alternating verses and chorus. Each chorus is the same, each verse a version of the last but subtly changed. There are no words. She simply sings a sound, a musical sigh, increasing in intensity. Other voices join in, hesitantly at first but with increasing confidence. They weave harmonies into the chorus while verses become louder, stronger. Meera appears carrying a drum, shallow wooden sides with an animal skin stretched tightly across it top and bottom. She sits beside Nan with the drum between her knees and picks up the rhythm of the song.

The music is hypnotic. Men are drawn from different parts of the ship. As they sing the women sway in unison, rise to their knees, swaying, rock backwards and forwards, sway and rock, sing, sway and rock then rise to their feet. Those in still skirts spin through each chorus while the others emphasise rhythm with heels and toes. For the verses they still their feet and reach up with arms, hands, fingers, their fingertips spiraling through the air, twisting invisible threads.

They glide into a line, the line becomes a circle. They move small, deliberate steps, emphasising the increasing speed of the rhythm, onto toes, onto heels, knees lifted they kick. They hold head and shoulders mysteriously still as they place their hands on their hips, then transfer movement to a lifting of shoulders, neck and head. Up and to the side, down and to the centre, up and to the other side they lift their heads. Then the arms weave snakelike, hands almost together, across their bodies and up, a momentary stillness then back down and the whole movement is repeated in reverse. Now they step towards the centre of the circle, clasping right hands, and reach up together forming a star above their heads, facing out, unblinking, their left hands the curling limbs of a mesmerising creature.

Men have been drawn to watch and now an outer circle is forming around the dance. The star explodes as women step, hands on hips half a pace forward then back with a flick of each hip, a swirl at the waist and a lifting of shoulders that draws the men in with their own hands outstretched. One by one the women step forward to draw a man in. Swirling skirts glide around them, weave in and out of them. It becomes impossible to tell whether the dancers follow the music or lead it.

The circle unravels as men and women circle each other then step on to another. Still singing, the women turn back to the centre, link hands and pull themselves together then push apart stepping in to, away from the centre, reforming the circle alongside a different man. Men's voices join the singing as the whole circle turns and each pair spins.

Watching them Ria feels a surge of excitement, a desire to be with Randal, for him to dance with her, at the centre. But he is not among the dancers. Turning back she sees that it is Jen at the centre, the heart of the circle, now the edge, as she passes from man to man then out of the circle to sidestep a partner, swinging to step back in to face someone new.

Now the women stand and the men step around them. She realises that the men are singing words… *were there words all along and I simply didn't hear them or have they just begun?*

'Turning and turning and turning again
Yes this way, no that way
Now move on young men
Now high tide, now low tide

Tide turning again,
Now summer now winter
Now turning again
Now morning, now evening
Now turning again.'

Looking for Randal she suddenly sees Kierle and instantly her thoughts are of Jen. Kierle, his face red with fury, strides over to Nan and seizes the drum, wrenching it from her as she tries to hold on to it. Singing and dancing stop as he roars his disgust and flings the drum out into the sea.

'This will end now and will never happen again on board this ship.' As he strides through them, his eyes are fixed on Jen and he reaches out to grab her as if into a foul swamp. Seizing her wrist he pulls as if he expects the circle to have some magical power to resist him and hold on to her.

He says nothing more as he turns his back on the men and women who stand and watch and drags Jen past them.

Randal's calm and quiet voice reassures them. 'Women, Go to your quarters, now. All of you. Men, prepare the sails. The New Hope is moving once more.' Randal is standing, feet apart, hands at his waist, watching them disperse. Ria notices the dark colour of his skin, the pulse beating in his neck. 'You also, Ria.' he says quietly as the others move quietly away. 'Return to your cabin.'

....

Blood and Milk

One of the women, Laan, is telling Ria her recurring dream:

'I am in the dark, feeling my way. My fingers trace the shape of an old cot, the covers, the face of a child. The child is asleep. I hold her face in my hands. I whisper 'Wake up.' She opens her eyes. I look into her eyes and it is me looking up at me.' *They sit quietly for a moment.* Ria is becoming a good listener. 'It was me, looking at me.' Ria listens without speaking. *Listen and wait. Wait. Give her time.* 'I have had this dream so many times since we sailed away from Sanctuary. I felt we were sailing away from safety. And now I know. All that time I was slowly waking up. Thank you Ria.' *They come to me now as they used to go to my grandmother.*

Now Ellie sits with Ria and reaches out to take her hands. 'I know I am the oldest woman on the ship but I am not so old that I should be losing my sight. Laan said you would know what to do. My eyes are weary, dried out. It is as if I am looking out through a web of dry threads.'

'Lie down on my bunk and I will scrape a little soap into your eyes. This will be uncomfortable. You will feel I have made your eyes worse. They will be redshot and sore but I will give you something to ease that. Lie back and be ready to lay the palms of your hands over your eyes. I know, it is sharp but it will work. Lie still. Let them sting. Let the tears run. Do not rub.'

'I think you will have to hold my hands to stop me rubbing.'

'I can do that.'

'It helps. Your hands are calming.'

'Take this with you. It is a mixture of spirit and honey. I can only give you a little, so use it sparingly, a drop in each eye morning, mid-day and night until your eyes are comfortable again. Bring any that you have left back to me.'

....

Randal has called Ria to his day cabin. 'I need your help. I have heard several of the men coughing. It is a sound I recognise having heard it at sea many times. My people call it the saltair cough. You and Zak must prepare whatever they need before it worsens and spreads further. Before they start spitting blood. Do you know what to do?'

'I will talk to Zak. My grandmother treated coughs in Sanctuary but this may be something different.'

'Yes, talk to Zak and do what needs to be done.'

....

Zak has been thinking about it already. 'Yes, I have heard the coughing. It only needs one to bring lungwaste on board. It sleeps inside a person until it gets the conditions it needs, then it wakes and spreads. We must act quickly. Randal is right, we need to prevent the spitting. Spitting spreads the waste. We will have to kill the second calf.'

'Must we kill her? We have lost one calf already.'

'We were lucky to have had calves at all and at least this will mean we can use all the cow's milk as long as it continues. And a little fresh meat can be made to go a long way to revive weakening spirits. Don't worry Ria. There will be other calves. You will have to help me. We will slaughter the calf and take the pluck. It will give us sufficient for two small barrels of balsam and that must be enough. Go down to the hold and collect balm, mint, lungwort and sage. I will make the preparations and talk to Nan. We will need her help.

....

This is the most terrible thing I have ever done. How can he kill a creature he brought into the world, cared for?

'Don't turn away, Ria. I know how hard it is. I wanted to turn away as a child but my mother would always say the same thing. 'You need to watch. One day I will not be with you and you will need to know.' She was right. Look the calf straight in the eye and thank her. She should not be afraid and neither should you. Hold her firmly and know exactly what you are going to do. It must be quick. I do not need to tie her up because she trusts me. She knows I will not hurt her. She knows that this is important and right.' *All the time he is talking he holds her, strokes her and says she knows and the speed and strength of the knife and the grunting collapse of her and the hot smell of blood.*

Zak is talking to the dying calf. 'Thank you. Thanks from all those who will benefit from what you give.' His voice changes, 'Now Ria. Be quick, while it is still warm.' *So efficient the way the knife slits the body open, the blood smells thick, I want to...*

'No time to leave me now Ria' says Zak quickly. Take the heart and cut it in two. Take care not to lose the blood. Let it run into the stills. Here, these are healthy and plenty of blood around them.' *Liver, lungs, words I have heard but things I have never seen and so much steaming blood.*

'Good, this is what we need. Cut it up while it is still warm and stir in the herbs. Cover it. Quickly now, we must carry them up to the galley. Nan will be waiting there.'

They each carry a pot up the stairways to the galley. No one pays them any attention.

How is it possible that they do not know? That just a few moments ago there was a trusting, living creature where now there is just meat and blood. That we have killed. That we are carrying the heart of a beautiful animal past them.

'Nan, you have the boiled milk?' Zak has taken charge. 'Still hot? Pour it over and we will stir. Now I must go back and see to the meat. I will bring it straight to you. Keep these boiling. Only lift the lids three times to stir and make sure it does not burn.

Ria stays in the galley with Nan until Zak returns. He is not gone long. 'Now take these' he says. *Hooves, teeth, tongue, jaw.* 'Stew them long and slow with the liquorice root to make the broth.' *And I need liquorice root for Grandmother's remedy* thinks Ria as she begins to feel calm again *which we can give them in water; liquorice, sliced root of elicompane, hyssop sprigs, boiled gently in ale then honey added.*

....

'The balsam is almost ready. Anyone with the cough must come to us: Men to Zak, the women will come to me, first thing in the morning and again at night. We will also give it to anyone who suffers a coughing fit. If we had a plentiful supply they would live on this alone but as this is not possible we are preparing a strong broth and a drink which we will give to anyone who is not responding quickly.'

....

'I cannot sleep, Ria. Ellie told me to come to you. She said you would calm me. I cannot rest. Sitting still is impossible. But there is nowhere to go. My body is beginning to twitch and jump against my own will. My mind turns again and again to jumping. I am afraid that the jumping will take over. However afraid I may be of what lies beneath us, I am afraid that my body will leap from the ship.'

'Sit with me and chew this root. It is valerian. You only need chew this tiny amount. No, take it. It will not harm you. Chew it now, while you sit here with me. Rest awhile and when you are ready, tell me how you feel. We will sit quietly together *Let yourself drift away see where it takes you from up here we can look down at the ship and see how tiny it is and see the men and women, tiny creatures moving about as in a complicated dance. They move around, in and out of each other's pathways, alongside each other, they meet and part and sometimes meet again. They climb the rigging, climb back down. They move and rest and move again. And there, she sees herself, sitting with this woman. And this woman's head hangs heavily. In her lap her fingers twine and fret, but less so now, and less. She is closing her eyes and breathing slowly. Breathing in. Breathing out. Breathing. Breathing.*

'I notice a difference in my mouth. Where my tongue is so tired and sore. from constantly moving, rubbing the backs of my teeth, the roof of my mouth, now it has stopped. I feel how tired it is. Such a relief, to rest. And the ache in my throat.' Rhona stops talking and closes her eyes. Briefly she covers her face with her hands then pushes back her hair, massages her forehead, eyes, cheeks, chin, and throat. She sighs, looks up at Ria and waits.

Ria gives her a few more tiny pieces of valerian root. 'Use it wisely and this will be enough. It will help you sleep. Chew it, just one piece, in the evening. This is enough for seven nights. Each day its effects will last a little longer.' She closes the woman's hand over the root, helps her stand, and guides her through the doorway.

Out here, with nothing but sea and sky if it is as if life has stopped all around us. Everywhere is blank. Not dead and yet not alive – swelling gently but hardly moving, barely a line where sky meets sea and always all the way around us. Only on the tiny spot, which is the ship can we feel, see, hear life. Even our own growing older is so slow we cannot know it. Looking out I can see no signs of birth, life or death. It is only we. It would be so easy to let go, slip away, to float, just a murmur away from a dream. And once I have entered a dream, and know I am dreaming, I can choose to fly. Climb up there to the highest rail to stand for one exalting moment before I leap

'Ria!' Zak's call brings her back. *Through a rush of changing energy and back to the deck, both feet firmly planted and he is right to bring me back. This is where our lives continue, where I must apply my strength. It is this life I must consider. Settled. Light at my head. Life at my feet. I will immerse myself in it.*

'Ria, come down to the hold. I will wait for you there.'

'Is it one of the animals?' *Already he has gone.*

She hurries down and moves quickly between the rows of animals checking them as she goes until she finds Zak standing amongst straw bales. *We have already used most of the straw. What if ...*

'I told her you would come.' He gestures. *Someone must be sitting there. Jen?* She glances around. *No one else? Not Kierle?*

'Ria. I was looking for you.'

'I brought her down here,' says Zak. 'The hens and goats on top deck were making an awful noise so I went up to investigate and found her disturbing them.'

'I was looking for you.' Jen's voice is accusing.

'I was down on the next deck,' begins Ria. 'Looking for ...' But she stops herself. Jen stands up and rushes towards Ria. She is thin and very pale. *She is pregnant.*

'You have to help me, Ria. No one else can help me. What can I do?'

'Does he know?'

'Who?'

'Kierle. Does he know you are carrying a child?'

'I cannot tell him.'

'But when he knows...'

'He must not know.'

'But he will take such care of you. He will be so ...'

'Ria' Jen screams Ria's name. Zak steps forward and puts a hand on her arm.

He speaks quietly. 'We can help you Jen but please ...'

She shudders but nods her head and speaks more quietly. 'Ria, you do not pay enough attention to what is going on right next to you. You see many things but you do not see the facts. You have heard the men and their superstitions. You know how pure we must always be. They will blame me for everything. For the ship's not moving, for Beth's attack and Kris's death. Everything. They will throw me overboard. And as for Kierle taking care of me, he will blame me too. He is terrified of them. His constant fear is that they will join together against him. He has to be above blame, the purest of the pure. I am so afraid of him, of what he might do to keep them under control.' Her breath is hot on Ria's face. *Sour with fear.* 'This pregnancy cannot be and I cannot allow him to know of it. Please, Ria. He must not know. There has to be a way.'

She moans, falls onto her knees and leans forward to let out the hot yellow bile, so strong smelling that Ria steps back.

'The third time. If he sees me like this he will know.' Seeing the difficulty she is having getting up Ria offers her hands to Jen who seizes them and pulls herself up to look straight into Ria's face. 'You must help me. If he finds out I think he will kill me.' *Step on this stone, your babe will be sorry. Crush it completely he'll not see tomorrow. But eat it lady before he is born and dead from a tomb he'll surely be torn.*

'Go back to your cabin. I will tell Randal that you have the coughing sickness, that you are coughing blood and no one must go near you until you are cured. Randal will tell Kierle.'

Zak nods in agreement. 'Kierle will be afraid of the disease. He is a coward.'

'And I must go before he misses me. Ria, will you come with me?' They do not speak as they climb the stairways and skirt the decks. *What are the questions I want to ask her? I know they are there but I cannot...*

As soon as they are in the cabin, although her strength seems to be deserting her so that she has to lean against the door, and half closes her eyes, Jen begins to speak. Her voice is quiet, almost a whisper, but urgent. 'There is more, Ria.' She looks up, meets Ria's eyes and gathers herself, 'It is not Kierle's child. I tell you this because you must see that I cannot carry the child of another man.' *Now I must listen. Now I must know what my questions are. Take care. Ask her.* 'He would kill me. Better for me if I can never have a child and no child should have him for a father. He is evil. I can endure this voyage, even endure his attentions, my 'responsibilities', you have no idea, being his chosen brings more than privileges in its wake. You should go now. He must not become suspicious. Please go now.'

'I will come to you again tomorrow. Take one more day to think about what you are asking. If we do this, your suffering will be terrible. Your body may never recover. You may never be able to carry a child to full term.'

'This has come as a surprise to you but I have had long days thinking of nothing else. I suffer every day at his hands. This ship is a prison to me and he is my jailer. Bad enough for me, but for a child, to be his, never. It is this or I will die.'

'But there may be another answer. Be sure that you have considered everything before we do this. I will come to you tomorrow. Wait for me in your cabin.'

'I cannot go anywhere else.'

Ria returns to Zak. 'It is not your decision.' He says, 'It is hers.'

'But to help her – that would be me.'

'No. The plant exists. We have it in the hold and she knows of it. She will use it if she decides to.'

'So why come to me?'

'She came to you for help but not for the decision.'

'I don't know.' *Impossible to think clearly. Perhaps grandmother will help me. I must go to my cabin. Perhaps if I rest my mind will be clearer. I know what grandmother would say. 'Listen to the question. The answer lies in the question.' What is the question? Why am I all confusion? Nothing is clear. I cannot see. Trying to listen to words like a net holding me down. I reach through holes and cannot grasp anything. Need to crawl out, creep away, climb above the confusion. Need to get higher. If I can get high enough to look down I can look for a pattern. Watching them creep along their tunnels, climb their stairs, trapped inside their little kingdom. The order seems to have broken down. The biggest, strongest are staying in the inner chambers with the ruling one. The weaker ones have abandoned their duties of caring for her and fight amongst themselves. They fight in silence and now I see why as the victors pull out the tongues of those they have defeated. Those who are unwilling, or unable, to fight creep downwards, away from the fighting, away from light and air, out of sight, to wait. They will have no say in their own fate. The victors enslave their speechless foe and turn to find the ruler. The egg layer. Where is she? They send their slaves down dark tunnels to search for her long secret hiding place while they themselves look up to see that she has not flown. And as they look up the air is filled with their high buzzing song but it is not enough to hide me. They have seen me and I have nowhere to go. I need to fly to escape them. Grandmother, teach me to fly. But to fly would be to abandon the weak ones, the women, the animals. Grandmother what must I do? I know she is here but she stays just out of reach, smiling, out of reach.*

When Ria wakes it is dark. She listens to the sounds of the ship, the waves licking the hull, the whisper of the breeze in the sails and the answer from the rigging. She notices the absence of voices, hears the tread of the night watch and knows that dusk was long ago and dawn will not be for hours. *I must go to Randal.* She knows the deck well now and moves silently in the darkness stepping over coils of rope, disturbing nothing. *voices?* She leans against the door and strains to hear. *They think they are whispering. They do not realise how clear their voices are, how far they carry.*

'This cannot be the truth.'

'It is. I swear.'

'How can you know that the child is mine. Surely it is your husband's.'

'He is not my husband.'

'And you chew the root.'

'No. He forbids it. He wants his child to be the first.'

'And so it will.'

'No. It is not his child.'

'Of course it is his child.'

'No. It cannot be and he will know it is not his because I have never allowed him... he has never...'

'Then the solution is simple. Allow him now and the child will be his.'

'I came to you for help. You command this ship and this is your child.'

'You tricked me into this.'

'No. You came to me and this is the consequence.'

'Yes, I came to you. But I came looking to help. You led me to believe...'

'I led you to believe nothing. You came to me when I was desperate, terrified. You offered me love.'

'I repeat, my intention was only to help.'

'Help me now. Make me your wife. Ria can have her choice from all the other men.' *No, no, no, this is not for me to hear. Must go back to my cabin and wait. However long it takes I will wait. He will come to me.*

....

'I am so sorry, Ria…' *He says he is sorry but I want to know everything. When it happened, why, every detail. But these are questions I will not ask.* 'I want to tell you. It was the night after you came to tell me that she needed help. I went to see her in her cabin. It was late, the last watch. The ship was quiet, a gentle sea under a cool breeze. When I knocked at her cabin door and she whispered, 'come in,' she sounded like a frightened child. She was sitting on her bunk, half dressed. She was hugging her legs, resting her chin on her bent up knees. Her hair was loose. I thought how beautiful sadness could look on a woman.

'I told her what you had said to me. That you were concerned for her safety, that she seemed frightened. I apologised, said that was not how it was meant to be.'

'But that is how it is,' she said. 'And I am lonely and afraid.'

'When she wept her whole body shook. I felt responsible. I sat beside her, put my arms around her and she lay her head against me. There were tears, huge tears, but she cried silently.'

She began to whisper. 'You would not be cruel like him. You would be loving and kind and gentle. That's all I ask, someone loving to care for me. I could bear it if I could turn to you.'

'She kissed me then and ... I am truly sorry in wishing I had not allowed this to happen. It was a moment's foolishness and I will regret it forever. Whatever you think of me now I will understand. I ask nothing of you.'

'You have been honest with me, and I will be honest in return. For the moment I am not sure how I feel. I need some time to think.'

'Of course. And I will go. Whatever you decide, I would not rob you of your privileges. They remain yours. Take the time you need and I will honour your decision. Whatever it may be.' He backs stiffly towards the door, half turns to life the latch, then lowers it again and returns to her side. 'Truly, I *am* sorry Ria. You are still my choice. Of all the women on this ship, of all the women I have ever known, it was you who called me across the ocean. For you I crawled out of the sea.'

As he leaves she sees that it is almost dawn and the first light draws her out on deck. At the rail she raises her hand to acknowledge the sea dwellers swimming alongside and hears the last notes of their quiet song before they dive below the surface and out of sight. Her breath is snatched by a gust of wind and she has to steady herself. Her hair lashes her face and she gasps.

The calls go up for the new watch and for hands to the rig for the changing wind. She returns to her cabin and is surprised to find Randal there waiting for her.

'The winds have changed,' she tells him.

'They know what to do.'

'What will you do?'

'For the winds?'

'For Jen.'

'What would you have me do?'

'Make your own decisions.'

He smiles, 'and what about Jen?'

'Jen must know what is true for her. I cannot.'

'And you, can live with Jen's decisions and my mistake?'

'I can do nothing else.'

'And my decisions?'

'You will make your decisions too and if those decisions change what is here, now, for me, then my here and now changes, my life changes. Things are constantly changing.'

'You talk in riddles.'

'No, I speak the answers to my own questions. Only when answers try to fit other people's questions do they become riddles.'

'Well you are right when you say that things are constantly changing.' They sit in silence. 'But I don't know what to do.'

'You will know the answers to your own questions. What question is in your mind now?'

'I want it to be about you.'

'But what is it about?'

'It is the ship.'

'Then consider the ship. We all need you to keep the New Hope moving safely on.'

'Then I will go and do what I can to ensure that.'

Their kiss is brief but loving.

Exhausted but I must go to Jen.

....

'Ria.'

Jen is sitting on the edge of her bunk when Ria enters the cabin.

'I have come to make sure you understand about the plant. To tell you what will happen, what to expect. Once I have told you the decision is yours.'

'But you will help me?'

'I will be here. I will tell you what I can and I will not try to influence you. That is the best that I can do.'

'And after that?'

'What happens afterwards will be what happens.'

'Is it easy for you to torment me with riddles? Don't you think I am suffering enough?'

'Not riddles. Plain speaking. And I tell you plainly now that this will be nothing to the suffering that the crimson lady's purse will cause you and the child.'

Jen's eyes widen. *I hear her breathing, feel her stomach fall, but I have passed responsibility back to her if she can accept it will give her strength*

'You are right, this is plain speaking. Tell me about the plant and I will decide.'

'I will bring you two corms. You must grind each one to a very fine powder on the day you will take it. Divide the powder from the first into four parts and take it mixed in a small amount of food or drink when you wake, mid-morning, mid-afternoon and in the evening. Do not rush it but do not spread it over more than one day. Once you have tasted it you will never want to put it in your mouth again but you must. Once you have swallowed even a tiny part of the plant you will poison your, poison the...'

'It is not a child to me Ria. It never could be after all that I have been through. Think of it as a seed. But a seed that cannot thrive. By helping me you are saving a child who is not meant to be. Imagine the fate of a child at Kierle's hands – bad enough...' her voice breaks, 'But then the day that he realises it is not his child...' Her voice is now barely above a whisper. *She is forcing herself to speak.* 'He would be unbearably cruel. I cannot do it and you must help me prevent it.'

'Taking the powder will be the beginning of a courageous act. But it will be so hard, so painful. Are you sure you will have the strength?'

'This is what I have to do. It is letting go of something I should never have. I should never have tried to grasp it. It is what I must do.' She is trembling, crying, *but she is determined.*

'By the end of the first day...' Ria hesitates, then tries again to speak the truth plainly to Jen, 'By the end of the first day the...' *The weight of this in my chest would drag me down, I do not know how I can do this but I do not know how I could refuse*

'It will be dead?'

'It will be dead.' *My own grief would overwhelm me, and hers, hers is impenetrable*

They sit in silence. Ria holds Jen's hands in her lap with her right hand. Her left arm rests firmly across Jen's shoulders. Each tries to calm herself but both are racked by shudders, their thoughts refusing to become clear.

'What - after the first day?'

'You will have days of terrible sickness, pain and bleeding.'

'How long will it go on?'

'Three days, maybe five. You will feel as if you are dying.'

'Yes, I am a part of me die, a part that I might long keep if I let myself think of it as mine. But it is not mine. It does not belong with me. I know that. I have thought of nothing else for days and nigh on end. It is either this or death and I don't want to die. And after, I will be stronger and wiser.'

'On the day that the bleeding begins you must crush the second corm. Swallow it in any way that you can. It will seem impossible. Your mouth will refuse it. Your throat will close. I do not know how you will find the strength but there can be no turning back. Without the second corm your body will cling to the dead child and it will poison you. It would be a terrible death.

'Give me one corm now. Keep the other until it is time'

'You must have them both. You must have the second ready to use as soon as the bleeding begins.'

'Then give them to me now.'

'I have not brought them.' Ria's jaw is so tense she has difficulty speaking. She massages her throat. 'I will bring you some milk.'

'Fresh milk? Jen is giggling, 'Fresh milk?' She puts her hand to her mouth but the laughter gains a hold. 'Is it pure?' she splutters between bursts of painful laughter, tears streaming from her eyes, thick mucus appearing in her nose, slipping away as she sniffs, reappearing. The desperate laughter grips Ria too and they cling to each other laughing and crying together.

....

Zak speaks without looking up from the cow he is milking. 'You have decided to help her then?' *He is not surprised*

'I don't know if it is helping her but you were right, the decision is hers, not mine. Tell me where to find the corms and I will go and get them.'

'You stay here with the animals and I will go. Take some milk. Have some yourself. You look as if you need it.'

Ria turns to the cow she has come to think of as a friend. 'Well, Cow, will you let me have some milk? Even after everything that has happened we are friends aren't we? I don't know which of us was more afraid in that first storm. I didn't guess you were carrying a calf, two calves, did I? There is so much that I have not seen. I must have been going about with my eyes half closed.'

Zak returns with his hands closed over the two small corms. 'The hay down there is starting to smell a bit sour. I will have to bring it up.'

'Do you think there will be enough for the rest of the voyage?'

'When we were loading the provisions on board I reckoned they were bringing enough for a year. So I did the same for the animals.'

'You think we might be on the ship for a year?'

'My guess is they thought a year would be long enough for us to reach our destination, leave us with a little, and have enough for the ship to return. Then they would bring more from Sanctuary on the ships that are to follow.'

'I don't think the New Hope will sail back to Sanctuary.'

'And the animals wouldn't be going back anyway so they are better provided for than the people.' Zak grins as he speaks.

A storm is building as Ria returns to Jen. Everyone knows what to do. Already the sails are furled and the men are busy securing anything on deck that might move. The women are below where Meera and Nan have distributed the tiny pieces of twig to chew for warding off sickness.

Ria is glad of the storm. The changing air lifts her spirits and everyone is occupied, too busy to notice her making her way up to the top deck carefully carrying a bowl of precious milk.

She taps on the cabin door and, when there is no reply, opens it cautiously. Jen looks up anxiously. 'Ria, come in.' She is hunched over the table but it is not until she is inside and has closed the door behind her that Ria sees that Jen has found a bowel and pestle.

'I'm ready.'

The ship lurches and Ria is pitched across the cabin and thrown against the side of the table. She manages to keep the bowl upright and only a little milk slops out. Jen reaches over to take the bowl and hold it firmly on the table. Ria does not let go.

'Do you want to wait until the storm is over?'

'I cannot wait. I am afraid that I might lose the strength

She holds the bowl of milk steady while Ria reaches into a pocket for the corms. *I cannot do this and yet it is not for me to decide. I would see the child and yet there is no child for me to see. There is only confusion. The confusion is my own. I cannot see whether there is truly a child or not or who the child may or may not be. I see only my own blindness and it is the storm and I am tossed by relentless waves and the voices in my ears are daemons and my eyes are full of salt and my lungs are heavy and filling.... And yet...my fingers have fastened on a stone and I pull it out and give it to her. She takes it and the storm eases a little. She is far away from me now. She is grinding the stone and all I can do is watch. She is talking and I am trying to run away but there is nowhere to run.*

'Will you stay with me?'

'If that is what you want. Here, drink a little milk first. It will help your stomach hold on to the powder.

'I need you here to make me go through with it all. You will see me go through with it won't you?'

A screaming wind in the rigging, in my head, but no it is my voice. 'Because it is Randal's child?' *I am screaming! I had not meant to say it.* Ria clenches her jaws to prevent herself saying more. Her fingernails pierce the skin of her palms in her fists but she cannot hold herself back. She seizes Jen by the shoulders, 'Because you are carrying Randal's child? Killing Randal's child?'

Jen stands motionless as Ria slaps her face, pummels her chest with small, desperate punches until she is exhausted and falls against Jen, sobbing. Jen puts her arms around Ria's shoulders and speaks softly through her hair, 'Because I trust you.'

Without speaking, and in spite of the lurching of the ship, she takes a smaller bowl from her bunk and tips part of the powder into it then stirs in some milk. She lifts the bowl, tips it quickly to her mouth and drinks the contents. She is silent but her face is contorted as she throws the bowl down and grasps at her throat.

Ria steps forward with the last of the milk. 'Drink this.' She says. 'I will bring more.'

Jen tries to speak but cannot. She sips the milk, pushes it away, lifts it again and sips then tips and drains the bowl. She holds both hands firmly over her mouth as if trying to hold everything in but a moan escapes and becomes a howl. She clings to Ria, her eyes wide with terror. The ship rolls again and they stumble onto the bunk where they lie together, Ria sobbing and Jen moaning and throughout the storm.

Several hours later Ria speaks gently to Jen. 'I have to leave you for a while. The storm is over. I must make sure no one disturbs you and get you more milk. Lie still. I will be back as soon as I can.'

She is relieved to meet Russell as she emerges from the cabin. 'Mr. Russell, Jen is very sick with the lung waste sickness. There is blood. It is very important that no-one goes near her.'

'I understand Miss. I will make sure Mr. Kierle knows.'

'Yes, thank you. Please tell him that I will take care of her and will let him know when it is safe for him to visit her.'

'Of course. It is very important that we safeguard the health of our Guardian. I will be sure he understands how serious the illness can be.'

A good man. 'Thank you, Mr. Russell. Your help means a great deal to me.'

He bows very slightly and smiles. 'Thank you, Ria'

Ria goes straight to Randal's cabin. He is there alone. *Waiting for me?*

'How is,' he begins then stops himself. 'How are you?'

'She is losing the child. She will suffer terribly. We are letting it be known that she is coughing blood. No-one must go near her.'

'I will issue an order and ask Kierle to speak to the crew and other women about the disease. Already the ship is full of rumours.'

On her way back down to Zak Ria sees that the women are anxious. She seeks out Nan and Meera. 'Tell the other women that there is nothing to worry about. We have caught the coughing early and Zak has the herbs and berries to treat her. But no one must go near her. We must avoid the disease spreading through the ship.' When Ria gets back to the cabin

Jen is asleep. Ria mixes more milk and powder then gently rouses her. 'I'm sorry to wake you Jen but it is time.'

At first Jen appears confused and then panic shows in her face, as she realises what Ria means. 'No,' she groans. 'I cannot.' Ria sits patiently, saying nothing. Jen speaks again, more quietly, 'I know I must, but how?' Her hands tremble as she reaches for the bowl. 'And how did I let this happen?' She tries to raise the bowl to her lips. 'I can't do it.' Her trembling becomes more violent and threatens to spill the milk. Ria leans forward and offers to take the bowl but Jen reacts by suddenly lifting it to her open mouth. She tips her head back as if to open her throat and pours the liquid down then drops the bowl and uses her hands to close her mouth, forcing herself to swallow. Droplets of milk spray from her nose as she struggles with a choking desire to cough. Her fingers slide across her face, easing her cheek muscles, closing her eyes. Still she does not open her mouth *as if she is afraid that somehow the vile liquid could find its way out.*

'There is a little more milk' Ria whispers taking Jen's hands to give her the bowl. As she sips the milk Jen opens her eyes. She cannot smile.

'At least there is no pain,' she replies.

'That will come.'

Jen curls up on the bunk and lies silent but she reaches out to take Ria's hand.

'I dare not stay.' Ria tells her quietly. Kierle has called us all together. He knows that you are sick but he will expect me to be there. Try to get some sleep.' Jen's grip tightens slightly *but she has no real strength* and Ria lifts the fingers one by one away from her own hand. 'I will be back as soon as I can.'

....

Kierle stands confidently, waiting for their full attention, 'Gentlemen, ladies, good afternoon. We sail in peace and in purity.

'In purity.'

'I have called you together at this unusual hour because there is important information which we must share at the earliest possible moment. Through no fault of our own we have a coughing sickness on board. As you already know a few men and women have had the disease and recovered. You may also know that my wife, Jen, has developed a severe case of the illness and is therefore confined to her cabin. As your surgeon I will obviously oversee her treatment while our commander's wife, Ria, will care her for. This sickness is extremely contagious and very dangerous. It is essential therefore that none of you enter the cabin. We must be extra vigilant in our protection of purity.

'Be watchful of yourselves and others. Anyone with a persistent cough should be reported to me so that I can ensure the necessary action is taken. Do not approach me yourself, particularly if you have produced any blood with your cough. Take yourself to Ria. She will tell you what precautions to take.'

'How has this cough come to be on board?' a man's voice calls, just loudly enough to be heard. Several others agree with him while trying not to be noticed. Many look at their feet and mutter;

'Who brought it on board?'

And a woman's voice, 'Why should Ria have to deal with it when we have a surgeon whose duty it is to cure us and care for us?'

Ria stands. 'With Mr. Kierle's permission,' Kierle nods briefly in response, 'I am happy to help anyone with illness as far as my knowledge will allow. We have herbs and berries in the hold and I have books that tell me how to use them. I am happy to care for Jen because she is my friend but I offer to do the same for anyone else. I hope we can prevent the sickness spreading to anyone else and that is why we ask that no-one approach Jen's cabin until she has recovered.' *I do not need to tell them that Kierle is such a coward he would not even approach his wife for fear of falling ill himself.*

'And will she recover?'

'I am hopeful.'

....

When she returns to Jen's cabin, Ria finds her sitting at the small wooden table gripping it so tightly her that knuckles are white.

'He won't come near you. He is terrified of the sickness.'

'Thank you Ria.' Jen loosens her grip on the table.

'But now you must swallow the third portion and I have no more milk, only water.'

'I know. I am ready.'

'The third is the worst. Your body knows what has gone before and will not want it. With the fourth you have some comfort in knowing that it is the last.'

'For the moment.'

'True. But when the time comes for the second corm you will be ready for it. It will represent a way of ending the pain. Pain that will soon begin.'

'There can be no going back Ria. We both know that. Bring me the mixture and I will do what I must.'

She takes the small bowl with trembling hands. 'Hold it with your strongest hand,' says Ria, 'and give me the other.' She turns Jen's left hand over and strokes the inside of her wrist. From her pocket she takes a small sharp stone which she places on the wrist. She searches around a little with the stone until it seems to settle in a small indentation. Without warning she presses the stone sharply into Jen's wrist with her thumb. Jen gasps as a sharp pain shoots up her arm and down towards her stomach as Ria shouts, 'Now!'

Jen tips back the bowl and opens her mouth. Her throat is about to close when Ria jabs the stone into her wrist again. Jen gasps and the liquid seems to be sucked into her stomach without her willing it. Now Ria holds the stone firmly in place while Jen's retches violently. 'Hold onto it!' says Ria firmly. 'Close your throat to it. You must keep it down. Imagine your stomach holding it in, forcing it on down. Only you can keep it there.'

Jen moans. She falls back onto the bunk, lies on her side and curls up tightly.

'It hurts me Ria. It's hurting me.'

Ria speaks gently. 'This is just the beginning. I will do everything I can to ease the pain but I cannot prevent it.'

For a while, Jen cannot speak. She gasps, flinches, and groans quietly. Sitting beside her Ria knows that she can do nothing else. *I will sit through the night. It will be her longest night and she will think that she is dying and she may be dying. Some talk through their dying and some are silent*

And as darkness falls, Jen begins telling her story. Racked by pain she hovers around consciousness, drifting in and out of the world. She talks in brief spells, stopping when the pain overtakes her breathing, and speaking again as soon as she is able *Let her speak. She would talk whether I was here or not and anyone hearing her would say it was the delirium of her sickness.*

'My mother and I lived in a chapel house. I never knew my father. I was told that he died when I was very young, maybe even before I was born. She never wanted to speak of him. I never asked. But there was always help. It came from the committee. She worked for them. Cooking, cleaning, always at their beck and call. They called her a chapel wife and I hated them for it. But she knew things, knew about history and laws and secrets. She even went to the rooms of the elders. She always said I would take over from her one day. I never argued.

Of course the day came that one of the elders asked for me in her place. 'Clean his rooms,' she said to me. She let me go there, knowing. She must have known. Of course I never spoke to her of what happened there. She never asked. He was cold and hard until he got what he wanted and afterwards, as if he was sorry, he would soften, sit quietly watching me dress, then take my hand.' Jen's eyes open and fill with tears that sparkle briefly but she closes her eyes again. She is unaware of the tears on her cheeks but they trickle onto her lips and tasting them seems to rouse her for a few seconds. She opens her eyes and tries to lift herself. 'The sea. They are calling me. I could join them in the sea with Beth,' but the effort is too great. 'Too heavy,' she says and slips away again.

'He used to take my hand, so gently. He liked to show me things. He showed me the beetles. His was old, many years old. My friend the beetle. Pinned in a box. It waved its legs, very slowly. It was terrible, that slow waving. Always trying to move away but always pinned in that box. It was a beautiful box – polished wood – I polished that wood, over and over again, polish the wood, polish the wood, lift the lid, see the beetle, and under the lid, the colours, changing colours, more beautiful colours than you could imagine. I see them now, all around me, like the sky and I am flying. Live all your life in that beautiful box of polished wood and changing colours but all you want to do is fly. He said he would give me one. I didn't want it. I didn't say. He didn't ask. He took me to the inner chapel, said no woman had ever been there before. And I was dizzy, almost sick with the beauty – the colour, the perfume – so rich, so thick I could hardly move and the sound, the buzzing, like sick blood throbbing inside my head. I hear it now, buzzing, throbbing. It fills my head. And the smell is here and I am lost, slipping under their perfume. He should never have shown me. I should never have known. Then I would not have this burning knife inside me tearing me apart. I know I am dying. I have killed it all. It looked so wonderful and it was all so dead.

'All the places he took me. Every one slipped to the ground he even the inner chapel. He said it was safe but I knew it would fall.

'I never asked. I didn't want to see their secrets, hear their lies. It was all lies. But he would never leave me alone. He would never stop. He would call for me. He told my mother he loved to watch me work. I lied. I said I never stood naked because I didn't want to believe it. I thought I could make it untrue – refuse to believe in it – I thought I could make it go away. I want it all to go away. What is it about these men that they can be so cruel? To have such beauty, such power, in their grasp? He knew that once I had known it I would always want it. Again and again. More and more.

'He called me his transhue girl. My skin would change colour. He had me pinned down and I waved and tried to crawl away but the shifting colours weighed down my arms and legs and I grew harder and harder, developed a shell. I had to keep going back. I couldn't stop.

'Kierle knew that too. They must have told him. He thought he could keep me pinned on this ship but he can't. I've hardened myself beyond his reach, I see further than all of them and now I can speak of things I never spoke of before.

'I have had a transhue beetle crawl across my skin, trailing its colours across my body. He has it on a pin and he is pitiless. He removes the pin and lets the creature crawl itself to exhaustion. He gives it this tiny torment of hope and watches it crawl, crawl over my body. He thinks he has me pinned but now I am crawling away.

Just before dawn Ria tries to rouse Jen. But Jen is not ready to be woken.

'Leave me to sleep. I would sleep more deeply.'

'Wake up Jen, and listen to me. Come back to me just this once and then I will leave you to make your own decision. You are not yourself. You are too far way and I need you to be here.' Lifting Jen into a sitting position Ria shakes her gently, rubs her back, and whispers to her. 'You made this decision for yourself. Remember this. Remember your own strength that you have hidden for so long. It is your own action. You are taking responsibility for yourself. Come back and finish the task.'

Jen's eyes flicker open and she seems to smile. Ria lifts a small bowl to her lips and she sips the liquid. As soon as she tastes the contents she is jolted awake. Screaming 'No, you are poisoning me' she knocks the bowl out of Ria's hand and it falls to the cabin floor. Fully awake now she is sobbing.

'No, no, Ria how could you let me? The last of the powder. Is it gone? Can we save it? She tries to throw back the covers, to get out of the bunk and retrieve the bowl.

'I'm sorry Jen. I had to be cruel. That was ivy you tasted, to shock you awake. The last of the powder is here.'

'You are a terrible and wonderful friend' she says, smiling a thin smile, 'and I am ready.' She takes the bowl in her right hand and offers her left to Ria.

....

Zak has come to Jen's cabin. 'Ria, the animals are quiet. I can manage here. Go back to your own bunk. You need some rest.'

'I know but she is in a lot of pain and terrified. I think she worries that Kierle will try to see her. At least if I am with her I can sleep whenever she does.'

'Are you sure you sure not hiding?'

'Why would I be hiding?'

'You might be hiding from Randal, or from having time to think about him.'

'I cannot seem to think about it. I'm not sure that thinking about it would be helpful.'

'All the more reason to give yourself some time.'

'There will be time enough later. In the coming days Jen is going to need all my strength but if you will stay with her now

I can go down, see the animals and collect the herbs I will need.'

A short while later, having gathered the herbs she needs Ria is climbing the stair past the women's quarter and up towards the deck when she meets Nan. 'Ria, I am glad to see you. How is Jen?'

'It is too early to say, but I am going back to her now.'

'Can you spare just a little time? There is something I...'

'I'm sorry Nan; I am exhausted I have to rest. I will find you later.' Almost as soon as she reaches her cabin there is a tap on the door.

'Ria.' *His voice.* She expects him to come in but he does not. He taps again. 'Ria?' his voice is softer, *anxious.* As she walks towards the door she is aware of her own trembling. She has difficulty finding the strength to lift the latch and although she wants to speak she can find neither her voice nor the right words. Once in the cabin with her he too is silent. He sees that she is crying and his own eyes fill with tears. As if with a single thought each steps forward and puts out a hand, touches the others' face gently. They lean their foreheads together and slip into a kiss, tasting each other's tears. *We do not need to speak of it.*

It is as if they both speak and yet neither speaks and they both know the same words. *We are meant to be together.* Without turning away from her he reaches back and secures the latch with its chain and pin. They move to the bunk without words or thoughts.

Much later Ria wakes from a deep and comforting sleep. Hearing her sigh he covers them both with the sheet. 'Are you cold?' he asks softly.

'No,' she replies.

'We must talk.'

'I don't think so, at least not about things that have passed.'

'Are you sure?'

'Only as sure as I can be.'

'Then what must we do?'

'We must help each other, if we are meant to be together?'

'We are.'

'Then we must work together. But not here, like this.' She turns to face him and kisses him. 'This is for ourselves only and we both have work to do. Let's save this for each other. We should dress and go to your day cabin to begin our work together.'

'I will go. You need to rest. It is enough for me to know that you are going to be with me. That I have not lost you.'

....

But Ria cannot rest any longer. She returns to Jen and finds her curled up and whimpering with pain. 'Jen, can you hear me?' Her quiet cries falter a little and Jen tries to lift her head but fails. 'You have a fever. I will go to Zak, find something to help if I can, but first we must cool you.' Outside the cabin door Russell has left a pail of water. Ria dips and fills a bowl and brings it over to Jen. Pulling back the cover as she speaks, 'I have some water. I will…' She gasps as she sees that Jen is already bleeding heavily but before she has time to think or even cover Jen again the door opens and Nan comes in.

'I'm sorry Ria but I am desperate.' She too gasps at the sight of Jen lying in a pool of blood. 'Jen! Ria, this is no cough. This is something much... Is she pregnant?'

'She was but she is no longer.'

'Do something, Ria. Stop the bleeding. Save the child.

'The child cannot be saved.'

'And Jen?'

'I am doing everything I can for Jen.'

'I see now that you could not leave her. But, Ria, please, I cannot wait any longer. I need your help.'

'I'm sorry, Nan. I have been so taken up with thinking about Jen. Sit down here and tell me.'

'It's Taylor.'

'What has he done?'

'He says he chooses me to be his wife.'

'And you?'

'I cannot believe you have not noticed. Of course I cannot be Taylor's wife.' She shivers. 'I have made my own choice. We, Russell and I, have agreed. But he told me yesterday that Taylor plans to make an announcement after this evening's prayers. You have to help me Ria.'

'But surely you can say no. No-one will be forced to agree.'

'You say that because you are happy with Randal's choice, but how can you not have seen Jen's misery? She must have tried to say no to Kierle.' *Has she? Has she tried to say no? Why have I not seen?*

'I will talk to Randal.'

'Go now. Please Ria. I will stay with Jen.'

18

Fears

'Taylor would not, by the rules set out by the elders before we sailed, be allowed to force himself on Nan or anyone else. But it would be better for everyone if he could be dissuaded from making an announcement. That way he would not have to deal with others knowing that he had been turned down. Are you sure about Russell?'

'Nan is sure.'

'I will speak with Russell first. If he confirms what Nan has said I will talk to Taylor. But this will not be a simple matter.'

....

When Ria returns to the cabin, carrying a pail, extra linen and clean clothes, straw and a collection of herbs and dried berries, she is not surprised to find that Meera has joined Nan there.

'Randal will speak to Taylor. There will be no announcement.'

Speechless with relief Nan rushes over and puts her arms around Ria.

'Ria,' says Meera 'Jen needs you.' Crossing the cabin, Ria places the pail at the foot of the bunk, the herbs, linen and clothes on the table and the straw under it then bends over Jen. Nan follows her.

'She has been so quiet,' she says.

'Silent,' agrees Meera 'But never still. She is in so much pain.'

'We have padded her with rolls of linen,' Nan adds, 'but they need constant changing. It is all wrapped in straw but you will need to get rid of it soon. It is already beginning to smell.'

'And there will be more,' says Ria quietly. 'Thank you, both of you. I would have cared for her myself but now that you are here I cannot tell you how glad I am. But you must not stay. We must take care not to arouse suspicion. Tell the other women that Jen is worse, that it does not look hopeful,' she says, and then adds, in explanation, 'we must keep Kierle away.'

'Word will reach him,' says Nan. 'Taylor knows everything that the women know and everything that Taylor knows, Kierle knows.'

'Then go and tell the women that Jen is gravely ill, that there is a lot of blood, that we fear we may even lose her.' Jen groans and Ria turns to her and speaks softly, 'The worst will soon be over.' Jen gasps, clutches at her stomach and cries out. Turning briefly back to Meera and Nan she says, 'You must go.' then all her attention is with Jen and she is not even aware of them leaving.

'Jen, it's me, Ria, I know that you have swallowed the whole of the second corm and I understand why you did it. And now you will have to fight for your life. I will not leave you until it is over. What you must do now is concentrate all your thoughts on saving yourself. Part of you is dying, that is true but it is only a small part and you can prevent it dragging you down with it. You must save yourself. Let go of death and save yourself. Trust me. Understand that if I bind your mouth it is only to save you from crying out so loud that he might guess. Take this,' she puts a small roll of linen between Jen's teeth. 'Bite on it, the pains are coming, free yourself, let yourself go to another place. I will do what I can.' She rolls Jen onto her stomach and pulls her down to the end of the bunk. *So light. I expected her to be heavy. There is so little of her. Sounds from her throat, her lungs, her heart. So much pain. But she is still strong. The pain rattles in her but she is resigned, as if she has known it all her life, is accustomed to it.* Jen's body relaxes.

'Sleep a moment,' Ria whispers. 'It will not be long.'

She goes to the cabin door and secures it with its pin and chain then looks around for something more and sees Jen's heavy wooden chest. It takes all her strength to pull the chest across the doorway. Before she can find anything else Jen stirs, moans and begins to cry out. Ria returns to her side. 'It will soon be over. I'm sorry Jen. Here, take a little water.' She reaches for the small bowl and holds it to Jen's lips but Jen can do nothing for herself except softly moan 'No'. Dipping two fingers into the bowl Ria gathers a few drops of water then allows them to trickle onto Jen's lips. The second time, Jen manages to part her lips a little. But the third time her eyes suddenly open, her back arches, a deep throated moan escapes. 'Bite on this.' Urges Ria. 'Jan, you must. Trust me. Soon it will all be over.'

Now she drags Ria further down the bunk until only her upper body lies on the mattress. Her legs hang over the edge of the bunk with her feet almost reaching the floor. Ria tears open Jen's blood-stained skirt and removes the sodden padding.

'Let it go Jen. Let it go.' She speaks softly while kneading Jen's back with her fists

'You can do it. You are strong. It is leaving you now and you must push it away. Deep, deep in you, you have the strength. The child is dead now Jen and it has no wish to poison you. You can do this. Let go Jen. Only you can do this. Only you. Push it Jen. Push it now.' *Her whole body is emptying.* Jen screams, just once, a short, desperate scream. Ria pushes down with the palms of her hands. There is blood, hot, brown and stinking. Ria remembers Zak and the calf, and hears a chorus of voices, Zak and her grandmother, speaking the same words, *Don't turn away Ria. This is no time to leave. I know how hard it is but hold her firmly and know exactly what you are going to do. She should not be afraid and neither should you.* And her own thoughts, her own words: *Liver, lungs, Words I have heard but things I have never seen and so much blood.*

Then she hears Jen's voice and it is like waking from one terrible dream into another. *'I need you here to make me go through with it all. You will see me go through with it won't you? The wind screams in the rigging, its sound is filling my head, but no...* Horrified, Ria realises that she is hearing her own voice, she is screaming uncontrollably, 'Because it is Randal's child, because you are carrying Randal's child?'

Again Jen's voice breaks into Ria's thoughts, 'Because I trust you'.

It is over.

As she helps Jen cover herself with a sheet she realises that Zak is tapping on the door and calling her name. 'Ria, it's me. Meera told me.'

Wearily she drags the away the chest, lifts the pin and opens the door just enough to let him in. His arms are full of straw which he uses to cover the pools of blood then he gathers up the soiled linen. He works without looking at Jen. 'I will take it,' he says, 'And this,' picking up the bucket. 'Bar the door.' As soon as he has gone, she replaces the pin and chain. She looks at the chest but knows that she does not have the strength to move it again.

Losing all sense of time, she washes Jen, pads her with clean linen and wraps her in a clean skirt. She helps her crawl from the bunk, and tries to get to her to the chair, but Jen crumples and lies at her feet, waving a hand as if to say 'It doesn't matter.'

Now Ria works as quickly as her exhaustion will allow. She cuts open the hessian mattress cover, drags out the blood-stained straw and replaces it with clean, scrubbing the cover with another handful. She pulls off her own bloodied clothes and tears them up, saving a few of the least stained pieces for washing herself. When she has gathered everything up, and stowed the bundle near the door, she hurriedly dresses in clean clothes.

The most difficult task is getting Jen back up into the bunk. She tries in vain to wake her. *I cannot lift her. She cannot stay there. I will have to get help* and is startled by someone trying to open the door. *Kierle?* But the voice is Randal's 'Ria, let me in.'

As she opens the door Zak comes up the stair. He follows Randal in and looks at Ria as if asking her a question. 'Just that.' she answers pointing at the bundle near the door. He nods, gathers it up and is gone. Randal secures the door then turns to Ria.

'I had to know.'

'It is over.'

'And she?'

'It is impossible to say. She has the weight of the dead. I cannot lift her' but Randal lifts Jen easily, puts her gently onto the bunk and pulls the cover over her. 'It is not her weight. It is your exhaustion. You must rest. Is there no-one else who can sit with her?'

'Meera and Nan. They understand.' He looks at her with unspoken questions showing in his eyes and the way he tilts his head. 'I have told them a little, only as much as they needed to know.'

'Well, you must rest. I will speak to Russell, he will bring them to her.'

As Ria allows him to guide her back to her own cabin she hears the singing of the sea dwellers. 'Do you hear them singing?' she asks as he lowers her gently onto the bunk.

'I hear them. But what you hear as singing is something different to me.'

'What is it, if not singing?'

'Guidance, encouragement, sometimes a warning.'

'They speak to you?'

'Not to me, to each other. But I listen. I have learned to understand them. My people call them Lodencroam, or Loden, it means guides without knowing.'

'I knew they were trying to help us. Why do they do it?'

'We have a story which says that the Lodencroam are the last remaining few of a race that once lived both on land and in the sea. They argued amongst themselves and, rather than fight, they split into two groups; those who loved the sea and those who turned against it. Most chose to remain on land. They lost the ability to breathe in the water and turned their backs for ever on the sea. The Loden are the descendants of those who chose the sea. We rarely see them, even from our ships, but sometimes they will swim with us in the hope of rebuilding friendship.'

'I would like to swim with them again.'

'That would probably not be wise. Last night their voices changed. It was a note I had not heard before. I felt that something was wrong, that they were displeased with us. I was surprised to find them still nearby at dawn this morning.'

'Perhaps you misunderstood them. I will go out on deck this evening. If they will sing for me I might understand them.'

'But first you must rest. You are exhausted. Close your eyes and I will sit with you a while.'

....

When Ria wakes she finds that he is still sitting beside her. 'How long have I slept? Have you been here all the time? I must go to Jen.'

He shakes his head. 'You have slept for three days,' he says, smiling. 'And I have not been here all that time. Jen is sleeping. Meera and Nan take turns to sit with her. Zak has given them everything they needed. How do you feel? Are you refreshed? Now Russell will bring you food, and Zak has already sent you this milk, still warm.'

'I am hungry,' she says as she sits up to take the milk. There is a gentle knock and Randal opens the door just enough to take a bowl of steaming broth from Russell.

'This will do you good. It even has a little meat in it. Eat the biscuits too, and the apple will be good even though is looks a little shrivelled. I believe we will be in sight of land soon. Then we will be able to go ashore and we will have fresh food.'

'Can that be true? Is that what the Loden people have told you?'

'The Lodencroam are distressed. They have been so for several days. I am sure they listen to us, watch us.' He pauses. 'They are not happy. I think they may be angry with us, with me perhaps. I cannot tell. Their voices no longer make sense to me.

'I have come to you now because I hoped you might be ready to return to us. I think the women need you. I let it be said that you contracted the coughing sickness and that Meera and Nan have been brought up to the top decks, to care for you and Jen. But people are uneasy. This new calling of the Loden is making them more and more anxious. They had grown accustomed to their song and were even beginning to accept their presence but this is different and old fears are being stirred up again.'

'What about Kierle?'

'Constantly preaching the dangers of the deep.'

Suddenly Ria remembers Nan. 'What about Taylor? Has he...'

'Taylor realised that he could not press Nan into being his wife although it was clear that he was angry. Of course he did not want anyone to know that he had been rejected but somehow a rumour arose that he was looking to make a choice and it seems that Nina presented herself to him. Nothing has been announced.'

'Do you always know what is happening below decks in such detail?'

'It is important, which is why I have come to you. The women need reassurance. Meera and Nan tell them that you are recovering but there are stories of you diving into the sea, swimming with the Loden. Some say you are one of them disguised as a woman; that you came on board to lure us into danger. It is important that people see you. Come to prayers this evening. Can you do this for me?'

Her reply is to pull his head towards her own and kiss him.

'I would like you meet my people,' he whispers through her hair, 'Especially my mother. She would understand everything if she were to meet you.'

'Do you think you will ever be able to take me there?'

'It is my constant hope.'

....

When Ria reaches Jen's cabin she finds Jen sitting up talking to Nan. She is thin and very pale, but composed. 'I want to thank you Meera, and Nan and Zak too, of course. But I need to put this behind me. Can you allow me to forget?' She is looking directly at Ria and it is Ria who answers.

'I think we should all forget or at least live as if we had forgotten. We can return to the decks this evening, go to supper and prayers. Do you think you are strong enough?'

'I am ready.'

Ria turns to Nan. 'How are you, and how….'

'Russell says all will be well. He expects Taylor to make his announcement this evening and then Russell will be free to do so.'

'Then we must be there.'

....

In the animal hold Zak questions Ria without turning round from the milking. 'Jen is recovering?'

'She is.'

'And you?'

'My strength has returned.'

'And you can put this all behind you?'

'We must all do so. We must be ready for…'

'For whatever happens? Something *is* happening Ria. The animals are restless. And have you heard the singing of the Loden? It has changed.'

'I mean to go on deck at dusk to try to understand them.'

'I think they see the dangers that we do not.'

'Surely you are not beginning to believe Kierle's teachings?'

'Of course not, but I do understand the animals and I believe they have a new fear. It may be that they and the sea dwellers know something that we do not.'

....

At supper the women are discussing their fears.

'The sound – I cannot call it singing – was terrible through the night.'

'It came up from below the ship as well as alongside us.'

'They must go down and swim right underneath us to send up their horrible wailing.'

'They do it to terrify us.'

'And it works.'

'This is what they meant: the Guardian, the elders. This is the terror of the deep. Now that we are far away from Sanctuary, out here where no-one can help us, we will be dragged down.'

'There will be something down there – some unimaginable creature from the depths clinging to the bottom of the ship.'

'Or maybe something has crawled inside.'

They are terrifying each other into madness Ria stands up slowly and speaks calmly

'I think you know me well enough for me to speak?' Most nod, or murmur agreement. 'It is my firm belief that we have nothing to fear from the sea dwellers. They mean us no harm.'

Nina stands abruptly on the other side of the table and almost at the other end. 'What do you know?' she asks angrily.

'It is true that I know nothing for certain. None of us can. But we all know that these creatures have been swimming alongside us throughout our journey. They sang to us in friendship. In all this time they have done nothing to harm us. They even tried to save Beth and they have mourned our losses with us.'

'So what are they doing now?' demands Nina. 'Their 'singing', as you call it, does not sound like friendship to me. I say they are threatening us. How can you deny it?'

The women look again to Ria. 'I can only tell you that I believe they are trying to help us.'

'But they *are* frightening many of us, Ria,' says Meera calmly. 'Surely you can understand these fears?'

'I do understand.'

While Ria sits, Nina angrily remains standing. 'You understand and yet you do nothing. These women have come to you for help. Will you give them nothing?'

Meera looks up. 'Sit down Nina. You are too hard on Ria. She is exhausted. She has been…'

'Oh, yes, the coughing sickness,' Nina sneers. 'Let us hope that the worst we have to endure is the coughing sickness.'

Eyes flicker towards Jen who remains silent. Nan rises slightly, as if to stand, but having drawn attention away from Jen she sits again as she speaks. 'The sickness is bad enough and no-one would wish to suffer it. We should all continue to be on our guard against it. There is balsam left for anyone who finds themselves coughing and I suggest we ask Ria to help us all she can. Perhaps she has something to help those of us who are most anxious?'

What they need is not something to dull their minds. They need to be awake, alive to reality. They are going to have to make decisions. And yet it may help them, for the moment, to believe that I can ease their fears. 'I will go to the hold this evening.'

. . . .

Zak interrupts Ria's thoughts as she is making her way to the hold. 'What are you looking for down there?'

'I don't know. I thought that if I just went down there, to smell the herbs, surround myself, maybe hold some dried berries, feel them, smell them, taste them, perhaps my grandmother would speak to me. The women have asked me for help and I don't know what I can do. The only place on the ship I can think of to go is the hold. What can we do for them Zak?'

'It is you they have asked Ria, not me. Of course I will help you if you need me but I can think of nothing to offer them. It would be no real help to give them roots to chew, or dried mushrooms to alter their thoughts for a day or two.

Those things are not what they need. They will not alter the facts nor remove whatever is causing the fear. I do not mean to be unhelpful, Ria. You spoke of going to the hold. Go. And call me if you need me.'

What am I doing? Do I really believe I can find an answer here? And yet I feel that I am in the right place. If they are right and there is some danger just below the ship, I will be closer to it here.

In the lowest, smallest, hold, Zak has neatly stowed row upon row of hessian sacks. The top of each is neatly stitched. Those that he has cut open he has tightly retied with strong cord. Closest to Ria, at the entrance, are the smallest sacks piled three, four, or even five deep while further back in the darkness are larger sacks one on top of another. As her eyes grow accustomed to the darkness she tugs at the cord of a nearby sack. Pulling it apart she breathes in a wave of its dusty scent. Words almost come to her. Her grandmother's voice hovers, just out of reach. She plunges her hand in amongst the fine grain gathering a handful to hold up to her face. She struggles but cannot grasp a memory that seems to taunt her. She puts a few of the tiny grains onto her tongue *Bitter* but she does not recognise the taste and as she chews she is disappointed *Nothing*. Bending close over the sack she breathes in deeply but cannot recapture the scent or the memory it hinted at. She re-ties the sack and moves deeper into the hold where she can now see clearly.

Wherever she sees that a sack has been opened she unties it and looks inside. She picks out tiny dried mushrooms, hardened berries, seeds still encased in shrivelled red pods, pungent onion-like fruits, but they tell her nothing.

Deciding to make her way through to the larger sacks which have lain, untouched, since the ship was loaded, she pulls out some of the smallest and is surprised to uncover a line of wooden boxes. *Surely these have been hidden here.*

Lifting their lids she thinks, at first, that they are full of sand. *Randal told me about ballast but why would it be here and why in boxes?* She kneels to put her hands into the sand. Just below the surface her fingers settle on something round and firm. *Vegetables.* She discovers turnips, parsnips and when she uncovers carrots she cannot resist eating one. She brushes off the sand then closes the box. As she turns to sit on it her thoughts turn to the mill with the familiar creaking of the wheel and the murmur of the water. Tears fill her eyes as she is overcome by the delicious rush of the carrot's sweetness and a longing to be off the ship, back on the land again, digging in her father's field. 'Earthing up treasures,' he used to call it as, every year, they dug the first crop of potatoes which seemed to be ready to burst from the ground. *Soon the first plate of potatoes, steaming hot from the pan in my mother's kitchen, and grandmother calling me. Strange, grandmother never came to the mill. But no, I am not in the mill, and my grandmother will never call me again.*

Ria wipes the tears from her face and looks around. *The answer does not lie in these boxes.* She stands up and pushes her way through to where the largest sacks are piled, one on top of another. Leaning with all her strength against the top row she pushes one sack back far enough to be able to climb onto the bottom row. Here all the sacks are unopened and it is impossible to unpick the stitching with her fingers. She bends to try with her teeth and, when she tugs almost loses her balance as the hessian itself splits apart. Tearing the opening wide enough to see what is inside she discovers that the sack is full of twigs. She pulls one out to look closely at it and does not recognise the hard red wood, which is so brittle that it snaps between her fingers. *Dead wood?* These twigs seem to have been packed very carefully in neat layers. Ria pulls at them gently. *Cool, hard, brittle twigs. Why a sack full of nothing but twigs?* She works her hand down into the sack. *Something is changing. These twigs are softer. They feel warm, almost damp, sticky, as if this were some kind of nest. And not just a nest, inside the nest, a cocoon.* She knew before she saw, before she heard. And even as she knew, the smell, the sickly sweet smell of decay and then the mesh of decaying twigs became the congealing mesh of the beetle's cocoon.

Shuddering, and fighting the retching in her stomach, Ria piles the twigs back into the sack and ties is as firmly as she can with the straggling threads at the top. *I must tell Randal.* Hurrying through the animal hold she notices that Zak is not there. *Prayers. I am late. Randal will be there.* But as she rushes in the direction of the prayer meeting she trips at the bottom of a stairway between decks and Randal, striding in the opposite direction, finds her there. 'Zak told me you would be coming this way' he says, lifting her to her feet. 'There is no time to lose.'

'Randal…' she interrupts him, 'There is something I must tell you, show you.'

'No, no, not now,' he replies, 'I have realised what they have been trying to tell us.'

But Ria cannot wait. 'There is no time.' Words spill from her lips, so close together it sounds like a single, long, and urgent question. 'How can I make you see that it cannot wait, that I have been through this before, I thought I was to blame, that it was all my fault but now I know what is happening to the ship, I know what the Lodencroam have been telling you all this time. I must show you. You must come now. How much do you know about the beetles that the committee wear?'

'Ria, listen. The Loden have been trying to warn us that there is danger here on board the New Hope.'

'I know. It is the beetles. I found them nesting in the hold.' As she speaks she takes his hand and pulls him in the direction of the sack. 'Come down and I will show you.' Her stomach heaves at the sickly scent as they approach. 'Can you smell it?'

'Bilge water?'

'Something else, sweeter. In that sack.' She hesitates then steps back pointing out the sack. 'You... you look... they.. look in there.' She shudders. 'I don't want to see.'

When he reaches the opened sack, he drags it out and slightly away from her before bending to open it but now she steps forward and puts her hands over the opening.

'Don't open it. Not here. Let me tell you.'

'There is no time. You said so yourself.' He has opened the sack and is pulling out the twigs. 'Tell me as I...'

'Not here!' She stops him again. 'It was their precious beetles that were destroying Sanctuary. This is Kierle's secret hoard.' She waves her arm over the boxes. 'He has food here, fresh vegetables and their precious wood chewing beetles.'

'He has brought their beetles on board?'

She nods.

'I should have guessed.' He swings the sack over his shoulder and they go up to the top deck where he pushes an anchor down amongst the twigs. When he throws it overboard he swings it in a wide arc so that it soars as far away from the ship as possible.

'There are probably more,' says Zak who has silently appeared behind them.

'Find Russell,' says Randal quietly. 'Ria, bring Meera and Nan but do not mention this to anyone else.'

19

Trust

The others are still at prayers. No one notices Ria as she slips into the back row. All attention is fixed on Jen who is with Kierle beside the lectern. She is speaking, but so quietly that Ria cannot make out her words. *She looks strong.* Kierle is responding with fury. His tiny eyes bulge in his red, screwed up face. He has hold of her wrist and pulls her savagely towards him as he shouts, 'You cannot do this. You do not have the right.' The words seem to slither out, between his clenched teeth and bluish lips. Turning away from Jen but keeping the fierce hold on her wrists, he continues shouting, partly at Jen, partly at the shocked assembly. 'She does not have the right. She was given time to consider. You all heard, you all knew. She, you, were happy enough to accept the privileges. You have therefore accepted the responsibilities. There is no question. You are my wife.'

Jen shakes her head.

Ria moves as if to push her way through to them but is instantly aware of Russell's hand on her arm, holding her back. Jen is trying to move towards the group of women nearest to her and as Kierle tightens his grip, repeating 'She does not have the right. You do not have...' but it is Randal's authoritative voice that stops him.

'Excuse me for interrupting your meeting, Mr. Kierle, but there is something of the utmost importance which I must discuss with you without delay.'

As Kierle hesitates, Jen wrenches herself away and, seeing Meera and Nan coming towards her, begins to fall in their direction. They each take an arm and support her through the crowd. Men and women step back to let them through and close the space again behind them to prevent her being followed. Ria leads them to her cabin. 'Jen, you must stay here and rest. But we have to go. There is something we must do. Secure the door as soon as we leave.'

'We cannot leave her here alone,' says Meera. 'Kierle will come looking for her.'

'If not him then Taylor' says Nan. 'And I am not afraid of either of them. I will stay with Jen. Come back to us as soon as you can.'

'We will. Bar the door,' says Ria as Meera follows her out of the cabin.

....

They reach the day cabin at the same time as Zak and Russell. Randal is waiting for them and speaks as soon as the door is closed. 'We can stay on board the ship no longer. The New Hope is not safe. I don't know how much time we have but it cannot be long.'

Zak interrupts 'Shall I search the sacks and boxes for more beetles?'

'No, it is too late for that. I think they may have colonised the hull itself. That is what the Lodencroam have been trying to tell us. Mr. Russell what can you report?'

'The upper decks and rigging appear sound. The ship's boats are high. They should be dry and therefore safe. Shall I check below the waterline?'

'It is not necessary. I have heard enough to know that the hull cannot last long. I want everyone off the ship as soon as possible. I believe we will be saved. I believe we are close to land; land where there are people who will be looking for us; looking for me. All we have to do is get people into the boats.'

'They will not be easily persuaded' says Meera.

'We can do this together. If you all trust me?' Randal looks directly at each of them in turn. 'You are the people they trust.'

Zak fights to keep his voice from cracking as he speaks, 'And the animals?'

'As soon as the women are in the boats you can begin bringing up the animals. Then we will release Gosse. I have instructed the men to prepare the boats. Now we must persuade the women to use them.'

....

Randal leads them to the top deck. He moves calmly but Ria sees the tightness between his shoulders and the stiffness in his neck. *He is afraid.*

The men have already lowered the first boat to the deck and Laran and Ellie, the youngest women on board, lead a group of women, mainly the young like themselves, who seem ready to climb in, but Kierle blocks their way by standing in the boat himself with a grim-faced man on either side. They are armed with heavy wooden clubs. Between Kierle and the women stands Taylor grim faced and trembling. Kierle lifts his hands as if single-handedly holding back the surge of women pushing towards the boat. He grows taller and the force of his voice silences the murmuring crowd and holds them motionless.

'This is madness,' he roars. 'The New Hope is your Sanctuary. You will not step from it until we reach land. It is written…

'Wake up Ria.' *Grandmother?* 'It is time to wake up.'

'No, it is you who are mad, Kierle,' Ria does not shout but her voice is loud and strong. She moves through the crowd, towards the boat as she continues, 'you with your secret supplies and your cruelty and if that were not bad enough you bring on board the very thing that has been destroying the community itself. That beetle you wear as a sign of your power, and the others hidden away in the depths of the ship, they have been eating away at us from the beginning. It is your doing that we must now choose between the sea and a sinking ship.

And now there is a new sound from Lodencroam who surround the ship swimming openly in a swelling sea. They rise and fall with the waves, lifting their heads to call, turning to swim out of sight to reappear a short distance away, calling again. Patiently they repeat this swimming towards the ship, calling, swimming away and calling again. The ship lists slightly.

When Ria reaches the space in front of Taylor and his men she turns her back to them fearlessly and faces the women.

'Wake up,' she calls 'It is time to wake up.'

Voices shout back from the crowd. 'She's right. Get him out of the way.'

'Let's go!'

More of the men are arriving now and join in the shouting. Among them is Gosse.

'Sanctuary, committee, guardians, all that is over, we have to get off this rotting ship.'

Russell speaks, nodding calmly in agreement. 'If the commander says the boats are safer than the ship then it's the boats for me.'

'Do not trust yourselves to the perils of the deep' Kierle intones *but he is less tall now. He is losing his power over them.* 'You must remain on board the New Hope. There is no other way. We must continue our journey as it is written in the book: The time will come. There will be a new shore. You will be the first. Yours will be the honour. You will be remembered.'

A few of the youngest women try to step onto the boat but Taylor's men move forward, threatening those nearest to them. 'You will not leave this ship. I forbid it,' Kierle continues but his tone had changed. He is almost pleading with them now. 'It is for your own safety. We do not know the horrors that await us. Without Guardianship we have nothing to protect us.' This does not prevent the women struggling to get through. One of them calls out, 'Get him out of the way.'

'It's his own future he worries about,' shouts another.

'What are we waiting for?'

As the New Hope leans further a cracking is heard from the rigging. Men move towards the boat and, for the first time, there is a note of fear in Kierle's voice as he appeals for help, 'Mr. Taylor...'

Randal remains calm amid the confusion. 'Mr. Kierle I must insist that you step out of the boat. You must believe me when I tell you that the ship cannot remain afloat much longer. The larvae of the beetle have infested her timbers. It was those beetles that brought down the buildings of your Sanctuary, the beetles which you brought on board.'

'You may be the commander of this ship but you have no authority over me. I am the Guardian of this community and you are an evil liar.' He turns back to the men and women waiting on the deck. 'He is no normal man. By his own admission he came into our community out of the ocean.

'I see him for what he is – an evil creature with the power to change his form to suit his own needs. Who knows what terrible shape his body took under the waves: some creeping thing that wriggled in the cold and dark down there where there is no air, no light? And how long has he lain there, waiting, while his body slowly took shape, waiting for a time when he could crawl out of the water, learn to breathe, to walk, to speak, and come to tempt us? What better time for him to emerge than when the crumbling of our buildings distracted our Guardian and elders?

'He is a creature of the deep. We have no knowledge of their powers but we can see that somehow they have transformed one of their own kind into the shape of a man.'

Ria is about to move forward and answer him but Randal has reached her side and puts a hand on her arm. 'Let him speak,' he says softly, 'it is the raving of a mad man. Let them hear it.'

'Look closely at his limbs.' Kierle laughs as he speaks. 'Does he walk like you? And his speech – he had not fully mastered speech when he first crawled from the waves. Even now his words sound strange, like someone who learned language without a childhood among decent men and women. And his breathing – have you not noticed how he struggles to breathe in the air? How he tries to disguise it as a cough? This coughing sickness – did we know of it in Sanctuary? Is it not the final remnant of a creature struggling to breathe in the air when he was in fact created as a sea dweller? He is one of them.' He waves his arm, gesturing out towards the Lodencroam. 'Climb into his boats and you surrender yourselves to them.'

Russell has reached the front of the crowd and now stands facing Taylor. 'This is madness.' He calls out. 'These are the words of a madman. Of course our commander is an ordinary man. Listen to him.'

'Or listen to me,' says Ria. 'You asked me to find out the truth and this is my understanding.

Kierle attempts to interrupt her. 'She is....'

'No Mr. Kierle, you have spoken. I have as much right to speak as you – more, since I was asked to gather this information. These people have waited a long time to hear the history I am trying to tell. She turns to the women, 'We do not have long but I will tell you what I can.

'Our people arrived at Sanctuary in ships, and then chose to live only on land. They gave up their knowledge of the sea, and sailing and somehow knowledge gave way to fear. Randal's people and our people were once one and the same. While our ancestors left and discovered Sanctuary his remained in the old land. But they continued their relationship with the sea and its creatures, and always hoped that one day we would return. They even sent out ships to look for us.

'And, as you have seen for yourselves, he has guided us safely through many dangers in the hope of reuniting us with his people, with our own past, so that we might all make a new start – together.' There is a sudden drop at the other end of the ship, a loud splintering crack and the sound of rushing water. 'He has brought us this far and we must trust him now.'

'Does this sound like the truth?' Kierle shouts again, 'Does she sound like someone who is to be trusted? She too is evil. She has swum with these creatures, she may even be one of them herself. We are told that she too has had the coughing sickness. What more evidence do we need?'

Again Randal's powerful voice is calm. 'I do not need to argue with Mr. Kierle. I command your ship, and your safety was entrusted to me. Mr. Taylor, help Mr. Kierle out of the boat. To the rest of you I say that what Ria has told you is true. And we are now almost in sight of my home and my people who are also your people. I can promise you that they will be out in their own ships looking for us. Now each of you must make a choice.' As Randal speaks, Taylor turns to offer his arm to Kierle who refuses it and stands arms folded, rigid and red faced with anger. 'We will help those of you who choose to climb into the boats.'

Russell leads three men towards the boat and Taylor and his men move aside, allowing them through to Kierle from whom all power now seems to slip away. They guide him out of the boat and through the crowd towards Randal. As he reaches Randal, Kierle breathes in deeply, regaining some of his former stature before turning to speak once more.

'Those who choose to stay on board the New Hope will continue in the Guardianship entrusted to me by our elders and Guardian in Sanctuary. I will go to my own cabin and leave you to make your decision.'

Beside the small boat the young women hesitate.

'Meera,' says Ria, 'you must go in the first boat. These women know and trust you. They will follow you.'

'But…'

'We must show them that we trust Randal.' The ship lurches again. 'There is no time to waste.'

The men work calmly and efficiently and the women follow Randal's instructions in silence. The boat is soon full with just one man either side to take the oars. Meera waves as they are lowered and all but two of the Loden move away from the hull to clear a space on the surface. These two swim one each side of the boat as it moves steadily away from the New Hope. On the other side of the ship the second boat is already being lowered.

Ria stands beside Randal as he gives orders that the men hardly seem to need. 'Bring Jen and Nan,' he says to Ria, 'and gather anything you wish to save. Russell knows which of my maps and books to bring. Mr. Taylor,' he calls, 'you and Nina will go in the second boat please.'

When she returns to her cabin, Ria is not surprised to find Zak there. 'You will want this' he says, holding out her grandmother's book.

'Thank you. What will you do?'

'Stay with the animals and do whatever I can for them.'

'But the ship is sinking.'

'I will do what I can,' he says as he leaves.

By the time Ria returns to the top deck with Jen and Nan, all the other women have gone. Russell arrives with two small wooden boxes filled with maps and books. Only three boats remain. The ship is strangely quiet.

'Russell,' says Randal 'you and Nan will take Ria and Jen with you on the next boat.'

He thinks I will leave the New Hope without him

'I intend waiting for the last boat sir' says Russell. 'Nan can go with them.'

'I need you to go now,' Randal replies.

'Your experience and expertise may be needed by those already afloat. I can manage here.'

He thinks he may not survive – that Russell will lead in his place

'Mr. Russell, you have never questioned my orders. Please do not do so now. You will take your place in the next boat. Ria, where is Zak?'

With the animals. He will not be persuaded to leave them. 'I will go and look for him.' She leans in and passes her belongings to Jen. 'Take care of these for me,' she whispers. 'Goodbye.' As she walks past Randal she says, 'Let this boat go. I will go with Zak.' then she takes Russell's hand. 'Go with them. They may need you. Good luck.'

She does not want to go down into the hold. 'Zak' she calls softly from the top stair, 'Zak'. The thick smell of blood is rising from below. She goes down slowly and finds him sitting with his arms around a cow's neck. The animals lie around him as if asleep.

'I had to do it,' he says. 'I could not bear their fear. They trusted me.'

'How?'

'I have been giving them Valerian and hop for a few days. They were all very calm.'

304

'And you...'

'Slit their throats. It was the kindest thing to do.'

'Will you go in the boat?' she says holding out her hand.

He does not reply but takes her hand. She pulls him to his feet and leads him back on deck.

The last men left on the ship now are those who have been lowering the boats. They are ready to go and this last boat is the smallest, light enough for Randal to manage it himself. He is waiting for Ria and Zak.

'I will not go without you,' she says.

'I cannot leave the ship as long as anyone remains on board.'

'But it is only Kierle.'

'Even Mr. Kierle. I have a duty even to him. We cannot keep this boat waiting any longer. If it is still attached when the ship goes down these men will be dragged down with it.'

'Then let it go.'

'Zak?'

Zak looks at Ria.

'Go with them,' she says stepping forward to put her arms around him for a second then letting go. 'Go now.'

Now just one of the Lodencroam remains alongside the New Hope. The ship is low in the water and leaning badly.

'You knew about the beetles?' Ria asks.

'I heard stories about them as a child but never encountered them. We were taught that the last of them died out many centuries ago. I should have been more vigilant.'

'So the wood you used to build the ship was contaminated?'

'No. It was Kierle who brought the beetles on board, to be a symbol of his power in the new community.'

'He should be told that this was his doing.'

'I think he knows.'

'Then I want to hear what he has to say,' says Ria.

'Ria, the ship is sinking fast. You must go. Dive now while it is still safe to do so and leave Kierle to me.'

'I will not leave the ship without you. Your people may yet come. Let's talk to Kierle.'

But Kierle is not in his cabin. *He has gone down to his beetles.* Ria leads the way but as they approach the hold she stops. Water is now swirling around their feet but it is not that which has distracted her. It is the smell of decay and a sound she recognises. It seems to be carried on a whispering current of air that gains strength and becomes the hum of a swarm of beetles as it sweeps past them and up towards the air. As soon as it has passed she continues down, but stops just above the bottom of the stairway. Kierle's feet dangle in front of her and she steps back.

'Stay there,' says Randal as he passes her, grasping the man's legs and lifting him. Then, 'Come past us, loosen the rope.' The rope is attached to an anchor that has been dropped from a beam. She slips it off the anchor and Randal lowers Kierle and carries him back up the stairway so that they can get out of the rising water. He lays the body on the deck and checks but Ria is already sure that Kierle is dead.

'There is nothing to keep us on the ship now,' he says simply and, as the New Hope rolls and slips further into the water, they go back to the top deck, climb onto the rail, and dive into the sea where the last of the Loden is waiting for them.

. . . .

Acknowledgements

I would like to thank

Roselle Angwin

Lindsey Clarke

June Dingle

Lee Rolph

and The Arvon Foundation

for all their help, support and encouragement, and to acknowledge the following as sources of inspiration and information:

The Immigration Museum, Melbourne, Australia

The Australian National Maritime Museum, Sydney, Australia

A Kentish Herbal by Alison Revell

Cross Sections – Man of War by Stephen Biesty

New Chum by John Masefield

www.ingramcontent.com/pod-product-compliance
Lightning Source LLC
Chambersburg PA
CBHW070553260626
47161CB00002B/595